Nick knew better than to touch her.

He'd been around the block a few too many times to court the kind of trouble a touch would rouse. He didn't like the way he was reacting to her as it was. He knew if he touched her, if he learned her skin was as soft and warm and fragrant as he imagined, it would make dealing with her even more complex.

"You ought to have it looked at," he said stiffly.

"It's just a scratch. I'll take care of it."

Nick fought another rush of blood to his groin. He denied it. He cursed it. But his body betrayed his intellect, reacting with an intensity that left him incredulous and disturbed. Now wasn't the time. This wasn't the place.

And Erin McNeal wasn't the woman.

D1051704

Dear Reader,

The excitement continues in Intimate Moments. First of all, this month brings the emotional and exciting conclusion of A YEAR OF LOVING DANGEROUSLY. In *Familiar Stranger*, Sharon Sala presents the final confrontation with the archvillain known as Simon—and you'll finally find out who he really is. You'll also be there as Jonah revisits the woman he's never forgotten and decides it's finally time to make some important changes in his life.

Also this month, welcome back Candace Camp to the Intimate Moments lineup. Formerly known as Kristin James, this multitalented author offers a *Hard-Headed Texan* who lives in A LITTLE TOWN IN TEXAS, which will enthrall readers everywhere. Paula Detmer Riggs returns with *Daddy with a Badge,* another installment in her popular MATERNITY ROW miniseries—and next month she's back with *Born a Hero,* the lead book in our new Intimate Moments continuity, FIRSTBORN SONS. Complete the month with *Moonglow, Texas,* by Mary McBride, Linda Castillo's *Cops and...Lovers?* and new author Susan Vaughan's debut book, *Dangerous Attraction.*

By the way, don't forget to check out our Silhouette Makes You a Star contest on the back of every book.

We hope to see you next month, too, when not only will FIRSTBORN SONS be making its bow, but we'll also be bringing you a brand-new TALL, DARK AND DANGEROUS title from award-winning Suzanne Brockmann. For now...enjoy!

Leslie J. Wainger
Executive Senior Editor

Please address questions and book requests to:
Silhouette Reader Service
U.S.: 3010 Walden Ave., P.O. Box 1325, Buffalo, NY 14269
Canadian: P.O. Box 609, Fort Erie, Ont. L2A 5X3

Cops and... Lovers?

LINDA CASTILLO

INTIMATE MOMENTS™

Published by Silhouette Books

America's Publisher of Contemporary Romance

If you purchased this book without a cover you should be aware that this book is stolen property. It was reported as "unsold and destroyed" to the publisher, and neither the author nor the publisher has received any payment for this "stripped book."

To my husband, Ernest, for your encouragement and undying support—I love you always.

Special thanks to my editor, Kim Nadelson, for your wise insights and vision—and your faith in the story.

To my critique pals—Cathy, Jen and Vickie— for helping me find the magic.

 SILHOUETTE BOOKS

ISBN 0-373-27155-7

COPS AND...LOVERS?

Copyright © 2001 by Linda Castillo

All rights reserved. Except for use in any review, the reproduction or utilization of this work in whole or in part in any form by any electronic, mechanical or other means, now known or hereafter invented, including xerography, photocopying and recording, or in any information storage or retrieval system, is forbidden without the written permission of the editorial office, Silhouette Books, 300 East 42nd Street, New York, NY 10017 U.S.A.

All characters in this book have no existence outside the imagination of the author and have no relation whatsoever to anyone bearing the same name or names. They are not even distantly inspired by any individual known or unknown to the author, and all incidents are pure invention.

This edition published by arrangement with Harlequin Books S.A.

® and TM are trademarks of Harlequin Books S.A., used under license. Trademarks indicated with ® are registered in the United States Patent and Trademark Office, the Canadian Trade Marks Office and in other countries.

Visit Silhouette at www.eHarlequin.com

Printed in U.S.A.

Books by Linda Castillo

Silhouette Intimate Moments

Remember the Night #1008
Cops and...Lovers? #1085

LINDA CASTILLO

grew up in a small farming community in western Ohio.
She knew from a very early age that she wanted to be a
writer—and penned her first novel at the age of thirteen,
during one of those long Ohio winters. Her dream of
becoming a published author came true the day Silhouette called and wanted to buy one of her books!

Romance is at the heart of all her stories. She loves the
idea of two fallible people falling in love amid danger,
and against their better judgment—or so they think. She
enjoys watching them struggle through their problems,
realize their weaknesses and strengths along the way
and, ultimately, fall head over heels in love.

She is the winner of numerous writing awards, including
the prestigious Maggie Award for Excellence. In 1999,
she was a triple Romance Writers of America Golden
Heart finalist, and her first Silhouette release, *Remember
the Night,* took first place in the romantic suspense divi-
sion.

Linda spins her tales of love and intrigue from her home
in Dallas, Texas, where she lives with her husband
and three lovable dogs. You can contact her at P.O. Box
670501, Dallas, Texas, 75367-0501.

SILHOUETTE MAKES YOU A STAR!
Feel like a star with Silhouette.
Look for the exciting details of our new contest inside all of these fabulous Silhouette novels:

Romance

#1522 An Officer and a Princess
Carla Cassidy

#1523 Her Tycoon Boss
Karen Rose Smith

THE TEXAS BROTHERHOOD
#1524 A Child for Cade
Patricia Thayer

AN OLDER MAN
#1525 The Baby Season
Alice Sharpe

#1526 Blind-Date Bride
Myrna Mackenzie

#1527 The Littlest Wrangler
Belinda Barnes

Special Edition

Hot Off the Press!
#1399 The Stranger in Room 205
Gina Wilkins

A Woman's Way
#1400 Shelter in a Soldier's Arms
Susan Mallery

#1401 The M.D. Meets His Match
Marie Ferrarella

#1402 Invitation to a Wedding
Peggy Webb

#1403 Her Sister's Secret Son
Lisette Belisle

WYOMING Wildflowers
#1404 Almost a Bride
Patricia McLinn

Desire

Belle Terre
#1369 A Lady for Lincoln Cade
BJ James

MILLION DOLLAR MEN
#1370 The Millionaire's Secret Wish
Leanne Banks

THE FORTUNES OF TEXAS
#1371 A Most Desirable M.D.
Anne Marie Winston

#1372 More to Love
Dixie Browning

#1373 Wyoming Cinderella
Cathleen Galitz

#1374 His Baby Surprise
Kathie DeNosky

Intimate Moments

A Little Town In TEXAS
#1081 Hard-Headed Texan
Candace Camp

a year of Loving dangerously
#1082 Familiar Stranger
Sharon Sala

MATERNITY ROW
#1083 Daddy with a Badge
Paula Detmer Riggs

#1084 Moonglow, Texas
Mary McBride

#1085 Cops and...Lovers?
Linda Castillo

#1086 Dangerous Attraction
Susan Vaughan

Prologue

Erin McNeal had always liked the taste of adrenaline. But as she stared at her partner lying on the floor with his hands bound and a pistol at his nape, it sat in the back of her throat in a bitter pool. He knew better than to get himself into a situation like this. She sure as hell knew better than to follow him into this godforsaken warehouse. But not even the caution instilled by nine years of law enforcement experience was enough to keep her from going in after him.

Heart thundering, she slipped her service revolver from the holster at the small of her back, praying she wouldn't have to use it. She didn't want to get into a firefight with two men wielding semiautomatic weapons and displaying a complete lack of conscience. But the cop in her wouldn't allow her partner to die simply because she was outgunned two to one.

Never taking her eyes from the men, she eased the hammer back with her thumb. She'd radioed for backup, but knew her counterparts wouldn't arrive in time to stop the inevitable. She figured her partner had about a minute left to live—if he was lucky. That gave her about thirty seconds to come up with a plan.

"You gonna tell us who your snitch is, cop, or do we get to beat it out of you?" said a man in an ill-fitting suit.

Erin was too far away to recognize the thug, but she could tell by his calm demeanor and steady hand he'd murdered before. Probably more than once, judging by the anticipation resonating in his voice. Where the hell was her backup?

"We ain't got all night," the second man said. "Do him."

The man in the suit raised his gun. "Last chance, cop."

Moving out from behind the forklift where she'd taken cover, Erin raised her revolver and leveled it on the man in the suit. "Police! Drop your weapons and put your hands over your heads!"

The second man pivoted, his right hand slithering into his jacket. "What the—"

Erin shifted her aim to the man reaching for his gun. "Get your hands where I can see them!"

The two men exchanged looks. A sinking sensation rippled in her gut. In that instant she knew they weren't going to go down without a fight—not to a woman.

Her partner raised his head, drawing her attention. Erin saw fear in his eyes. She felt her own like a raging beast in her chest. She was outnumbered, and they all knew it. Not the kind of odds she wanted to stake her life on, not to mention someone else's.

Damn, this wasn't working out the way she'd hoped.

Panic threatening, she dropped into a shooter's stance, with legs apart, pistol cocked and level, but not quite steady. "Drop 'em!" she said, barely hearing her own voice over the roar of blood in her ears.

In her peripheral vision, she saw movement from above. Surprise jolted her when she saw a figure on the catwalk. Dark clothes. Tinted glasses. A glimpse of blue steel.

Terror fused with adrenaline and cut a path through her belly. She swung her weapon upward—and felt her blood turn to ice. The man on the catwalk was too *young* to be aiming a gun at a cop. Her police training told her to fire, but her finger froze on the trigger. An instant later, the sound of a gunshot rocked her brain.

The bullet slammed into her shoulder with the force of a cannonball. She reeled backward. White-hot fire seared down her arm to her fingertips. The ensuing pain sent her to her knees.

Through a haze of dizziness, she raised her weapon and fired twice in quick succession. The figure on the catwalk tumbled over the rail and hit the concrete with a sickening thud.

Another gun blast reverberated through the warehouse.

Erin screamed her partner's name, but she knew it was too late. She'd seen the bullet hit its mark. She tried to stand, but her legs refused to obey. An animal-like sound tore from her throat as she sank to the cold concrete. Her vision blurred, but she didn't lose consciousness. Through a haze of shock, she heard sirens wailing in the distance. Angry shouts. The shuffle of shoes against concrete.

Twenty yards away, her partner lay silent and still.

Rage and disbelief mingled with grief. Pain slashed her with brutal force, but it was nothing compared to the guilt exploding in her heart.

Please, God, don't let him die.

As the darkness caved in around her, she silently prayed her partner would live. In a small corner of her mind, she prayed he would be able to forgive her for what she'd done. As unconsciousness overtook her, she prayed she would someday be able to forgive herself.

Chapter 1

Erin McNeal pulled her car up to the parking meter outside the Logan Falls, Indiana, police department and stared at the two-story brick building, a sense of dread gathering in her chest like a thunderstorm.

"You can do this," she said aloud, ordering her fingers to release their death grip on the steering wheel. But the words did little to ease the rapid-fire beat of her heart or the suffocating clenching in her chest.

The realization that she was nervous sent a bitter laugh to her lips. She'd dealt with some of the toughest criminals on the street during her nine-year career with the Chicago Police Department. Yet here she was, reduced to a mass of frayed nerves over a job interview with the police chief of a town half the size of the beat she'd once walked.

But that was all over now, she reminded herself darkly. She was no longer a member of the Chicago Police Force. She was no longer the only woman who'd gone from beat cop to tactical officer to narcotics detective in the span of nine years.

The fact of the matter was that Erin was out of a job. The deputy position with the Logan Falls PD was the best prospect in sight, especially for a cop with a bum shoulder, a tarnished reputation and a duffel bag full of personal baggage. Small town or not, she'd damn well better make a good impression.

Her nerves snapped like lit dynamite fuses as she got out of the car and approached the august portals of the police station. Her purse slung over her good shoulder, she clutched her résumé in one hand, raised her chin and took two deep breaths. The ritual should have calmed her, but it didn't. The laugh hovered in her throat again, but she didn't give in to it. Six months ago, bursting through the door of a deserted warehouse with an armed suspect holed up inside hadn't scared her this much. Of course, back then she'd had that addiction to adrenaline and the knowledge that she was damn good at what she did to back her. Now, with her confidence shattered and her career down the proverbial drain, she figured she'd be lucky to get through this with her dignity intact.

Vowing not to let the past interfere now, Erin put on her cop's suit of armor and headed toward the door, praying the man on the other side wasn't particularly discerning.

Police Chief Nick Ryan brooded over the résumé. On paper, the career of ex-detective Erin McNeal left no room for disappointment. Two department commendations. The Blue Star Award. The Award of Valor. She'd come recommended by Commander Frank Rossi of the Chicago PD—a man Nick had called a friend since his academy days. A man to whom Nick owed a favor.

Erin was a good cop, Frank had assured him. Streetwise. Tough. A little too confident. A little too cocky. Well, up until the night she'd botched a sting operation—and her partner paid the price. Frank had been forced to take her off the street. She had ended up resigning in disgrace.

Hell of a note that the situation had ended up in Nick's lap. He needed a damaged cop working for him about as much as he needed a tornado ripping through his town. Why didn't Frank just ask him to jump off the bridge down at Logan Creek?

Nick had been looking for a deputy for nearly a month. Tarnished reputation or not, Erin McNeal fit the bill. The fact that she was Frank's niece pretty much sealed the deal. Damn Frank for calling in the chips now.

Nick stared at her résumé, troubled and more than a little annoyed by the situation. He knew better than to get involved in this woman's plight. He didn't care about Erin McNeal or her problems. He didn't care that she'd once been a good cop. McNeal had committed the ultimate cop's sin: she'd frozen up at a crucial moment. In Nick's book, a cop who couldn't back up her partner didn't deserve to be a cop.

But Nick owed Frank. Frank had been there for him after Rita. He'd been Nick's best man when he'd married her. Twelve years later, Frank had been a pallbearer at her funeral.

Blowing out a sigh, Nick leaned back in his chair and raked his fingers through his hair. He didn't want to deal with this. He didn't want to take a chance on a damaged cop, even if Logan Falls was a small town where the crime consisted of petty theft and the occasional domestic dispute. But he'd promised Frank he'd keep an eye on her. Keep her out of trouble. Give her a chance to get back on her feet. Nick figured he'd probably live to regret it. But then, he was good at living with regrets. What was one more heaped atop a pile that was already sky-high?

"Heck of a résumé." Hector Price, Nick's only other full-time deputy, whistled. "Best one we've seen, Chief. This guy has credentials out the bazoomba. Six years on patrol. Two on the tactical team. A year in narcotics."

"McNeal is a woman," Nick said irritably.

Hector looked dumbstruck. "Shoot, Chief, she's good. A black belt in karate. Holy cow, her marksmanship is better than yours. She's *good*." Catching Nick's dark look, Hector added, "I mean, for a woman."

Good by a man's standards, too, Nick thought sourly. Too good, in fact. He wondered what she had to prove, who she needed to prove it to. He wondered if all those skills had anything to do with guilt.

He'd known her partner, Danny Perrine, from his days in Chicago. He'd heard the rumors about the shooting. The night Erin McNeal forgot about her marksmanship, her black belt in karate and everything else she'd learned at the academy. Danny had paid a steep price because of her.

"As long as she doesn't mind putting those fancy credentials to use down at the school crosswalk," Nick said.

"We've never had a woman cop in Logan Falls, Chief. That ought to be interesting."

Nick could do without the interesting part. He could damn well do without the headache. He hadn't even met the woman and already disliked her on principle alone. He knew it wasn't fair, but he didn't care about that, either. Of course he didn't have to *like* her to appease Frank—just put up with her until she figured out small-town police work wasn't to her liking.

The bell on the front door jingled. Nick looked up. Something went soft in his chest when he saw the woman standing at the door looking as if she'd just walked into a lion's den—and wanted to personally kick him out no matter how big his fangs. Her expression was an odd combination of raw nerves and don't-mess-with-me tough. McNeal wasn't due for another two hours. Besides, he would know a cop on sight. This woman wasn't a cop, but a piece-of-fluff civilian. He wondered what she was selling, and if this was her first day on the job.

She wore a nicely cut pantsuit that sacrificed curves for style. Even with low heels, she was tall, just a few inches short of his six-foot-two frame. Nick could tell by the way she moved that she was athletic. He groaned inwardly when he imagined her lugging in a trunkful of office supplies and offering him the deal of a lifetime.

Not bothering to rise, he made eye contact. "Can I help you with something?"

"I'm here to see Nick Ryan."

She had the greenest eyes he'd ever seen. Cat eyes, he thought, large and cautious and full of female mystery, all framed by lashes as dark and lush as mink. High cheekbones and a full mouth were set into a face that was a little too pale, a little too serious. Freckles dusted her small nose. Her reddish-brown hair was tucked into an unruly bun at her nape. She looked like she'd driven for a long distance with the windows down.

"You probably missed the No Soliciting sign posted on the door," he offered, hoping to save both of them some time.

"I'm not selling anything," she said. "I have an appointment."

Nick stared at her, taking in the folder in her hand, the determination in her cool green eyes, and felt a sinking sensation in his gut. He didn't embarrass easily, but the back of his neck heated. Suddenly, he found himself wanting to throttle Frank Rossi.

"You're Erin McNeal," he said.

She nodded. "I'm a little early."

"You're a lot early." He glanced at his watch. "Two hours to be exact."

"The drive didn't take as long as I thought it would." She strode forward, eyes level on his, hand extended.

Rising, he rounded his desk. "I'm Nick Ryan."

She wasn't what he'd expected the ex-detective to look like. He'd expected hard eyes that were tired from too many years of seeing too much. This woman was anything but hard. She was young and slender and way too…soft to be a cop.

"Frank said to tell you hello," she said.

Frowning, Nick extended his hand, wondering if Frank was back in Chicago having a good laugh. But the moment her fingers closed around his, Nick's concentration wavered. The force of her grip surprised him. It was a little too quick. A little too firm. He hadn't expected to feel calluses on her palm. A weight lifter, too. How on earth could he have mistaken her for a solicitor? Soft or not, this woman had "cop" written all over her.

"I brought my résumé," she said.

"Frank faxed me a copy."

Belatedly, he remembered he was still grasping her hand, and released it. Even though she wasn't standing particularly close, he caught a whiff of her scent, some exotic spice tempered with the essence of clean hair and female. How could a woman with calluses on her palms and a cop's eyes smell so good?

Realizing he was staring, Nick gave himself a mental shake and looked at Hector, who had yet to close his mouth—or take his eyes off her. "This is Deputy Price."

Erin extended her hand. "It's a pleasure, Deputy."

"Ma'am." Hector jumped to his feet, wiped his palms on his uniform slacks and stuck out his hand.

Nick was still struggling with the fact that Detective Erin McNeal wasn't the hardened, cynical cop he'd expected, but a woman who smelled like heaven and looked like she'd just stepped off the set of some high-drama police TV show.

She wasn't beautiful in the classic sense. Her hair was too red to be brown, too brown to be truly red and struggling valiantly to break free of that bun. Her mouth was a tad full and too wide for his taste. He'd never cared for freckles, either. But she was attractive in an earthy, girl-next-door sort of way—the kind of girl who'd played with slingshots instead of dolls.

She studied Nick. "Frank tells me you two are old friends."

He frowned, not liking the way she'd used the word *old*. Just because he felt a lot older than his thirty-eight years didn't mean it was fact. "We go back a few years," he said.

All too aware that his deputy wasn't the only one having a difficult time keeping his eyes off her, Nick cleared his throat. "Frank and I partnered up for a couple of years in Chicago."

"He speaks well of you," she said.

"Only when he needs a favor."

Her gaze sharpened, and he knew she was wondering if he'd just slighted her. Perceptive, too, he thought, and felt a glimmer of hope that she wouldn't take this job, after all.

"I'm really early," she said. "If you're in the middle of something, I don't mind waiting."

Great, he'd been staring again. He was acting like a pimply-faced teenager who'd just come face-to-face with his favorite centerfold. Erin McNeal was a cop—and a bad one at that. He'd worked with plenty of female cops back in Chicago. This one shouldn't be any different.

Noticing that Hector's eyes still hadn't settled back in their sockets, Nick motioned toward his office. "We can talk in here, Ms. McNeal."

She started for the door with long, confident strides. He followed, refusing to let his eyes peruse what he instinctively knew was a nice derriere. He didn't want to know that she was built just the way he liked. He'd just as soon not like anything at all about this woman.

Once in his office, he slid behind his desk, then watched her take the chair opposite him. Her jacket gaped slightly when she crossed her legs, and he caught a glimpse of lace and the swell of her breasts beneath her blouse. Determined to keep his mind on the interview, he forced his gaze to the file in front of him. "Your credentials are impressive," he said. "Frank gave you a favorable recommendation."

"Frank was a good commander."

"It's probably no handicap that he's also your uncle." Nick looked down at the file, wondering if she realized Frank had told him about the shooting. "You scored high on your detective's exam. You transferred out of tactical to become a detective after only two years. Says here 'because you like to think.' Your solve rate is high. Your marksmanship is outstanding." He raised his eyes to hers. "Those are some pretty remarkable achievements considering there are over thirteen thousand sworn officers on the force."

Her gaze never left his. "I like being a cop."

Despite his resistance to her, the answer scored a point with him. Nick had a pretty good idea how many hurdles this woman had had to leap to reach detective status. He knew plenty of men who couldn't match half her skills. He knew plenty of others who would do their utmost to hold her back just because she was the wrong sex. Yet she'd prevailed. Nick admired tenacity almost as much as he admired guts. He wondered if she was gutsy enough to bring up the subject neither of them wanted to discuss.

"We don't get much action here in Logan Falls," he said. "A few juvenile delinquents. Domestic disputes. The Brass Rail Saloon got robbed last Friday, but that sort of thing is pretty unusual. Think you can handle that kind of excitement?"

"If I can handle the South Side of Chicago, I'm sure I can handle anything that happens in Logan Falls."

He'd asked the question lightly, but she'd taken it as a personal challenge. An ego to boot, he thought. He studied the file, irritated with her for not being what he'd expected, annoyed with Frank for not warning him how good she was to look at—and downright ticked off at himself for noticing.

"I see you've had a couple personnel problems," he said.

"They were relatively minor—"

"It's my responsibility to ask you about them." He flipped to the next page. "You've been written up for insubordination."

Eyeing him warily, she shifted in her chair. "I didn't like an assignment, and I let my lieutenant know about it."

"What was it about?"

"Cases involving unpopular victims that were shoved aside in lieu of the more affluent ones. Prostitutes mostly, because nobody cared about them. I didn't think that was fair."

Nick nodded noncommittally, not liking it that he agreed with her. He didn't miss big-city police work, or the politics that went along with it. "Any problems with your shoulder?" He could tell by the way her eyes widened that he'd caught her off guard. "Frank told me about the shooting," he clarified.

"I have a little arthritis," she replied. "Nothing I can't handle."

"Did you pass the physical?"

She nodded. "I'm left-handed, so the injury didn't affect my marksmanship. I lost some strength in my right hand."

On the surface, her answer seemed adequate. To the point. Acceptable. Just the way she'd planned, Nick thought. But he was observant enough to notice the other signs that weren't quite as apparent. He didn't miss her white-knuckled grip on her purse. The slight tremor in her hand. The tight clench of her jaw. All signs of stress; all signs that the shooting had affected her much more profoundly than she was letting on. Just like a cop, he thought, and inwardly groaned. He knew intimately the signs of personal baggage—he was an expert on the subject, after all—

and bet his bottom dollar the woman across from him had a truckload sitting on those rigid shoulders.

"Frank said you were lucky to get out of that warehouse alive," he said.

She looked as though she wanted to argue for a moment, but didn't. "I was very lucky."

Her partner, Danny Perrine, hadn't been as lucky. The thought sent a flare of irritation through Nick. He wondered if she was going to come clean with the entire story, or if he was going to have to squeeze it out of her one question at a time.

"Did you spend any time with the department shrink afterward?" he asked casually.

Her gaze snapped to his. He could tell from her expression she knew it wasn't a casual question. Though she tried to shutter her reaction, Nick saw the flash of emotion in the depths of her gaze.

"I saw Dr. Ferguson for a couple of months. It's department regulation for any cop involved in a shooting. She gave me a clean bill of health."

"So if the shrink gave you a clean bill of health, why did Frank fire you?"

"Frank didn't fire me. I resigned."

"On paper maybe. It's obvious you were on your way out. Only you knew a resignation would look better than a termination on your résumé, didn't you?" Nick didn't look up, but rather felt the rise of tension. He let the silence work for a moment, then met her gaze. "You didn't think I wouldn't ask you about the shooting, did you?"

Erin stared at him, her expression guarded. "Of course not."

"I have your complete file," he pointed out. "I was wondering if you wanted to give me your take on what happened."

"Frank said—"

"Why don't you stop wondering how much of this Frank has already told me, and just lay it out?"

For the first time, her composure wavered. She blinked, then looked down at her hands, twisting in her lap. Quickly, she relaxed them. "He had no right to give you my entire file. Some of it's confidential."

"You don't think he's going to let you waltz in and dazzle me with your test scores and solve rate when we both know you've had some serious problems in the last six months, do you?"

"Frank knows I'm a good cop."

"He also knows you're wobbly on your feet. You were involved in a shooting. There are repercussions to that sort of thing whether we like to admit it or not. Frank didn't expect me to walk in blind. Not after what happened to Danny Perrine."

She flinched. "I'm not wobbly. I made a mistake—"

"A very serious one that nearly cost a man his life."

"I'm fully aware—"

Nick's throat squeezed out a short, incredulous laugh designed to let her know just how he felt about cops and mistakes. "Just because you're aware, Ms. McNeal, doesn't mean it's going to go away or that it won't happen again."

"I screwed up," she said. "I went back to work too soon after...Danny. But I'm better now—"

"Ah, I'll feel a hell of lot better going through a door with you, knowing you're all better."

Her eyes heated. "I can do without the sarcasm."

Ignoring her anger, maybe even enjoying it a little, Nick continued, "This isn't personal, McNeal. I'm just trying to decide if you're still suitable for police work."

"Why don't you give me the chance to prove it?"

"Because I'm afraid you'll freeze up when I need you. I can do without a bullet in my back."

She stared at him, her eyes wide, nostrils flaring slightly. "I'm solid."

"If that was the case you'd still be in Chicago."

"Frank's assessment of me was incorrect."

Nick leaned forward. "You mean he lied? Why would he do that?"

"I'm his niece. He's overprotective. He thinks I ought to be home baking cookies, for Pete's sake."

"Maybe you should have considered administrative work when he offered it."

"I'm a police officer. I don't want to sit behind a desk."

"You'd rather play Rambo, and freeze up on your partner."

"That's not how any of this happened."

Nick knew he was being hard on her, but he figured since this was his town he had every right to put her on the hot seat.

"I know what happened in that warehouse," he said. "I know about Danny Perrine. You froze up, McNeal. Were you going to bother mentioning that to me?"

She stared at him, her jaw tight, her eyes shooting fire and ice.

"So before you come in here trying to dazzle me with your assorted bragging points, why don't you explain to me why I ought to hire you?"

Erin wanted so badly to tell him to go to hell she could taste it. Of course, she didn't. Six months ago she would have laughed in his face. Today, shaken, uncertain and a little desperate, she could do nothing more than stare at him and wonder how the interview had gone from bad to downright catastrophic in less than ten minutes.

He knows, she thought. *He knows I can't hack it anymore.* The familiar pain cut her and went deep. Doubt and guilt slashed her, and she felt the blood well like a fresh wound. She looked down at where she held her purse with a death grip. Forcing her hands to relax, refusing to let this man reduce her to a bumbling rookie, she looked up and met his gaze levelly.

"I think we both know this isn't working," she said.

Lowering his head, Nick pinched the bridge of his nose. "That's an understatement," he growled.

Disappointment burned, but she raised her chin in spite of it and rose. "I won't waste any more of your time, Chief Ryan."

"We're not finished yet."

"Yes, we are." She slung her purse over her shoulder.

He rose. "Look, I told Frank—"

"Don't do me any favors, Chief. Just because my uncle is your friend doesn't mean you have to feel obligated to hire me. I don't need your charity." She didn't need this job, either, she assured herself. There were other opportunities. She just needed to find the right one. She sure as hell didn't need a jerk like Nick Ryan humiliating her at every turn.

For the first time he looked chagrined. "Don't make this personal—"

"Don't sweat it, Chief. I'm used to being underestimated. Besides, my skin's a lot thicker than it looks." She offered a crisp smile, hating that she had to bite her lower lip to keep it from quivering. "I've got some other prospects lined up, anyway."

"Do you?"

"Corporate security. That sort of thing."

"Uh-huh."

"I prefer working in a larger town, anyway."

"Sure you do."

She was going to have to figure *something* out, considering she hadn't made her car payment last month. Maybe security work wasn't such a bad thing, after all.

"Thanks again for your time." Without looking at him, Erin started for the door. She couldn't remember the last time she'd felt like such a failure. Maybe the last interview she'd screwed up. Or the day she'd walked out of the precinct for the last time. Or maybe the day she'd frozen at a crucial moment and realized she wasn't as strong as she'd once believed.

"McNeal."

She didn't stop until she reached the door of his office. Even then she didn't turn around. She wasn't sure what would happen if she did. She wasn't a crier or overly emotional, but for the first time in a long time, she felt on the verge of a crying jag the likes of which the world had never seen.

"Frank Rossi doesn't recommend just anyone," Nick said.

Erin's hand froze on the knob. Furiously, she blinked back tears.

"I trust his judgment," he said. "You worked for him for nine years. Maybe you should trust him, too."

The meaning behind his words registered slowly, like an easy rain falling over a drought-stricken land. Hope jumped through her with such force that her knees went weak. One breath. Two. She turned and looked at him, trembling no matter how hard she tried not to. "Frank is my uncle. He's probably not objective when it comes to me."

"Taking that into consideration, is there any reason I should doubt your ability to perform police work?"

"I was a good cop," she said a little breathlessly. "I'm still a good cop."

"I need a deputy. You came with a recommendation. You've got the credentials. Are you interested?"

Erin stared at him, wondering if he would be offering her the job if he knew about the nightmares. Or the flashbacks that swooped down on her like a giant bird of prey when a car backfired and her memory transported her back to that warehouse.

"You mean you want to hire me?" she blurted.

He hit her with a piercing stare. "Logan Falls is a small

town. It might be a good place for you to get back on your feet and decide if you want to stay in law enforcement, or move on to something else.''

Her heart thrummed against her breastbone as if she'd just run a mile. Hope and fear roiled in her chest as his gaze burned into hers. ''I want the job.''

''Maybe you should sit back down so we can finish our interview.''

Six months ago, her pride would have dictated she tell him to take a flying leap into whatever body of water Logan Falls had been named after. Today, she figured they were both too hard up to look a gift horse in the mouth. Either Frank had done a number on him, or Chief Nick Ryan was desperate to get a deputy hired. She wasn't sure which scenario bothered her most.

''All right.'' On numb legs, she walked back to the chair and sank into it.

She watched him take the chair behind his desk. Judging from the crow's-feet at the corners of his eyes, she guessed he was probably in his late thirties. His brown hair was cropped short and so dark it was almost black. Even though it was barely past noon, a five o'clock shadow darkened a jaw that was lean and strong. He wasn't handsome—well, not exactly—but then pretty boys had never appealed to Erin. She preferred rugged over perfect. Character over charm. This man possessed generous amounts of both in the hardened planes of his face.

From the scar on his right eyebrow to his hard eyes and uncompromising mouth, Nick Ryan was as rugged as a man could get and still look civilized. He stood well over six feet, so that even with her lofty height of five-nine, she had to crane her neck to look up at him. He possessed the lean build of a distance runner tempered with the brawn of a boxer. But despite his physique, it was his eyes that emanated power. They were the color of strong coffee and as coldly sharp as the wind off Lake Michigan in January. His mouth was a straight slash she instinctively knew didn't smile much.

"How soon can you start?" he asked.

She blinked, realizing with some embarrassment she'd been staring. "Monday." How she would move from Chicago to Logan Falls in two days when she didn't even have an apartment yet was a mystery to her, but somehow she'd pull it off.

"You'll need to fill out these forms." He passed several sheets of paper to her. "The pay isn't as good as it is in Chicago, but the cost of living is a lot less."

Numbly, she took the papers, starkly aware that her hands were shaking. "I don't have an apartment yet." She'd made the one-hundred-mile trip from Chicago in less than two hours just that morning. Once in town, she hadn't taken the time to sightsee, but headed directly to the police station.

"There's a two-bedroom apartment for rent above the florist shop on Commerce Street." Nick opened his pencil drawer, pulled out a business card and handed it to her. "Mike Barton is my neighbor. He's been trying to rent it for two months. You might want to give him a call."

She was still trying to absorb that he'd hired her when he hit her with the bit about the apartment. "I'll do that."

"Are you staying in town tonight or heading back to Chicago?"

"I'll find an apartment today, then drive back tonight for my things. If all goes well, I'll move in the day after tomorrow." Erin rose, feeling as though she'd just stepped off a roller coaster.

"Good, then I'll see you Monday morning."

She started toward the door, but paused halfway there. Taking a deep breath, she stopped and turned to face him. "What made you change you mind?" she asked.

Rising, he approached her, his expression inscrutable. "You wanted to tell me to go to hell. You almost did, but your pride wouldn't let you because you didn't want me to know I'd rattled you. I thought that ought to count for something.''

''I wasn't rattled.''

He had the gall to look amused. ''Really?''

Her cheeks heated. She didn't like having her dignity toyed with. She didn't have that much to spare. ''I was ticked off that you felt the need to grill me when I clearly have the credentials to handle the job.''

''That remains to be seen.'' Surprising her, he extended his hand. ''Just don't make me regret hiring you.''

''I won't.'' She raised her hand to his.

The contact jolted her like a mild electrical shock that jumped from him to her and wreaked havoc on every nerve ending in her body. She felt herself give a little jerk, praying he didn't notice. Vaguely, she was aware of his grip—firm, but not painful. All the while his gaze bored into hers, sending pinpricks of awareness rippling through her like a flash flood.

The knot in her chest unraveled only to be replaced with another kind of tension. Erin wanted to think it was because she'd waited a long time for this moment, but in the backwaters of her mind she knew the weightless feeling had more to do with the fact that he was standing so close she could smell the clean tang of his aftershave. She told herself she was crazy for noticing something so irrelevant. She'd learned a long time ago that police work and relationships were about as compatible as gasoline and fire—and just as combustible.

Shaken by her reaction, she broke the connection and stepped back. Nick gazed steadily at her, but he wasn't smiling. He looked taken aback and as annoyed as she felt. If his jaws clenched any tighter, he was going to need dental work.

Clearing his throat, he opened his office door for her and stepped back. Erin used that moment to escape. She barely looked at Deputy Price as she headed toward the safety of the front entrance. She wasn't sure what had just happened between her and Nick Ryan, but knew it wasn't good. It sure as hell couldn't happen again. This job was her last chance.

Her hand was closing around the knob when Nick's baritone voice cut through the air. "McNeal."

She froze, a dozen scenarios tumbling through her brain. He'd changed his mind. He wanted to talk to Frank again. He wanted to hear the details about what had happened to Danny. He wanted to know why her hands were shaking, why he could hear her heart hammering against her ribs. Taking a deep breath, she turned and forced her gaze to his.

Nick stood just outside his office door, his face as expressionless as a stone. "Tell Frank I owe him one."

Chapter 2

Nick stared into his coffee cup and called himself a fool a dozen ways. He wanted to think he'd caved in and hired Erin McNeal because he owed Frank a favor. Because of her impressive credentials, or maybe because he felt the need to lend a helping hand to a fellow cop. But Nick knew his decision to hire her probably had more to do with the desperation he'd seen in the depths of her gaze—and the fact that she would have walked out of his office and not looked back in spite of it.

He glanced at the wall clock, annoyed that it was the fourth time he'd done so in less than twenty minutes. He told himself he wasn't thinking about her, that he wasn't anxious because this was her first day of work and she was going to be riding with him. But he was honest enough with himself to know that wasn't quite true. In the three days since he'd hired Logan Falls's first female police officer, he'd found himself thinking about her more often than he wanted to admit. He assured himself it was because she'd been involved in a shooting, and it was his responsibility, as her direct supervisor, to know her mindset. Only Nick knew his interest in her wasn't as impersonal as he wanted to believe.

What bothered him most was that he'd reacted to her on a personal level. Not as a superior or fellow cop, but a man who saw a deep well of vulnerability beneath that veneer of toughness. A man who'd been willing to go against his better judgment the moment he laid eyes on her and saw the damaged pride and go-to-hell attitude—and the kind of curves that made his pulse pound.

He wondered how Frank would feel if he knew his good friend was ogling his niece, who was nearly ten years his junior.

Grimacing, Nick took a drink of coffee. He'd often wondered how long it would take for the celibacy to get to him. After Rita, he'd believed he was as immune as a man could get when it came to women. That was fine with him; the lack of distraction left him able to focus all of this attention on his daughter. Then Erin McNeal had walked in and proved him wrong. This was a hell of a time for his hormones to tell him he was still human.

So what if she was attractive? Nick had more self-discipline than he knew what to do with, and a whole lot more common sense. He certainly knew better than to court trouble. Erin McNeal had trouble written all over that shapely body of hers. Not that he'd been looking, of course. But there were times when a man couldn't help but see the finer points of a woman, no matter how staunch his resistance.

Nick was truthful enough with himself to realize the woman intrigued him. But he assured himself he could handle it. Even after three years, he was in no frame of mind to take on a relationship. After losing Rita, he'd sworn he'd never put his heart on the line ever again. The consequences were too dire. Besides, he didn't even *like* McNeal.

The bell on the front door jingled. Nick jumped, cursing

when some of his coffee sloshed over the top of his cup. Even without looking, he knew it was Erin. Steeling himself against the anticipation winding through his chest, he glanced out his office door. His heart kicked against his ribs when he spotted her striding toward him through the outer office.

He watched her approach against his better judgment, knowing his slow perusal of her would probably cost him later. The navy jacket and skirt she was wearing should have been conservative, but the sway of her hips and the shape of her thighs beneath the material were anything but. She reminded him of a sleek panther. Graceful. Wary. A little dangerous. A hint of tightly wound energy lay behind that smooth gait. Her legs were long, her strides confident. She returned his gaze levelly.

"Morning," he said.

"Morning." She entered his office.

"You're early. It's barely eight."

"I like to get an early start."

Even as an inner voice warned him against it, Nick found his eyes seeking out the silk blouse beneath her jacket. Before he could look away, the outline of lace and curves he had absolutely no business noticing scattered his concentration.

Silently cursing himself, he motioned to the chair opposite his desk. "Have a seat."

"Thanks."

Her eyes seemed darker today. They were the color of a rain forest, filled with shadows and secrets as mysterious as the forest itself. Taking the chair he'd indicated, she crossed her legs.

When her jacket parted, he looked down at his paperwork. "Did you find an apartment?"

"Actually, I took the one you recommended."

"Good. I think you'll find Mr. Barton is a fair landlord." Nick wasn't sure why he felt so off-kilter. In the ten years he'd been chief of police, he'd never felt awkward with his deputies. What was it about Erin McNeal that had him acting like a tongue-tied juvenile?

Disgusted by his behavior, he rose and walked to the metal file cabinet behind his desk, where her uniforms, service revolver and badge lay in a neat pile. He scooped it up and set it on the desk between them.

"You and I are riding together today," he said. "We'll be together until your probationary period is up in thirty days. I'll show you around town. Point out the trouble spots, the city limits, the landmarks. Clyde Blankenship's horses got out this morning. We'll drive by and make sure he fixed the fence. He's over ninety years old and doesn't always do a good job."

"Horses?"

Nick frowned at her, wondering if the lady hotshot cop from Chicago considered herself above such menial law enforcement tasks. "School started last week. Hector drew crosswalk duty. We'll drive by and see how he's doing."

Erin nodded.

"There's a locker room next to the water cooler," he said. "You can change there. Locker number five."

"It'll just take me a minute to change clothes."

The image of her slipping out of that skirt came to mind unbidden, but he ruthlessly shoved it away. "Assignments and shifts are posted weekly on the board above the time clock."

Rising, she gathered her uniforms, revolver and badge from his desk. "How many other deputies work for you?" she asked.

"Hector and two part-timers." Nick caught a whiff of her sweet, exotic scent—and nearly lost his train of thought. This was becoming downright annoying.

He studied her, trying not to notice the softness of her mouth or the delicate slant of her jaw. "Any questions?" he asked, rising.

"I'll just get dressed."

Rounding his desk, he started toward the main office, starkly aware that she was behind him. "Locker room's there." He motioned toward the hall leading to the rear of the building.

"I'll be five minutes."

"Take your time."

Erin's hands shook as she stepped into her uniform slacks and tucked in her shirt. Her service revolver lay on the bench beside her, reminding her that after six months and four interviews she was once again a police officer. She should have been ecstatic now that she was finally getting her life back on track. But the reality of what she faced was as disconcerting as it was thrilling. The responsibility of it pressed down on her like a lead weight. As she slipped the revolver into her holster, she tried not to think about whether she'd have the guts to use it.

Erin refused to second-guess herself. Not when she'd already passed the point of no return.

Smoothing her shirt, she picked up her extra uniform and started for the door, all too aware that her heart was pounding. "You can do this," she murmured, determined not to let the uncertainty rattle her.

The sound of a child's voice coming from the outer office broke into her thoughts. Curious, she continued down the hall and stopped on entering the main office. A little girl with hair the color of a wheat field sat at Hector's desk, tugging a coloring book from her backpack. She looked to be only eight or nine years old, but possessed the most adult eyes Erin had ever seen on a child.

Nick had come out of his office and was walking toward the girl. "Why aren't you in school, honeybunch?" he asked.

The child shrugged. "I wanted to ride with you today."

"It's a schoolday."

"I don't want to go to school today."

Stooping, he pressed a kiss to her forehead, then stood back and regarded her with an expression of stern amusement. "I thought you liked school this year. Isn't today library day?"

"Mrs. McClellan doesn't like me."

"Doesn't like you? What's not to like?" He tousled her hair, his hand lingering. "Just between you and me, Mrs. McClellan told me you're her favorite librarian."

The little girl looked at the coloring book spread out on the desk. "Can't I just stay here awhile? I brought my coloring book, see? I'll be quiet."

"Honey, I'd love to spend the day with you, but you can't miss any more school and I've got work to do." Digging in her backpack, he pulled out a box of colorful markers. "Who brought you here to the station?"

The little girl leaned over and shot Erin a less-than-friendly look over Nick's shoulder. "Who's that lady?"

Nick glanced at Erin, then turned back to the girl. "Her name's Erin. She's my new deputy—"

"That's a boy's name."

"Steph, I want you to tell me who brought you here."

"No one." She selected a marker and began to color. "I just left. Mr. Finn sent me to the office for talking to Kimmy Bunger during attendance. The hall monitor was in the bathroom, and nobody was paying any attention, so I just left."

Erin saw Nick's shoulders go rigid. "Wait a minute," he said firmly. "You just left? An adult didn't drive you here?"

"It's not that big a deal, Daddy. The school's only two blocks away."

"I'm afraid leaving school without permission *is* a big deal, Steph. You know I'm going to have to call the school and talk to the principal again, don't you?" Gently easing the marker from her fingers, he rounded her chair and pulled it back from the desk.

That was when Erin noticed the wheelchair. She stared, trying valiantly to curb the resulting shock.

"You know you're not allowed to leave school without permission," Nick said, picking up the phone and punching in numbers. "Why didn't you tell your teacher you wanted to go home? Why didn't you call me?"

In some small corner of her mind, Erin heard him ask for the principal. She stood frozen in place, telling herself the sight of the wheelchair hadn't upset her, hadn't made her remember.

Images from the night of the shooting burst forth in her mind's eye. She fought the flashback, but it pressed down on her, a solid weight of fear that stole her concentration and threatened her control. Danny lying on the floor in a pool of blood. The churning in her gut. The smell of gunpowder.

The folded uniform she'd been clutching slipped from her hands and fell to the floor in a heap. Nick looked up, his eyes narrowing. Terrified he would misinterpret her reaction, Erin quickly scooped up the fallen uniform, then backed into the relative safety of the hall. Her chest felt as if it was being squeezed by a giant vise, but she forced air into her lungs. She was going to be okay, she assured herself. It had been a while since she'd had a flashback, but they still came on occasion. Whenever a sound or smell or sight reminded her of the night she'd been shot, it all came rushing back....

Ordering herself to calm down, she smoothed the front of her uniform and watched Nick kneel to tie his daughter's shoe. The little girl wore a pink sweatshirt and matching pants, with polka-dot sneakers. It was a happy outfit, made for climbing trees and playing hopscotch. But Erin could plainly see by the look in this child's eyes that she wasn't happy. She certainly wasn't going to get up out of that wheelchair and play hopscotch anytime soon.

"Get your books and markers together, kiddo," he said. "I'm taking you home."

"I don't want to go home."

"It's either school or home," he said firmly. "I'll let you choose."

"Please, Daddy, I want to go with you."

Erin didn't miss the pain that knifed across Nick's features. Jaw clenched, he looked down at the floor, then slowly straightened, as if the effort cost him more energy than he had to spare. "Put your books and markers in your book bag, honeybunch. I'll take you home."

Huffing in displeasure, the little girl wheeled closer to the desk and started throwing markers one by one into her book bag.

Erin hadn't even known Nick Ryan had a family. He didn't wear a ring; she'd assumed he was unmarried. That his child was handicapped struck a chord within her. Pain broke open in her chest—a slow ache that burgeoned until it enveloped her entire body. And her heart silently wept when she remembered another wheelchair, and a man she'd sentenced to the kind of hell she could only imagine in her worst nightmares.

"McNeal."

She started at the sound of Nick's voice, and forced her gaze to his.

Standing at the end of the hall, he shot her a look cold enough to freeze acid. "In my office."

Pressing her hand against her stomach, she walked past him and into his office. Oh, Lord, she hadn't intended to react to the wheelchair. She couldn't imagine what he must think of her.

Nick entered behind her and closed the door. When he turned to her, his eyes were the color of a force five tornado that was headed straight in her direction.

"If the wheelchair bothers you I suggest you go back to Chicago and forget you ever set foot in Logan Falls," he snapped.

"It doesn't—"

"You look like you just saw a ghost. I can't have you falling apart every time you see my daughter, for crying out loud."

Erin stared at him, heart pounding wildly, while the words built in her chest like a sickness. "I'm sorry. I was...distracted—"

"You were about to come apart at the seams," he interrupted.

"I was...thinking—"

"Thinking?"

"I was thinking about...Danny," she said, knowing it would be professional suicide to tell him about the flashbacks or the nightmares.

"What does he have to do with this?"

When she trusted her voice not to betray her, she raised her chin and met Nick's gaze. "He's in a wheelchair. I'm the one who put him there."

Because he had an eight-year-old daughter, Nick didn't usually curse, but today he made an exception. Of all the explanations Erin could have offered, the bit about her ex-partner knocked him speechless as effectively as a set of brass knuckles.

He was accustomed to negative reactions to his daughter's wheelchair. Some people stared. Others ignored her. Some people just smiled too much because they were uncomfortable with the prospect of a child who couldn't walk. No matter how innocent, those reactions invariably upset Stephanie—and set his own temper ablaze. He would never forget the day she'd come home from school crying so hard she couldn't speak. His heart had broken into a thousand pieces when she'd told him the kids had made fun of her.

He couldn't count the number of times he'd wished it was him in that wheelchair instead of her.

He wasn't sure why, but he'd expected Erin to be different. She was a decorated cop. She'd seen a lot over the years. He'd hoped she'd be somehow above it. Then she'd hit him with that bit about her partner, and he'd realized her reaction didn't have anything to do with a lack of character, but with her own private hell.

Damn, he didn't want to have to deal with this.

"It was wrong of me not to tell you I'm still…dealing with what happened to Danny," she said.

"Frank didn't bother," he said dryly. "Why should you?"

"Frank doesn't hold me responsible. It's not an issue for him."

"He didn't clean up your file, did he?"

"He wouldn't do that."

"Internal Affairs cleared you?"

She looked at him as if she were about to walk the plank—and he was the one holding the gun at her back. "Yes."

Nick didn't like the way this was playing out. It was clear this woman had been exonerated by the department. The problem was she hadn't yet exonerated herself.

"The police department isn't the place for personal baggage," he said. "Even in Logan Falls."

"I'm working through it."

Even from three feet away he could see she was shaking. What in the world had happened to this woman? What had Frank gotten him into? Whatever the case, Nick wasn't happy about the situation. He sure didn't like the way he was reacting to her. At the moment, he wished he'd never heard of her. Wished he'd never hired her, for God's sake.

But another part of him knew that wasn't completely true. She might be an attractive woman who was affecting him in all the wrong ways. She might have let her partner down in a crisis. But she was still a cop. A cop who'd been cut down in the line of duty and needed a chance to get back on her feet.

Frowning, Nick crossed to his desk, but he didn't sit. His temper was still lit, but he knew it would be wrong of him to take it out on Erin. He didn't know all the details of what she'd gone through. Frank had told him the shooting wasn't directly her fault—she'd followed procedure for the most part. But her momentary hesitation had cost her—and her partner—dearly. The ensuing Internal Affairs investigation irrevocably damaged her career. She'd lost her confidence. In the end, she'd resigned voluntarily, to keep herself from getting fired.

"I hope this doesn't affect your decision about hiring me," she said.

He turned and looked at her, taking in the rigid shoulders. The high chin. The gaze that was level and a little too intense. His chest tightened uncomfortably when he realized it was taking most of her nerve just to maintain eye contact. Whatever happened in that warehouse had taken a heavy toll on her. She blamed herself, he realized. Nick knew firsthand how easy it was to accept blame when the real culprit wasn't able to.

"This isn't going to work out if you can't handle being around the wheelchair," he said.

"I can handle it."

"You sure about that?"

"It just...caught me off guard. I didn't mean to upset her."

"I don't think she noticed. But she's sensitive about her handicap. I don't want it to happen again."

"It won't." Guilt shimmered in the depths of Erin's eyes. "I overreacted. I'm sorry."

Once again, Nick couldn't take his eyes off her. She gazed steadily at him, her green eyes dark against her pale complexion. Relief flashed through him when he realized she wasn't a crier. Female tears were the one thing he'd never handled well. Thank God he didn't have to deal with *that* heaped on top of those bottomless, troubled eyes and soft mouth.

"We don't have time to discuss this right now," he said. "But you owe me a more detailed explanation."

A breath shuddered out of her. "I know."

He glanced toward the door, beyond which Stephanie waited. He'd always been protective of his daughter. Especially since the car accident three years ago that had taken her mother from her and injured her spine. As of late, it seemed his protective instinct had grown into something even Nick couldn't control.

"I need to take her home," he said. "You can ride along. Then we'll start our shift, and we can talk."

"Look, Nick, I'm a good cop—"

"This has nothing to do with whether or not you're a good cop. The question is whether or not you're ready to return to the field."

"I'm ready," she snapped.

He contemplated her, trying not to notice the way the sunlight brought out the red in her hair and made it shine like Oriental silk. Damn her for complicating things by being a woman. Damn him for noticing.

"I hope you're right," he said, and headed toward the door.

Erin watched Nick scoop his daughter out of the wheelchair and settle her onto the back seat of the Suburban, where he strapped her in place. He didn't speak, didn't even look at Erin as he folded the wheelchair and stowed it in the rear. Crossing in front of the truck, he slid behind the wheel and started the engine.

Erin got in beside him, hating that she'd reacted to the wheelchair so intensely. She'd thought the flashbacks were over. But the moment she saw Stephanie's wheelchair, the

night of the shooting had rushed back like a deluge of ran-
cid floodwater. The man on the catwalk. The blue steel of
a gun. The split-second hesitation that would haunt her the
rest of her life.

Shoving the memory aside, she leaned back in her seat
and gazed out the window, determined not to let the incident shake her. So she'd overreacted. If Erin had learned
anything in the last several months, it was that she couldn't
change what was already done. Another mistake heaped on
top of a dozen others wasn't going to make a difference
now.

Two slow, deep breaths and her nerves began to calm.
For the first time since she'd climbed into the truck, she
noticed the scenery outside her window as they drove toward Nick's house. She'd never lived in a small town before, but had fallen in love with Logan Falls the moment
she'd arrived. Surrounded by endless fields of corn and
wheat, neat white farmhouses and pastures dotted with cat-
tle, Logan Falls was a typical Midwestern town. Cobble-
stone streets and brick storefronts distinguished the downtown area. A silver-roofed bell tower graced the top of the
courthouse. Across the street, a fountain punctuated the
center of the business traffic loop. Beyond, a redbrick
school surrounded by maples and stately oak trees sepa-
rated the downtown area from a well-kept residential neigh-
borhood.

They rode in silence to a more rural area, the only sound
coming from the occasional crackle of Nick's police radio.
In the back seat, Stephanie stared out the window, her face
pulled into a sullen mask Erin couldn't begin to read.

"It looks like Mrs. Thornsberry's home."

Nick's voice jerked Erin from her reverie. She looked
over at him just as he turned the Suburban down a gravel
drive lined on both sides by a white rail fence. Ahead, a
white frame house with black shutters and a wraparound
porch beckoned. Erin wasn't sure where she'd expected

Nick Ryan to live, but it wasn't here. The home spread out before her looked like a happy place where children played and adults barbecued in the backyard. But on closer inspection, she noticed the signs that no children had played in this yard for quite some time. A swing set sat like an abandoned ship in a sea of lush grass. A basketball hoop mounted above the garage door was rusty, its netting torn and swinging in the breeze.

Erin smiled when she noticed the spotted horse grazing next to the rail fence. "Whose horse?" she asked, hoping to land on a subject that would brighten Stephanie's mood.

"That's Bandito," the little girl replied. "He's an Appaloosa."

"He's beautiful," Erin said. "Do you ride?"

"I used to be in 4-H and show in western pleasure and trail." Stephanie sighed. "But I don't anymore."

"How come?"

A sound of disgust emanated from the back seat. "As if you haven't noticed, my legs aren't exactly strong enough to stay in the stirrups."

Turning in her seat, Erin smiled at her. "Have you ever heard of therapeutic horseback riding?"

The little girl studied her with soft, intelligent eyes that held a lot more interest than she was letting on with her responses. "No."

"That's where kids with disabilities ride horses, work out their muscles and, basically, have a lot of fun."

"My dad says we're going to retire Bandito."

Erin risked a look at Nick. "Have you checked with her doc—"

"Steph is concentrating most of her time on physical therapy," Nick said firmly, then looked in the rearview mirror and smiled at her. "Aren't you, honeybunch?"

"Yeah, but I still miss Bandito," she said.

Deciding it might be a good idea to steer the conversation away from the riding aspect of horse ownership, Erin tried another approach. "Well, since you don't ride anymore, Steph, maybe you could just show him to me one of these days."

"Bandito doesn't like strangers," the little girl said.

Nick shot his daughter another look in the rearview mirror as he parked the truck. "That's enough, Steph. Deputy McNeal is trying to be friendly."

"Well, she keeps asking dumb questions."

He shut down the engine and opened his door, terminating a conversation Erin wished she'd never started. She got out of the truck, and watched as Nick unloaded the wheelchair. He opened the rear passenger door, scooped the little girl into his arms and set her in the chair.

"I don't mind waiting out here," Erin said quickly, when he started for the house.

Nick paused and frowned at her. "You may as well come in. Mrs. Thornsberry will want to meet you."

"Mrs. Thornsberry?"

"Stephanie's nanny."

"Oh." Feeling awkward, Erin fell into step beside him as he wheeled his daughter toward the front door. Being a cop in Logan Falls was definitely going to be different than being a cop in Chicago.

The farmhouse was set on several acres. A big maple tree shaded the side yard. Beyond, a small barn with Dutch doors and an adjacent circular pen stood as if in testimony that Bandito had once led a very busy life. The fact that Stephanie no longer rode her horse bothered Erin. Childhood was precious and she didn't want to see this little girl miss out on any of it.

The front door swung open. "Nick? Stephanie? For goodness sakes, what are you doing home this time of day?" A short, round woman with graying hair and bifocals greeted them with a maternal smile. "Do we have a guest?"

"This is Deputy McNeal." Nick looked at Erin. "This is Mrs. Thornsberry."

Relief trembled through Erin that Stephanie and Nick had a strong woman in their lives. Mrs. Thornsberry wasn't a day under seventy, but Erin could tell the instant they made eye contact that the woman was anything but frail. Mrs. Thornsberry might be only five feet tall, but behind that gentle facade and favorite-aunt voice lay the compassion and wisdom of a grandmother, and the iron will of a five-star general.

"I'm pleased to meet you," Erin said sincerely.

Mrs. Thornsberry's gaze was unwavering. "Welcome to Logan Falls." Her eyes settled on Stephanie, and she frowned. "Why aren't you in school, young lady?"

The little girl concentrated on her sneakers.

Nick squeezed his daughter's shoulder. "She showed up at the station. Said she wanted to ride with me today."

"Cutting class again, more like it." Though the nanny's voice was firm, Erin didn't miss the thinly concealed sympathy in it. Mrs. Thornsberry swung the door wide and walked back into the house. "Grab Steph's book bag, will you?" she said over her shoulder to Erin.

Erin lifted the book bag from Stephanie's lap.

Nick shot her a small, covert smile. "I think you passed inspection."

"I take it that's good?" Erin said.

"Took Hector a few tries."

Without waiting for a response, he pushed the wheelchair over the custom-made threshold. Erin followed with the book bag.

The first thing she noticed was the aroma of home-cooked food. Frank Sinatra's silky voice filled the air. The furniture was older, but of fine quality. A comfortable-looking sofa and matching easy chair sat in a grouping across from a console TV. In the dining room beyond, a sewing machine and bundles of fabric covered the length of the dinner table.

"You caught me mending," Mrs. Thornsberry said. "Stephanie, I expect you have homework." Without missing a beat she turned to Nick and looked at him over her bifocals. "Shall I call the principal this time, or do you want to?"

He grimaced. "I took care of it."

"Are you going to take her back to school?" the nanny asked.

"She wants to stay home today," he said.

"She's missed an awful lot this year."

"I'll see about getting her assignments, Em."

Nodding, Mrs. Thornsberry turned to Erin. "Would you like coffee?"

"We can't stay," Nick interjected.

"Oh, come now, Chief. Don't put me off. I just made a fresh pot of that hazelnut stuff."

"I don't have any homework," Stephanie complained.

Mrs. Thornsberry clucked her tongue. "Then why don't you go into your room and write me a nice letter explaining why you left school without permission again, honey?"

Stephanie rolled her eyes.

"I'll bring you some milk and cookies in a bit," the nanny finished. "Do you take cream, Deputy McNeal?"

The woman switched topics so effortlessly, it took Erin a moment to realize she was speaking to her. "Call me Erin," she said. "Cream would be fine. Thank you."

Stephanie turned her wheelchair and started down the hall. Something warm jumped in Erin's chest when Nick followed, stooping to kiss his daughter's cheek. "Do as Mrs. T. asks, Steph," he said softly. "I'll be home in time for dinner."

The little girl looked at him from beneath long lashes. "Will you teach me how to play chess tonight?"

"You already know how to play chess." He touched her

cheek with his knuckles. "You beat the pants off me last time."

She grinned. "I'll let you win."

"Deal." Nick held out his hand, and she gave him a high five.

"'Kay." The little girl wheeled toward her room.

Erin couldn't help but feel she'd intruded on a private moment, but she hadn't been able to look away. The grim-faced police chief who'd berated her just half an hour earlier seemed incongruous with the father who dealt so gently with this child.

She was still staring when he turned toward her. The warmth in her chest spread when his gaze met hers. For an instant, she thought she'd never seen a man look so sad.

"Hell of a way for you to spend your first morning on the job," he said.

"It's okay," she replied, realizing the situation was probably just as uncomfortable for him.

"I should tell you up front that most of my deputies have picked Stephanie up at one time or another." He grimaced. "She's been cutting school. Most times, I'm around. But if I'm not, I expect whoever's on duty to drive her home."

"I'll be happy to drive her home when you're not around."

"Steph's a good kid. She's just going through a tough time right now."

"How old is she?"

"She'll be nine on Saturday."

Erin didn't have any idea what kind of birthday gift a nine-year-old girl would want, but knew she wanted to get her something. Anything to bring some joy—no matter how minute—into that little girl's life.

"How long has she been cutting school?" she asked.

"About a year."

Remembering he didn't wear a ring, she said, "Divorce is tough on kids, but they're amazingly resilient."

His jaw tightened, but he didn't look away. "I'm a widower."

The shadow in his eyes came and went so quickly, Erin wasn't sure she'd seen it at all. Appalled by her blunder, she cringed. "I'm sorry. I just assumed—"

"It's a common assumption. Don't sweat it."

Considering Nick was a widower, Stephanie's behavior took on a whole new light. A pang went through Erin when she thought of her own mother, and how lonely a young girl could be growing up without one.

"Here's your coffee."

Erin looked up, relieved to see Mrs. Thornsberry coming from the kitchen with a tray. The coffee smelled like heaven.

"Thank you," she said, accepting her cup.

"Did you invite Erin to Stephanie's party on Saturday, Chief?" the nanny asked.

Nick shot the older woman a warning look over the rim of his cup. "No."

Judging from his expression, Erin deduced he wasn't necessarily glad the nanny had brought up the subject. Erin couldn't blame him, after the way she'd reacted to his daughter's wheelchair. Besides, she didn't know any of them well enough to expect to get invited to a party. Vowing not to take it personally, she moved to let him off the hook. "I'll probably be tied up unpacking—"

"Nonsense," Mrs. Thornsberry said. "It will be a good opportunity for you to get to know Stephanie and Nick. Hector will be here, too. We'd like you to come—"

"She's going to be on duty, Em," Nick interjected.

Mrs. Thornsberry barely spared him a glance. "Well, maybe you can stop in for a piece of cake after your shift."

Nick's cell phone chirped. Murmuring a quick apology, he set his cup on the dining room table, tugged the phone from his pocket and answered with a curt utterance of his name.

''When?'' he asked sharply.

His tone caught Erin's attention, and she set her own cup on the table.

''I'll be right there.'' Shoving the phone back into his pocket, he turned to Erin. ''We've got an emergency call.''

Linda Castillo

When he pulled elusively away. 'Nick—"

By placing caution and discretion aside, Nick knew she was right.

On the table, a half-finished cup of coffee grows cold. Eyes harsh, Nick stared. "Would you accept my answer if . . ."

Chapter 3

Nick sprinted to the truck and jerked open the door. Emergency calls didn't come often, but when they did, he took them very seriously. Sliding behind the wheel, he snatched up the radio mike. "What do you have, dispatch?"

Vaguely, he was aware of Erin settling into the passenger seat beside him, strands of hair streaming out of her bun. Hell of a thing for him to be thinking about when he should have his mind on the voice coming over the mike.

"Code three at the Brass Rail Saloon," the dispatcher's voice said. "Robbery in progress."

"That's the second time in two weeks. Who called it in?"

"Passerby saw a white male in a blue shirt kick in the front door."

"Well, that's real subtle." He started the Suburban and slammed it into gear. Dust and gravel spewed into the air as he sped down the driveway. "Put out a call to the sheriff's office," he barked into the mike. "Tell Hector to put on his vest and get over there, too. No one goes inside. I'm on my way." Once on the highway, he flipped on his emergency lights, no siren, and floored the accelerator.

"Juvenile delinquents?" Erin asked. "Domestic disputes?"

He looked over to see her strapping on her seat belt. Her cheeks were flushed, her eyes wide and alert. She looked excited. He wasn't sure that was a good sign. "Same place got hit last week," he said. "Patrick doesn't make his bank drops as often as he should. He lost over two thousand dollars. The perp carried a cannon."

"Are we going to go in?" she asked.

"I'm going to assess the situation."

"They could be gone by the time—"

"I'll go in if I think it's warranted."

"I'll cover you."

"I want you to stay in the truck." He whipped the vehicle around a corner at breakneck speed. "I want this low-key. No one gets hurt."

"You might need me to back you—"

"This isn't Chicago, McNeal."

"Last I heard perps with guns weren't limited to Chicago."

He glanced away from his driving and glared at her. He could almost feel the excitement coming off her. Uneasiness swirled in his gut. "If you've got something to prove, I suggest you do it elsewhere."

"I'm sure this will come as a shock, but I know what I'm doing."

"Why don't you prove it by following my orders?"

Nick ran the traffic light at Main Street. He'd wondered when her ego would enter the picture. He wondered what he was going to do about it. Damn, he didn't need this headache.

The Brass Rail Saloon was at the end of the block. He pulled into the side lot of the adjacent building, out of sight. Dust billowed as the truck came to a halt. "Stay put,

McNeal,'' he snapped. Pulling his revolver from his holster, he shoved open the door and hit the ground running.

The initial burst of adrenaline had kicked through Erin's veins the instant she heard the call come over the police radio. Now, as she watched Nick sprint across the parking lot toward the rear of the bar, she struggled to keep her frustration in check.

If you've got something to prove, I suggest you do it elsewhere.

That he'd ordered her to stay in the truck stung. She told herself he'd misjudged her. Just because she wasn't afraid to jump into a fray didn't mean she was overzealous. She merely liked police work. That heady rush that came with danger. The euphoria that followed an arrest that had been successful because of skill and police know-how. Nick didn't know her well enough to make blanket assumptions. She didn't have anything to prove—not to herself, certainly not to Nick Ryan.

Frustration choked her as she watched him disappear around the rear of the building. "Oh, this is just peachy," she muttered.

In her peripheral vision, she saw a car turn into the front lot. Not a sheriff's department vehicle, but an old Ford with wide tires and a loud engine. Erin held her breath as the vehicle stopped directly in front of the bar. The driver got out and looked around. He was the size of a bull and just as mean looking. An alarm jangled in her head when she spotted the butt of a pistol sticking out of the waistband of his jeans.

She told herself it was tension that had her hands shaking. But she knew intimately the many faces of fear. The heady rush of blood. The jitter of nerves. The coppery taste at the back of her throat.

It took her all of two seconds to realize she wasn't going to sit in the truck when there was an armed suspect in plain sight. Slipping her gun from her holster, she unlatched the door and stepped out of the vehicle. Adrenaline hummed through her muscles as she jogged to the building and pressed herself against the brick exterior. Except for the old Ford, the lot was empty. Nick was nowhere in sight.

Sticking close to the brick, she eased along the side of the building. The gun felt heavy in her hand. Sweat slicked her palm. Her heart beat out of control in her chest. She felt the flashback coming on and fought it, but the images rushed at her, playing in her mind's eye like a bad video. Danny lying bound and helpless. The blast of a gunshot. The smell of gunpowder and fear. Pain so sharp it took her breath.

Panting rapidly, sweating beneath her uniform, she shook off the memory, steeling herself against the deluge of emotions that followed. Not now. Not when Nick was relying on her. She couldn't let him down. Not like she had Danny.

Movement at the front of the tavern drew her attention. A second man had emerged from the front door carrying a brown paper bag. Nick's words rang in the back of her mind. She wondered if his orders included letting two armed suspects get away. On the other hand, two armed men against a single cop wasn't something she felt comfortable with—especially knowing what had happened the last time she'd faced those odds. She didn't have backup. She was still a probationary officer. She hadn't even been issued cuffs yet. But there was no way she could stand back and let them walk away with a bagful of money and the knowledge that they'd outsmarted two small-town cops. Erin figured she didn't have a choice but to stop them.

Heart pounding, she sidled toward the front of the building and waited. When the men started for the car, she stepped into view. "Police!" she shouted. "Drop your weapons!"

The driver spun, glaring at her with rodent-like eyes. He snarled a profanity, making no move to relinquish his gun.

"Drop it!" she shouted. "Now!"

He shot a look at his partner and muttered something, but Erin couldn't hear him over the thunder of blood in her ears.

"I didn't do nothin'," he spat.

"Drop the gun!"

He tossed the weapon on the gravel. "You're makin' a mistake."

"Get your hands where I can see them," she snapped.

Lips peeled back in a snarl, he raised his hands.

"Get on the ground! Facedown! Now!"

Muttering an oath, the man got down on his knees, then eased himself facedown on the gravel. Erin edged closer and kicked his gun away.

She turned to the second man. "You, too. On the ground."

He sneered at her. "What you gonna do if I decide I'd rather take my chances with you, lady cop?"

"Make you regret it," she said.

Never taking his eyes from her, he lowered himself to the ground and lay flat.

Relief vibrated through her. Lowering her weapon, she stepped back. Where in the world was Nick? The sheriff's deputies? Where was Hector? Without backup, there wasn't much she could do to subdue these men if one of them decided to test her. Cursing under her breath, she glanced over her shoulder toward the building where the Suburban was parked.

An instant later a hard body slammed into her with the force of a Mack truck. Erin's breath left her lungs in a rush. Dread and surprise punched her with sickening force when she realized her mistake. Oh, God, the second man. He'd moved so quickly she hadn't even heard him get up.

The impact of his body sent her reeling. Her legs tangled with his and she sprawled on her back, her head cracking against the ground, hard enough to make her see stars. A dozen scenarios raced through her mind, the worst being that he would get control of her weapon. She couldn't let that happen. If Nick showed up now... No, she couldn't bear the thought of another cop getting hurt because of her.

Feeling his weight come down on top of her, Erin lashed out with her boots. She smelled sweat. Bad breath. Her right heel connected with his shin. He cursed and grabbed for her gun. She gripped her pistol tightly, tried to wedge it between them, but he was stronger, and no matter how much training she'd had she couldn't keep him from over-powering her. Refusing to acquiesce, she wrenched free and rolled. Out of the corner of her eye, she saw the other man scramble to his feet. Her attacker made it to his knees, but Erin was quicker. She dropped into a shooter's stance. "Halt! Police officer! I'll shoot!"

Both men froze. The second man raised his hands. "I'm cool."

The driver glared at Erin. She was shaken, but by the looks of him, so was he. For several seconds they just stood there, breathing hard, staring at each other.

"Get on the ground!" Nick's deadly calm voice snapped through the air like a gunshot.

Relief poured through Erin with such force that for a moment she didn't trust her legs. Blinking the sweat from her eyes, she looked over her shoulder and saw Nick stand-ing less than ten feet away, his weapon leveled on the man who'd attacked her. Hector Price and two deputies from the sheriff's department flanked him.

"We'll take it from here, McNeal," Nick growled.

Trembling violently with the aftereffects of high adren-aline, Erin turned away and holstered her revolver. She heard the sound of handcuffs clicking into place. In the distance, someone recited the Miranda rights. Nausea roiled in her gut. Well, *that* hadn't ever happened before. Afraid she was going to be sick, she started for Nick's truck. It was silly, but she didn't want him to see her like this. Not when she was raw and shaking and still scared half out of her wits.

"McNeal."

Her nerves jumped at the anger in his voice. What in the world did he have to be mad about? She'd just bagged two armed suspects for him, and probably saved his neck to boot.

"In a minute, Chief." She'd intended for her voice to come out stronger, but it shook like plucked guitar wire.

"Now, McNeal."

Sighing, she stopped but didn't turn around. Just a few more seconds and she'd be steadier. She drew a deep breath, willing her hands to stop shaking. Behind her, she heard Nick approach. Her nerves wound tighter. Lord, why couldn't he give her a moment to pull herself together?

Slowly, she turned, realizing how it must feel to face a firing squad. "I can see from the look on your face you're not going to thank me," she said.

His eyes raked her like sharp instruments as he drew nearer. "Are you hurt?"

"I'm fine."

He stopped less than a foot away—so close she could feel the heat of his anger mingling with the heady aroma of male sweat and aftershave. By the looks of him, she was in for a major butt-chewing.

"Good," he snapped. "Because you've got two minutes to explain to me what the hell you were trying to pull."

Nick wasn't sure if he wanted to throttle her on the spot or embrace her for bringing down two suspects twice her size single-handedly—even if she had done it by the skin of her teeth. He wasn't sure of a whole hell of a lot at the moment because his own adrenaline had yet to ebb. The only thing he knew for certain was that she looked shaken and vulnerable and tough all at once, and he wasn't sure which facet ticked him off the most. To top things off she looked way too good in that blue uniform with her flushed cheeks and red-brown hair tumbling over her shoulders like strands of tangled silk.

"I told you to stay in the truck, not to take down two armed suspects like some kind of female Rambo," he said.

"I wasn't going to let two thugs get away in the name of decorum. I'm sorry if that ticks you off, Chief, but I don't operate that way."

"You're a probationary officer, McNeal. You haven't even filled out your forms and already you're jumping on suspects."

"I backed you up."

"You disobeyed a direct order."

"I used my best judgment," she retorted. "Where in the hell were *you?*"

"The guy in the rear kept me a little too busy to baby-sit you."

Anger flared in her eyes. "I'm a trained police officer."

"You're a loose cannon."

Her wince was almost imperceptible, but Nick saw it and knew he'd hit a nerve. His temper wouldn't let him back off. "I won't have you taking risks and endangering yourself and everyone else because you have something to prove."

"Maybe you'd rather Steph lost her other parent in there!"

The words struck him dead center. Nick felt himself recoil. Emotionally. Physically. He tried to squelch the reaction. He didn't want her to know she'd struck a geyser of guilt than ran a mile deep in his heart. He didn't want her to know he felt the depth of that guilt every time he looked at his daughter and saw that wheelchair.

"Don't push me, McNeal," he warned. "You'll lose."

She blinked, as if her own words had shocked her. "I'm sorry. That was uncalled for—"

"Frank warned me about that killer instinct of yours."

"I didn't mean—"

"Sure you did. Don't lessen the impact by trying to take it back now. Go for the jugular. That's your style, isn't it?"

"You don't have a clue what my style is."

He tried to curb the anger building in his chest, but it had already gotten away from him. He knew he was over-reacting, but this woman had a way of pushing all the wrong buttons. "You like stepping a little too close to the edge, don't you, McNeal?"

"I don't know what you're talking about."

"You got a death wish or something?" he asked.

"That's a ridiculous question."

"Maybe you're trying to make up for something you did or didn't do in that warehouse six months ago."

Her entire body jolted. "Go to hell."

Before he realized he was going to touch her, Nick took her arm and guided her to the truck, away from the curious eyes of his deputies and the crowd that had gathered in front of the bar. "You weren't straight with me."

"I never lied to you."

"Don't spew semantics at me. Your head being screwed up over that shooting was bad enough. But your little penchant for taking risks is a disaster waiting to happen."

"You're overreacting—"

"I always overreact when someone lies to me. It ticks me off!"

"I reacted like a cop, Nick. I did what I thought was right."

"Did you even bother to think that we didn't have backup? That you didn't have cuffs? That the suspect could have had another weapon in his freaking sock? That a civilian could have been shot in that scuffle?"

"Of course I did! I considered all those things."

Nick stopped when they reached the truck. "When I tell you to do something, you'd better do it. And I mean down to the letter. You got that?"

"I disarmed two dangerous suspects. I backed you up."

"You walked into a dangerous situation half-cocked. If we're going to work together, I've got to be able to trust you, McNeal. As it is now, I don't. I sure as hell don't trust your judgment."

"My judgment bagged two suspects—"

"You're not ready to return to the field!" Nick's hands shook with rage. He was unreasonably angry. He saw it clearly, but couldn't stop. He didn't want to analyze the reaction she'd unleashed inside him. He didn't want to name its source. But it hit close to home, and he felt it like a bad piece of meat stuck in his gullet, rotting him from the inside out.

He stared at her, the only sounds coming from their labored breathing and the traffic on Commerce Street. The realization of what she was struck him like a blow. Erin was a risk taker. An adrenaline junkie. After the way she'd put herself on the line just now, he wouldn't be far off the mark if he called her reckless. Nick couldn't deal with recklessness. Not after Rita. Not after the havoc her death had wreaked on his life and the life of his little girl.

Releasing Erin abruptly, he stepped back, stunned by the depth of his rage. "I want a full report on my desk, then I want you to clean out your locker."

"What's that supposed to mean?"

"You're a smart woman. You figure it out."

Incredulity filled her gaze. "You can't fire me."

"I just did."

She stared at him, her breasts rising and falling beneath her uniform as she sucked in oxygen.

"If you want to get yourself killed, do it on someone else's time, because I won't have any part in it. I don't care whose niece you are." Without giving her time to respond, he turned on his heel and stalked away.

Erin was still shaking when she opened the door to her apartment and let herself in. She told herself she wasn't upset. That Nick's harsh words hadn't shaken her. That she didn't need this job. She sure didn't need Nick Ryan.

She couldn't believe he'd fired her!

He'd overreacted, she assured herself. He couldn't handle the reality of a woman in a dangerous job. Just like Assistant District Attorney Warren Prentice all those years ago—a man Erin had given her heart to, only to have him hand it back to her in shreds because he couldn't accept her being a cop. The parallel left a rank taste in her mouth.

Nick had no right to come down on her so hard just because she'd taken a calculated risk. But deep down inside Erin wondered if there was a kernel of truth behind his accusations. If the underlying guilt she'd been fighting for months had compelled her to act recklessly.

I won't have you taking risks and endangering yourself and everyone else because you have something to prove.

His words rang uncomfortably in her ears as she stepped into the foyer and shut the door behind her. Closing her eyes, she leaned against the jamb and told herself he was wrong. She didn't have anything to prove. She didn't have anything to feel guilty about. Damn Nick Ryan and his Freudian cop psychology, anyway.

Shoving away from the door, she walked into the living room, trying not to notice the empty moving boxes, or the aches that had crept into her bones since her scuffle with the suspect an hour ago. He hadn't looked that big, but he'd hit her solidly. Not hard enough to cause serious injury, but hard enough to hurt, and she was feeling every single bruise.

Packing could wait, she decided. A handful of aspirin and a hot bath couldn't. If she didn't soak now, by morning she'd be too stiff to move. And she definitely needed to be able to move, since she'd be lugging boxes to her car and driving back to Chicago.

Gingerly, she unbuckled her holster and dropped it on

the coffee table, then toed off her boots. Lowering herself onto the sofa, she eased off her uniform shirt and checked the scrape that ran from her elbow to the top of her shoulder. The abrasion was shallow, but deep enough to ooze blood and burn like the dickens.

''Just what you need, McNeal,'' she muttered. ''Another scar.'' Ignoring the pain, she unclasped her bra and slipped it off, draping it over the arm of the sofa. She should have let Nick take the hit. Maybe he would appreciate her a little more if he knew that tussle had cost her a couple of layers of skin.

Pulling off her belt, she rose and headed toward the bathroom. She turned on the tap, tossed an herbal cube under the spout and stepped out of her uniform trousers. The aroma of lavender filled the air. She breathed in deeply and felt herself begin to relax. Adjusting the water temperature, she stepped into the tub and sank down to her chin. The abrasions protested, the cut on her knee came to life, but her muscles purred. Sighing, she closed her eyes. After surviving the proverbial day from hell, she knew it didn't get any better than this.

She'd just begun to drift when the doorbell blasted. Erin opened her eyes and blew out a sigh. Who would be at her door when she didn't know a soul in the entire town aside from Nick and Hector?

The doorbell rang again.

''Just a minute!'' Climbing out of the tub, she toweled off quickly, shrugged into her robe and padded barefoot to the front door. She looked through the peephole and felt her heart nose-dive into her stomach. Nick stood on the other side, still in uniform, looking as grim as when she'd left him.

An odd sense of uncertainty jolted her. Turning away, she pressed her hand to her stomach to keep it from jumping. She glanced down at her robe. It was modest enough, but not something she wanted to be seen in by her boss—

well, ex-boss in this case—especially since he'd probably stopped by to give her an exit interview she wouldn't soon forget.

"McNeal, I know you're in there," he said through the door. "We need to talk."

Determined to get through this with as much dignity as possible, she put her hand on the knob. She didn't give a hoot if the almighty Nick Ryan saw her in her robe. If he had a problem with that, to hell with him.

She took two deep breaths and yanked open the door.

Erin McNeal wrapped in a terry cloth robe and smelling like freshly cut flowers was the last thing Nick expected. He stood frozen, shocked speechless by her transformation from cop to woman. All the while his brain floundered to form a coherent thought that didn't have to do with soft skin or curves he knew better than to notice. He may as well have been splitting atoms for all the success he had.

She'd pinned her hair on top of her head, and dark, wet wisps clung to the creamy flesh of her neck. His eyes wanted to roam lower, but he quickly stopped the urge. He preferred not to know this woman had the kind of cleavage that could drive a man slowly insane. He held her gaze, vaguely aware of the color rising in her cheeks, feeling that same heat burn the back of his neck. He refused to think about what the sight of all those curves was doing to the rest of his body.

"I didn't mean to get you out of the tub," he said.

Her throat quivered when she swallowed. "I thought about not answering the door, but figured we ought to get this over with."

"If this is a bad time, I can come back."

She cocked her head. "If the robe bothers you, Chief, I can throw on my jeans. I think the outcome of this meeting will be the same either way."

Nick didn't want to think about her in jeans. Not when

she was standing before him with water glistening on her flesh and his body humming with interest. After three years, why did it have to be *this* woman to remind him that he was still a man, with a man's needs?

"I'll make this short, then," he said.

"I'd appreciate that. Do you want to come in?"

"I'd rather not."

"Look, if you came here to finish firing me, the least you can do is come in."

"I didn't come here to fire you."

She narrowed her eyes. "I thought you were under the impression that I was a loose cannon and a threat to the inhabitants of Logan Falls and mankind in general."

Nick couldn't help smiling. He dropped his gaze, only to find himself staring at her toes. Unfortunately, they were every bit as sexy as the rest of her.

He raised his eyes to hers. "You weren't the only one who overreacted today."

"Is that your idea of an apology?"

"Save it, McNeal. I may have overreacted, but you were out of line. I won't tolerate it." Hearing movement behind him, Nick turned to see Mrs. Newman, the town gossip, pause outside the adjacent apartment with a bag of groceries in her arms. She gazed at him for a moment, then peered into Erin's apartment with unconcealed curiosity. Terrific, he thought, this ought to get the tongues wagging.

Erin noticed and moved aside. "Do you want to come in?"

"I can't stay." He stepped into her apartment, realizing belatedly it would have been smarter for him to have handled the situation over the phone.

Turning away, Erin walked into the living room. Nick followed, struggling not to feel awkward—failing miserably—and trying in vain not to notice the curve of her backside beneath that robe.

The apartment was small, with high windows and gauzy

curtains that ushered in ribbons of yellow sunlight. The furniture was outdated, but functional. Nothing frilly for Erin McNeal. No photographs or mementos. It didn't surprise him she wasn't neat. She'd barely unpacked, and already there was a hint of feminine clutter. A towel tossed haphazardly over a box. Her boots lay next to the sofa, where she'd kicked them off. He spotted her holster on the coffee table. Then his gaze stopped on the scrap of lace draped over the sofa arm. Her bra, Nick realized. The same one he'd noticed through her blouse the first time he'd seen her. No, he thought, coming here hadn't been a good idea at all.

"Would you like something to drink?"

He tore his gaze from the bra. For crying out loud, what was the matter with him? He wasn't some sex-starved teenager who went brain dead over a woman's bra. Especially when that particular woman was off-limits for too many reasons to count—let alone that she worked for him.

"No." He cleared his throat and shifted his weight from one foot to the other to accommodate the rush of blood to his groin. "Look, Erin, it's not unusual for a cop to lose his or her confidence after they've been involved in a shooting."

"I haven't lost my confidence."

"You're trying too hard. You're trying to get something back that takes time. You're rushing it, and you're going to end up getting hurt. I don't want that to happen."

She flushed.

"I still need a deputy," he said. "The last thing you need is another termination on your record. What do you say we give this another shot?"

"If you're asking me to stay, the answer is yes."

Nick grimaced, not sure if that was what he'd wanted to hear. But he could live with it. "I'm going to level with you, McNeal. I've got my doubts about whether or not you're ready to come back to the field. I'm going to extend your probationary period—''

''I'm ready.''

''You went against my direct orders this morning. You took a stupid risk that could have turned out much worse. I won't tolerate recklessness of any kind from you or any of my other deputies. Are you clear on that?''

She gazed levelly at him. ''Those two men were armed and dangerous. I wasn't about to let them get away.''

''One of those suspects came within an inch of gaining control of your weapon. You could have turned a robbery into a hostage situation, or worse.''

''I know you're having a hard time believing this,'' she said, ''but I happen to be a professional. I'm good at—''

''So I've heard. That's not what's in question here.''

''But my judgment is?''

''Knowing what I do about you personally, and your past, I'd be a fool not to question your judgment after today.''

''I see.'' Her chin went up, and Nick knew he'd scored a direct hit. ''You're convinced I'm skewed because of the shooting.''

''Are you?'' he asked.

''You've already decided, so why does it matter what I think?''

''Look, Erin, cops react to shootings in different ways. Some retreat. Some quit. Some turn to alcohol. Look at the divorce rate. The suicide rate, for God's sake. You don't have to make up for something you did or didn't do in that warehouse.''

She crossed her arms in front of her. ''Now you're a shrink.''

''I'm the chief of police—and your superior. I have a right to know where your head is. My life—or my deputies' lives—depends on that.''

''I'm sure this isn't what you want to hear, Chief, but if

I were faced with the same situation right now, I'd react the same way.''

''That's fine. I'll assign you accordingly.''

Wariness flooded her gaze. ''What's that supposed to mean?''

''That means you've got the school crosswalks until I think you're ready for something with more responsibility.''

Nick didn't miss the minute jolt that traveled through her body when he hit her with the news. Couldn't she see he was doing this for her own good?

Heat flashed in her eyes. ''That's not fair.''

''Life isn't fair, McNeal. You of all people ought to know that.''

''You can't do this.''

''I just did. I suggest you get used to it. That's your assignment indefinitely. I'll decide when to change it. When I think you've come to terms with whatever's eating at you, we'll talk about it again.''

''I *have* come to terms.''

''Prove it to me.''

''You've no right penalizing me—''

''This has nothing to do with you personally. All I'm concerned about is your well-being and the safety of your fellow deputies and the citizens of this town. Take it or leave it. It's your call.''

Nick held his breath as he watched the inner struggle tear at her. He saw temper and restraint and a hefty dose of ego pulling her in different directions. He knew she wanted to tell him to go take a flying leap, but he also knew she had too much to lose to succumb to the urge.

After a moment, she squared her shoulders and looked him dead in the eye. ''All right, Chief. Have it your way. I'll take the assignment.''

Inwardly, he smiled. She'd passed the test. Restraint had

won. They might just get through this, after all. "Good," he said.

"That doesn't mean I have to like it." Frowning, she raised her hand to push a tendril of hair away from her face.

"Police work isn't about what we…" His voice trailed off when he spotted the nasty abrasion on her elbow. "What happened to your arm?"

She glanced down at her elbow. "I must have done it in the scuffle. It's no big deal."

Nick knew better than to touch her. He'd been around the block a few too many times to court the kind of trouble a touch would rouse. He didn't like the way he was reacting to her as it was. He knew if he touched her, if he discovered her skin was as soft and warm and fragrant as he imagined, it would only make dealing with her even more complex.

"You ought to have it looked at," he said stiffly.

"It's just a scratch. I'll take care of it."

She was so close he could smell the clean scent of her hair. The warm, flowery aroma of whatever she'd put in the tub. A droplet of water clung to a dark lock of hair behind her ear. Nick stared at it, wondering what it would be like to catch that droplet with his tongue and get a taste of the tender flesh beneath. He wondered if she would taste as good as she smelled.

He fought another rush of blood to his groin. He denied it. He cursed it. But his body betrayed his intellect, reacting with an intensity that left him incredulous and disturbed. Now wasn't the time. This wasn't the place. And Erin McNeal wasn't the woman.

Some inner warning told him to get out of there. Nick stepped back, breaking the spell he had absolutely no desire to explore. Shaken by his reaction, he turned away and started toward the door.

He felt her stare on his back, but he didn't stop. He knew he was running. But he didn't care. As long as he didn't let this woman get to him, he'd be fine. He'd had his fill of risk takers. A few months in Logan Falls, then she'd go back to Chicago, and Nick would be rid of her. He might like the way she looked; under different circumstances he might have liked to get her in his bed. But Erin McNeal was the last woman he wanted to care about.

He left without looking back.

Chapter 4

The Midwestern sky shimmered Caribbean blue as Erin strapped on her fluorescent orange vest and left her cruiser. Dressed in full uniform and toting her safety flag, she crossed the street to the Logan Falls Elementary School, prepared to drudge through an assignment she had absolutely no desire to complete.

Let Nick Ryan have his petty revenge, she told herself as she unrolled the flag and watched the school zone caution lights blink on. At least he'd changed his mind about firing her. That was something to be thankful for, since she was pretty much starting at ground zero when it came to her career. She'd get her problems ironed out here in Logan Falls. If all went as planned, in a few months she'd be ready to move on to a bigger town. Maybe even Chicago—if Frank would have her back.

A school bus breezed by. Erin mustered a smile and waved, taking her place at the crosswalk. A light breeze rustled the leaves of the maples and elms along Commerce Street. The drone of a lawn mower sounded in the distance.

She breathed in the scent of fresh-cut grass and felt a grow-ing sense of contentment as Logan Falls's version of rush hour commenced. Mothers dressed in housecoats dropped their children curbside. The older kids gathered on the side-walk where Erin stood, their soft voices and laughter sounding as foreign to her as another language.

After nine years of working some of Chicago's toughest neighborhoods, Erin had thought crosswalk duty would bore her to tears. Oddly, she found herself enjoying the simplicity of the assignment, watching the children, the fierce hugs of mothers as they bade them goodbye, and experiencing firsthand the wholesome goodness of small-town life.

She had expected to be disappointed by the lack of ac-tion, by the absence of the danger that had sustained her for so many years. To her surprise, she found herself feeling protective of the townspeople she'd sworn to serve and pro-tect. She felt as if she'd stepped back in time, to a place that was pure and simple, a place where people obeyed the laws of the land because they believed in doing the right thing.

Within the first hour of her shift, she'd chatted with the principal, Mrs. Helmsley, about the new bleachers she wanted to have built on the north side of the track. Erin had helped a fourth-grade student find her lost notebook. Her self-discipline had caved in when a first grader with missing front teeth asked her if she wanted to buy a grossly overpriced chocolate bar. Erin ended up buying two.

A far cry from Chicago, she mused, remembering too many other children whose worlds had been ravaged by poverty, their minds and bodies polluted by crack or heroin or whatever other poison they'd been unlucky enough to get introduced to. As she stood at the crosswalk, watching the scene unfold like something out of a Norman Rockwell painting, she wondered if Nick realized how lucky he was.

It wasn't the first time she'd thought of her surly boss

that morning. The fact of the matter was he'd been on her mind a lot during the last day. She told herself it was because she was annoyed with him. Not only about the way he'd handled the situation at the Brass Rail Saloon, but because he'd assigned her the school crosswalk.

But she couldn't deny there was more to her preoccupation with him than mere annoyance. As much as she didn't want to admit it, she'd found herself reacting to him on a level that had nothing to do with police work—and everything to do with good old-fashioned physical attraction.

Erin wasn't a sexual creature by nature. Having worked in a male-dominated profession her entire adult life, she was accustomed to working with men. She'd had dozens of male friends over the years, had always considered herself immune to hormones and the problems they presented—at least until now.

She tried to analyze her feelings—the quickening of her heart, her wet palms, the sensation of not being able to get enough oxygen into her lungs—and wanted to blame the symptoms on the fact that he went out of his way to make things difficult for her. But Erin was honest enough with herself to acknowledge the truth. He was an attractive man—and her body had taken notice. She didn't want to deal with it. Wouldn't, in fact, since he'd already proved to her he couldn't handle the prospect of a woman in a dangerous profession. Not that she was looking for his approval, or anything else, for that matter.

Regardless of his flaws, she couldn't deny Nick Ryan was something to look at with those coffee-brown eyes, his brooding demeanor and unforgiving mouth. He disturbed her. He infuriated her. He appealed to her more than any man had in too many years to count.

But even more disturbing was the fact that her attraction to him didn't stop with the physical. The flash of emotion in his expression when he'd told her he was a widower, the anguish on his face when confronted with his daughter's pain. Something had shifted inside Erin when she saw that sad little girl transform him from hardened cop to lonely widower struggling to cope with a devastating situation. She knew firsthand the many faces of pain, and Nick Ryan had it etched into every feature. No matter how hard she'd tried to resist, that part of the man touched her deeply. So how was she supposed to deal with that?

"By ignoring it, of course," Erin muttered as she lowered her flag and crossed the street to a group of children. Traffic stopped, and she motioned to the children. "Okay, kids, it's safe to cross! Have fun at school today!"

Just because the chief of police was drop-dead gorgeous and had a human side to boot didn't mean she was going to act on some banal impulse and blow this job. Quite the contrary. Erin could handle her hormones—she always had. The fact that Nick didn't even *like* her would undoubtedly help. They had completely opposite philosophies on law enforcement. That should keep them on opposing sides long enough for her to get over this...fascination—if she could even call it that.

The group of children crossed the street behind Erin. "Don't forget to look both ways when crossing," she said over the din of young voices.

The children had just reached the other side when a little girl in a pink sweater dropped one of her papers. "My picture!" she exclaimed as the breeze picked it up and tumbled it along the pavement.

The traffic remained stopped, so Erin wasn't concerned. Thank goodness road rage didn't exist here in Logan Falls, she thought wryly. She raised the flag higher, making sure she had the attention of the driver in the first car. The young woman behind the wheel rolled her eyes and smiled.

Erin looked over her shoulder at the child. The little girl scrambled for the paper, catching it just a few feet away from Erin. "I got it!" she said.

The low roar of an engine drew Erin's attention. A dark sedan broke from the line of traffic several cars back. She saw a chrome grille. The sun glinting off a darkened windshield. Anger pumped through her that an impatient driver would endanger innocent school children.

She raised the flag and angrily motioned for the driver to pull over. The car picked up speed, the engine whining like a jet engine.

"What the—" Her anger turned quickly to disbelief when the driver cut the wheel and came straight for her. There was no time to react. Her only thought was that she couldn't let the little girl in the pink sweater get hurt.

Spinning, Erin grabbed the child's arm and shoved her. The engine whined. She dove. A scream pierced the air— her own—followed by the sound of steel against flesh. The impact spun her in midair. Pain jolted through her right hip. An instant later, the pavement rushed up, and she tumbled into darkness.

Nick's pulse was still hammering when he walked into the Parke County Hospital and headed toward the emergency room. He hated hospitals on principle. He hated this hospital in particular, since it was in this very same emergency room three years before that his life had been turned upside down by another woman who'd taken one too many risks—and paid the ultimate price.

He hadn't wanted to make the connection between Erin and Rita. He hadn't wanted to bridge that treacherous gap. But he could no longer deny what disturbed him so much about his new deputy. Aside from the fact that he was attracted to her beyond reason, Erin was a risk taker. He'd seen it on her résumé. He'd heard it in Frank's voice during the recommendation. Nick had experienced it firsthand the day before, when he'd watched her fight off a suspect twice her size.

Only he had been too caught up in denial to acknowledge

the truth about her. The pain was too great, or maybe he'd just buried it too deep.

Rita, the woman he'd loved more than life itself for thirteen years, had been a risk taker. She'd been impulsive. Careless. Rash. She'd died because of it, and taken something vital and precious from Nick in the process. His heart. His daughter's happiness. His own. He couldn't tolerate recklessness. Not as police chief. Not as a friend. Certainly not as anything more.

He wanted to blame Erin for getting herself hurt. He wanted to condemn her. Hell, he wanted to *fire* her. What had happened today seemed like as good a reason as any. He didn't care about being fair. He wanted to get her out of his life and rid himself of this insane attraction to her once and for all.

The problem was that Nick knew the incident hadn't been her fault. He'd spent the last two hours investigating the scene. Witness after damning witness had absolved Erin of wrongdoing. No, he thought bitterly, she hadn't been at fault. And even though she hadn't given so much as a thought to her own safety, he couldn't condemn her for saving that little girl's life.

The nurse at the station outside the emergency room doors looked up when Nick strode past, but she didn't try to stop him. He figured she'd seen his sour expression too many times to try to keep him out. He shoved open the doors and paused in time to hear a familiar female voice utter a curse. Something resembling relief flooded him. He told himself he wasn't unduly relieved to hear Erin cursing the on-call doctor. Of course, that didn't explain why his hands were still shaking.

Frowning, he stepped past the floor-to-ceiling curtain and into the fray of the emergency room. On his left, a woman held a crying child while a nurse applied drops to his ears. To his right a small boy in a baseball cap received stitches in his knee, initiating him into the Little League hall of fame. Nick scanned the room, his gaze seeking a blue uniform and a mass of silky red-brown hair.

His breath lodged in his throat when he spotted her. She was lying on a gurney, looking more annoyed than injured. A doctor in green scrubs hovered over her. The cold knot in Nick's gut slowly unraveled. She still wore her uniform pants, but her shirt had been replaced with a hospital gown. He tried not to notice the way the soft material lay against her breasts. He didn't want to see her as a woman—she was his deputy, for God's sake. He sure didn't like seeing her vulnerable, either. His need to protect was too strong. He didn't want anything to do with the lofty task of looking out for a woman who hadn't the good sense to do it herself.

She raised her head. Her body gave a little jerk when she spotted him. Uncertainty darkened her gaze. A tentative smile pulled at the corners of her mouth.

He walked slowly to the gurney, where the on-call doctor was putting in the last of four stitches in a nasty-looking gash at her temple.

"McNeal." Why was it that every time he spoke her name his voice sounded like a rusty nail being pried out of a petrified tree?

"I was wondering when you'd come by to fire me." She looked at her watch. "Two hours. You're slipping."

He stopped next to the gurney and frowned at her. Her hair had come loose from her bun and lay softly against the pillow. Nick repressed the urge to touch it, just to see how it felt between his fingers.

"Are you all right?" he asked.

"Once the doc stops sticking me with that blasted needle I'll be just fine," she grumbled.

Nick looked at the doctor. "I take it she's going to be okay?"

"She's mildly concussed," the doctor said, his eyes never leaving the small head wound he was stitching. "A few abrasions and contusions. A deep bruise on her hip that's going to be sore for a few days. This is the only wound that needed closing."

"Good thing she's got a hard head." Nick glanced down at her. "You should have known the car would win if you got into a game of chicken."

"I must have missed that day at the academy."

"You going to keep her overnight?" he asked the doctor.

The other man shook his head. "Not necessary. Her pupils are fine, CAT scan is normal. Wake her every two hours. Make sure she's lucid. Make sure she knows her name and the date."

Alarm fluttered in the back of Nick's brain. He looked down at Erin. "You got someone to look after you, McNeal?"

"No, but I can get someone to call—"

"Out of the question," the doctor interrupted. "Someone stays with her or I'll keep her here."

"I'm not staying here all night," she snapped.

Nick felt a moment of panic. If it were any of his other deputies lying on that gurney, he would volunteer for the job. But because it was Erin—a woman who elicited all the wrong responses from him—he found himself hesitating. He did *not* want to be in this position.

"I'm not staying," she repeated.

"I'll admit you," the doctor warned.

If the situation hadn't been so dire, Nick might have laughed. As it was, he figured he'd be lucky to get through this without doing something he was going to regret.

"I'll keep an eye on her," he said after a moment.

She shot him a startled look. "I don't think—"

"I've got to finish your afternoon shift, anyway," he argued, cutting in. "It's no big deal for me to stop by your apartment every couple of hours."

The doctor tied off the last stitch and shoved the stainless steel tray aside. "Okay, Deputy McNeal, let's sit you up and see how you do." The doctor placed his hand against her back and helped her to a sitting position. "Any dizziness?"

"No. My hip hurts."

"You can ice it when you get home. Headache?"

"No." Then she looked at Nick and frowned. "You're not going to give me a headache over this, are you, Chief?"

The doctor shot an amused look at Nick. "She's all yours, Chief Ryan. No restrictions other than for her to take the afternoon off. She can take over-the-counter medication for pain. Call me if she experiences blurred vision or confusion."

"Thanks, Doc," she muttered.

Nick watched him walk away, then turned his attention back to Erin. "You know, McNeal, I didn't think even *you* could get into trouble working the school crosswalk."

"Sorry to disappoint you, but the guy in the sedan didn't give me much choice." She sat up straighter.

Nick squelched the urge to reach out to her when she winced. "I guess not."

She glared at him. "This wasn't my fault."

"I didn't say it was."

"You were thinking it."

"Why don't you stop trying to figure out what I'm thinking and concentrate on uncrossing your eyes, so we can get out of here?"

"Careful, or you're going to say something nice and throw me into a tailspin." She touched the bandage on her temple. "Did you catch the guy?"

"No." He frowned, hating the pale cast to her lips and the shadows beneath her eyes. "A couple of witnesses saw the car. A dark sedan with Illinois plates. That's all I've got. Do you feel up to answering a few questions?"

"Of course I do." Grimacing, she swung her legs over the side of the gurney. "Ouch."

Nick reached for her when she swayed, his fingers closing around her biceps. "I can't believe you lied to the doc about being dizzy."

"I'm *not* dizzy."

"If I hadn't been standing here you would have taken a dive right off that gurney."

"Would not."

"Damn, you're stubborn." Keenly aware of the soft flesh beneath his fingers, and the clean scent of her hair wreaking havoc on his concentration, he stepped back. "Ah, McNeal, what am I going to do with you?"

"Just don't yell at me. I do have a headache, and if you start yelling it's only going to get worse."

Nick didn't want to look into her eyes. He didn't want to see the vulnerability; he didn't like the way it made him feel. But he knew eye contact was inevitable. Once their gazes met, he couldn't look away. "Gladys Delaney wanted me to thank you for saving her daughter's life."

"The little girl in the pink sweater," Erin murmured.

"You got her out of the way just in time. Half the town saw you do it."

Erin looked away, made a show of scraping a speck of dirt from her trousers. "I'm glad she's all right."

Nick wondered why she found it difficult to accept praise. Some sixth sense told him now wasn't the time to pursue it, but he would eventually. "Get dressed, and I'll take you home."

She glanced down at her hospital gown, looking flustered for a moment. "Uh…my shirt is behind you, on the chair."

Turning, he spotted the shirt, lifted it from the chair and found himself staring at her bra. Terrific. Carefully lifting the bit of lace, he handed the shirt and bra to her. "Here you go."

"Thanks. Turn around a second, will you?"

Nick faced the curtain, every sense honed on the rustle of clothing behind her. "I need to ask you about the dark sedan that hit you," he said.

"It was blue or gray. American make. Chrome grille. Tinted windows. Bumper was hard as hell. It's got an indentation of my hip on it. You can turn around."

Nick turned and felt his pulse spike at the sight of her in uniform with all that hair tumbling over her shoulders. His brain stalled for an instant, but he managed to hang on to his concentration by a thread. "Did you see the driver?"

"The sun was glaring off the windshield. I didn't see faces, but I think there were two people in the car." Gingerly, she put her feet on the floor and stood.

"Two people?" At first Nick had thought they were dealing with a drunk driver, but something niggled at him. The car had Illinois plates, for one thing. The time of day didn't sit right, either. "What's your take on it?"

Erin straightened, then leaned heavily against the gurney. "Oh, boy…"

Nick moved before he even realized he was going to. His left arm went around her waist. "Don't pass out on me, McNeal," he growled.

"I'm not going to pass out."

His next words died on his lips the instant he registered the feel of her in his arms. Curves and softness and the mysterious essence of woman wrapped around his brain and squeezed until he couldn't form a single coherent thought. The bustle of the emergency room faded until all he was aware of was Erin. The warmth of her body against his. The clean scent of her hair. The weight of her breast against his forearm. He fought the slow spiral of pleasure winding through his body. But he knew it was a losing battle.

"You're just what?" he said, easing her to arm's length. "Weak? Dizzy? Hardheaded?"

"Just a little nauseous. Watch your shoes."

"Terrific," he grumbled. "I've a mind to call the doctor in here and tell him to keep you."

"He said to expect nausea," she pointed out. "I just got up too fast. Give me a break, Chief, will you?"

Nick's heart was still beating too fast, and an odd mix of sexual awareness and self-recrimination sat in his gut like a hot stone. He'd been without sex too long, he told himself. That's all there was to it. He was going to have to do something about it before long. Stephanie's third-grade teacher, Lindsey Burns, was nice enough. Pretty, too, with blond hair and smiling blue eyes. So why hadn't he called her back after their one and only date?

"Think you can walk out of here without passing out on me?" he asked.

Erin shot him a cocky smile. "Try to keep me here."

Nick almost smiled, but he didn't give in to the urge. He didn't want to get too close to this woman. She had trouble written all over her in big red letters. He'd had his fill of trouble. "Let's go," he said, and tried not to think about what he was setting himself up for.

Erin slipped on the sleeveless nightgown and reached for her robe, trying in vain not to jar her aching head. So much for heroism, she thought grimly. If she wasn't in so much pain, she might be embarrassed, having Nick baby-sit her like this. As it was, her head hurt too much to care about anything except downing a handful of aspirin and falling into a soft bed in a dark room.

Pausing at her bedroom door, she took a deep, calming breath, then swung it open. Nick stood in the foyer, looking like a nervous date, his expression relaying the fact that he'd rather be anywhere else than in her apartment. His eyes flicked down the front of her, and Erin felt an uncomfortable tug of self-consciousness.

"You don't have to do this," she said, pulling the lapels of her robe more tightly together.

"I told the doc I would. You know as well as I do you don't ignore a concussion, McNeal."

She wanted to let him off the hook and get him out of there—he was obviously as uncomfortable with the situation as she was. But Erin figured his sense of responsibility—and his need to protect—was too strong for him to leave her alone.

"How's the head?" Shoving his hands into his pockets, he approached her.

"Feels kind of like the drum set my brother got for Christmas when we were kids. He was a Led Zeppelin fan." She walked to the sofa, trying not to notice the moving boxes or the clutter, telling herself she wasn't embarrassed that her apartment was a mess. It had been a mess the last time Nick was there. She told herself it didn't matter. She was a cop. Nick was a cop. All cops had messy apartments, didn't they?

"You're limping," he said.

"That's because I'm too proud to crawl."

One side of his mouth hiked into a half smile. "Where's your aspirin?"

She risked a look at him, and almost wished she hadn't. His penetrating stare invariably unnerved her. What was it about those dark eyes of his that left her feeling stripped bare? Like he could look right through her and see all the things she spent so much time and energy trying to conceal.

"There's a bottle in the bathroom medicine cabinet," she replied.

He started toward the bathroom.

Erin breathed a sigh of relief at his departure—even if it was only for a minute. She felt unsettled. Jittery. She tried to blame it on the fact that she was still shaken up from the incident at the school, but she knew that wasn't the only reason. She didn't want to admit the possibility that Nick was the source of her uneasiness. If she acknowledged the problem, it would become real, and she would have to deal with it.

Being attracted to her boss was a mistake she had no

intention of making. Especially when he was the kind of man who couldn't handle the idea of a woman with a dangerous career—like police work.

Warren Prentice had taught her all she ever needed to know about the overprotective-male syndrome. After the way Nick had reacted to her taking down those two suspects, it appeared he had a terminal case. She refused to give up her career for the likes of a man or the fallacy of happily ever after. Erin McNeal simply knew better.

"Here you go."

She jumped at the sound of Nick's voice and turned to find him standing behind her with two aspirin in one hand, a glass of water in the other. She drew a breath, caught the scent of his aftershave and felt an instant of vertigo she knew had nothing to do with the bump on her head. Good heavens, standing next to this man was like riding a tidal wave.

Shaking off the sensation, she reached for the aspirin and tossed them back. His fingers brushed hers when she took the glass of water. "Thanks."

"Why don't you sit down?"

"Actually, I was thinking of taking a nap as soon as you take off."

Amusement played in his eyes. "Trying to get rid of me?"

"Letting you off the hook, actually."

One side of his mouth curved. "I appreciate that. But to be perfectly honest with you, I'd like to ask you a few more questions before I make my big escape. If you're feeling up to it, that is."

Something in the way he said it caught her cop's attention, reminding her that a serious crime had been committed, and she was right in the center of it. Common ground at last. No longer feeling quite as awkward, she sank down on the sofa. "Shoot."

Nick took the chair across from her. "Felony assault with

a motor vehicle isn't the kind of crime typical to Logan Falls.'' Leaning forward, he put his elbows on his knees and gave her a canny look. ''What's your take on this?''

''An impatient driver. Road rage.'' She shrugged. ''Maybe he was drunk.''

''He? The driver was male?''

''I think so. I only saw a silhouette, but it didn't look female.''

''You mentioned a passenger earlier. Are you sure?''

She nodded. ''I'm sure.''

''We don't get much road rage here in Logan Falls.'' Nick grimaced. ''I talked to several witnesses at the scene. Every one of them said it seemed deliberate. Do you agree?''

''Maybe. I don't know. It happened pretty fast.''

''Is there any reason why someone might want to hurt you?''

The question made the hairs at her nape stand on end. ''What are you getting at?''

Leaning back in the chair, he gazed steadily at her. ''You were a cop for nine years. Cops make enemies. Some criminals have long memories.''

Erin knew the possibility was there—she'd busted plenty of thugs over the years, and made plenty of enemies back in Chicago. She couldn't rule out the possibility, but she didn't believe it, either. ''The thought of some thug bent on revenge following me all the way to Logan Falls just to run me down at a school crosswalk—and miss—seems unlikely, Nick.''

''Probably. Still, it's something we have to consider. From now on I want you to be aware of what's going on around you at all times—''

''I'm always aware of my surroundings,'' she interrupted. ''I'm a cop, remember?''

''You're not invincible. You know better than to not take this seriously.''

"I'll take it seriously. But I still think you're overreacting."

"Just covering all my bases."

"Contrary to what you might think of me, I know how to take care of myself."

"That's why you've got a knot the size of Texas on your head."

Irritated that he was undermining her efforts to convince him that she could handle herself, Erin rose abruptly. A curse escaped her when the throbbing pain in her head sent her back down. "Ouch. This is annoying."

Nick was by her side instantly. His hand hovered over her shoulder, but he didn't touch her. "I should have told the doc to keep you," he growled, dropping his hands to his sides.

"Just a headache," she said. "As long as I don't start speaking in tongues or tell you I've been picked up by space aliens, I should be okay. Think you could fish another aspirin out of that bottle?"

Frowning, he picked up the bottle, tapped an aspirin into his palm and passed it to her. "If the headache isn't gone in twenty minutes, I'm taking you back to the hospital."

"Like that's going to happen." Erin took the aspirin and drank half the water. In her peripheral vision she saw Nick head toward the hall. Relieved, she set the water on the coffee table, leaned against the sofa back and closed her eyes.

"Okay, McNeal, I want you on your back."

She opened one eye to see him lugging her pillow and comforter from her bedroom. "You're kidding, right?"

He looked down at the comforter in his arms. "Do I look like I'm kidding?" He set the pillow against the sofa arm. "Lie down."

"But—"

"That's an order."

Rolling her eyes to hide her discomfiture, she eased the

robe from her shoulders. "Do you do this for all your deputies, Chief?"

"Only the ones who take on a ton of steel moving at forty miles an hour."

Easing the robe out from under her, she leaned back into the pillow, realizing just how badly she needed to lie down. "You know, Chief, you wouldn't make a bad nurse."

"Don't push your luck." Taking her robe, he draped the comforter over her. "You were damn lucky today. This could have turned out—" Nick froze, his eyes narrowing on her exposed right shoulder.

Erin realized her mistake an instant too late.

The scar.

Oh, God. He'd seen the scar.

Chapter 5

The sight of the scar froze him in place. It started on the outside edge of her shoulder and ran in a jagged line toward her collarbone. Not the work of a surgeon, but the violent action of a bullet and an emergency room doctor's frantic efforts to stop serious bleeding, he imagined.

Nick saw her stiffen, realizing belatedly he'd been staring. She jerked the comforter up to her chin, gripping the edge tightly. What was the matter with him? She was obviously self-conscious about the scar. He was only making things worse by sticking around and prolonging this. But he couldn't take back what he'd seen. As a fellow cop—and her superior—he damn well couldn't refrain from asking her about it.

He raised his gaze to hers, seeing far too clearly what she was feeling. "That's not the first time I've seen a scar from a bullet wound, McNeal."

"It's the first time you've seen mine." She looked away, no longer the tough-talking cop with a war story, but a woman faced with a disfiguring scar. "It's ugly."

The contrast between woman and cop struck him. As he watched the emotions scroll across her features, a fierce protectiveness rose up inside him. He couldn't let her statement stand, he realized. Even if the scar was bad, he wanted her to know it didn't detract from her in any way. Not as a cop. Certainly not as a woman. "It's nothing to be ashamed of," he said gently.

"How do you know?" she snapped.

The ice in her voice surprised him. Nick pulled in a breath, realizing for the first time the depth of her emotional wounds—and how little he knew about that night.

"You want to tell me what you mean by that?" he asked.

A dry smile curved her mouth. "Are you asking as my superior who needs to gauge my frame of mind, or as a friend, Nick?"

"How about a little of both?"

Sighing, she pulled one of the throw pillows against her and frowned at him. "I got hit the same night Danny Perrine was shot. Bullets do a hell of a number on flesh. End of story."

"I already know that, but why the guilt? Why won't you talk to me?"

She shot him a dark look. "I don't want to get into this. Not now."

"We work together. I need to be able to trust you. I deserve an explanation."

She looked down at her hands, stilled them by smoothing the pillowcase. "I froze up, Nick. I screwed up and got hit. I let Danny Perrine take a hit. How do you expect me to feel?"

"Frank said it wasn't your fault."

"According to Internal Affairs. But they weren't there."

"You feel differently?"

"If I'd reacted differently, Danny wouldn't be stuck in a wheelchair with a bullet in his spine. I'd still have my career. And I wouldn't be here in Logan Falls trying to get back everything I've lost. Does that answer your question?"

"It doesn't tell me why you feel responsible."

"I made a mistake. It's as stupid and simple as that."

"So you're trying to make up for your so-called mistake by putting yourself on the line? By taking unnecessary risks? We both know that's not going to change what happened."

"I'm dealing with this the only way I know how."

"What are you trying to prove, McNeal?"

Her eyes heated. "I don't have anything to prove."

"I think you do. Only it's not to me or Frank or Internal Affairs. You've got something to prove to yourself."

"You don't know me as well as you think you do."

"You're getting defensive," he pointed out.

"Damn right I am."

"Look, I know what it's like to feel responsible for something, even when you're not."

"You know, Nick, I've had just about all the cop psychoanalysis I can take." Jerking her robe off the back of the sofa, Erin rose abruptly and headed toward the kitchen, pulling it over her shoulders as she went.

Nick knew better than to go after her. She looked shaky at best. He didn't want to take a chance of her falling apart on him. But he'd reached the point where he needed answers about what had happened that night. "You can't let the guilt eat at you. You can't keep blaming yourself. You're going to end up getting hurt."

"What happened today wasn't my fault."

"I'm not talking about today."

At the kitchen entry, Erin spun to face him. "Wouldn't you be a little disturbed if you were responsible for putting your partner in a wheelchair? For ending a man's career? Wouldn't you feel a little guilty if he hated you so much he couldn't look you in the eye? That his wife couldn't keep the bitterness out of her voice when you called to check on him? That the only reason you continue to put yourself through it is because you feel so guilty you can't stand it? His kids look at me like I'm the devil incarnate, Nick. How would you feel?''

He crossed the space between them. ''Maybe I'd feel guilty. But I don't think I'd be blaming myself when I'd been cleared by a bunch of veteran cops who know the ropes.''

''I walked into a dangerous situation that night with one goal in mind—to make that bust no matter what the cost. I didn't consider the possibility that someone might get hurt. I didn't think about Danny. Or his wife. Or his two kids.''

''A cop can't be effective if he dwells on—''

''I froze up! I didn't react until both of us were down.''

''Why did you hesitate, McNeal?''

She blinked at him as if the question had stunned her. ''The shooter…he was just a kid….''

Another piece of the puzzle fell into place. ''You're not the only cop who's ever hesitated for that reason,'' he said.

''Look, Nick, I know you're trying to help. But you're not. I don't need your amateur-shrink bull. I'm handling this.''

He snorted. ''I can tell.''

Her nostrils flared. ''Spare me the sarcasm. This is hard enough without you—''

''All I'm trying to tell you is that you don't have to deal with this alone.''

''I'm the one who got my partner shot. Who else should deal with it but me?''

''Danny Perrine wasn't the only one who got shot that night, McNeal. You took a bullet, too. You risked your life and you've got the scar to prove it. Have you ever stopped to think that maybe *both* of you are alive today because of you?''

''That sounds really good, Chief. It even makes me

sound heroic. But we both know that's not how it really happened, don't we?''

Nick raked his fingers through his hair in frustration. ''You know, McNeal, if we were anywhere but Logan Falls, I'd yank you off the street so fast you'd get whiplash.''

A short laugh broke from her throat. ''Careful, my confidence is soaring.''

''You're not helping matters.''

''Leave it alone, Nick. I don't want to discuss this with you. I don't want to—''

''Deal with it? Level with me? Be truthful with yourself?''

''How about all of the above?''

''You'd rather wallow in guilt? Funny, but I didn't peg you as the wallowing type.''

''That's not fair. None of this has been easy to take.''

''Ah, there you go again, talking about fair. Haven't you learned by now that fair doesn't enter the picture when it comes to real life?''

''I'm not going to have this conversation with you.''

She turned to walk into the kitchen, but Nick stopped her by grasping her biceps and turning her toward him. Couldn't she see he was trying to help her?

''You're a good cop,'' he said. ''You're gutsy and brave, with a bright future. But you've got to give yourself time to heal. You've got to accept the reality that sometimes bad things happen that we can't control.'' The statement made him grimace when he thought of his own life, and the harsh reality of the last three years. But he knew now wasn't the time to address his own demons. Not when it was so much easier to address hers.

When she turned to him, Nick noticed the tears shimmering in her eyes. He stared at her, stricken, torn between the need to comfort and the stark, sudden need for distance.

''Don't cry on me now, McNeal.''

"I'm *not* crying." She tried to turn away to keep him from seeing her tears, but he held her fast.

"You're part of my team," he said. "Your safety is my responsibility. I'm not the enemy here. Do you understand?"

"I can't talk about this right now." She swiped at her tears with the back of her hand. "Let go of me so I can humiliate myself in peace."

He knew better than to let her tears get to him. But to see the strong woman before him reduced to a trembling bundle of raw emotions tore his judgment to shreds. He didn't like thinking of the physical pain the bullet had caused her or the mental anguish she'd lived with because of it. He sure didn't want to think about the way he was reacting to her. Not physically. Certainly not emotionally.

Damning the consequences, he reached for her. "Come here."

She resisted for an instant, then took a tentative step toward him. "Nick—"

"Shh." Her body came against his like a soft, liquid jolt of electricity. Pleasure wound slowly through him. The smell of clean hair and womanly flesh penetrated his resistance. Softness and heat tore down his defenses. Awareness spiraled through him when her arms went around his neck.

Nick closed his eyes against sensations and feelings he had absolutely no desire to examine. Not with Erin McNeal. A woman who could destroy every wall, every line of defense he'd built in the last three years. But the warmth of her body heated his blood. The softness of her breasts against his chest tormented him in ways he'd forgotten existed.

She murmured something against his shoulder, but Nick didn't comprehend the words. All he could think of was that he wanted her closer, wanted to feel her against him, caution be damned.

Helpless to keep himself from it, he tightened his arms

around her. Awareness and pleasure melded into need. His hand went to the back of her head. He stroked her hair. It felt like silk beneath his fingertips, and he marveled at the texture. Tilting his head, he pressed his cheek against her hair and took in her scent. Sweet. Mysterious. Titillating.

Arousal flared hot and deep in his groin. Need ate away at his resistance until it was little more than an annoyance he crushed with a single blow. All he could think of was that he wanted her body closer to his. His mouth against hers. Her flesh beneath his hands.

She sighed, and her body went fluid in his arms. His lips brushed against her temple. She shifted closer. Sensation crashed over him. Powerful. Shocking. He rode the wave, absorbing her essence, trying in vain to keep from falling into a crevasse he might not ever be able to climb out of.

Erin told herself it was just a hug. A comforting embrace given to her by a fellow cop who understood what she was going through. But she knew that wasn't the truth. And she wasn't brave enough to admit just how good it felt to be cocooned in his arms. Or how solid and arousing his body felt against hers. It had been so long since anyone had held her. Since a man had held her. Since she'd let anyone get close enough.

His hands skimmed down her back, and a shiver swept the length of her. She felt his lips against her temple. The warmth of his breath on her cheek. Her body tingled where he touched her. Warm. Reassuring. More erotic than a kiss. An alarm clanged somewhere in the back of her mind, but she silenced it. This embrace didn't mean anything to either of them, she assured herself. They were cops, bound by understanding and what might one day become friendship. It wouldn't hurt for him to hold her. It wouldn't hurt for her to partake in this one, tiny mistake.

He shifted closer. For the first time she noticed his quickened breath. The fact that his hands had grown restless, his body hard against hers. Erin knew she should pull away and stop this before things got out of hand. She knew better than to give in to something as foolish as the need to be held, or, heaven forbid, the desire to feel his mouth against hers. Not this man. Not now. But it seemed as if Nick had cast some kind of spell over her. She couldn't move. Couldn't bring herself to deprive her body of his, even if it was the smart thing to do.

She closed her eyes, fighting the sexual tug, but her body betrayed her, and there was nothing she could do to stop it. She felt his hands at her sides, moving upward, brushing the outer curves of her breasts. Another shiver trembled through her. Then he was cupping her face, his dark eyes seeking hers. She knew what would happen next, and she dreaded it even as anticipation rampaged through her.

His mouth met hers with devastating gentleness that sent an explosion of desire through her body. A pang settled low in her belly, and she felt herself become aroused. The sheer power of her reaction stunned her, sent a spark of panic to a brain that didn't want to believe she'd met a man who could kiss her with such utter perfection that she forgot who she was. Surely not this small-town cop who, as a man, could never deal with her career.

Breaking the kiss, Erin moved away from him and stumbled back.

Nick let her go, dropping his arms to his sides. ''I'm sorry,'' he muttered.

Embarrassment flooded her as the realization of what had just happened hit her full force. She stared at him, taking in the tightly clenched jaw, the knowledge darkening his eyes, all the while painfully aware that her body wanted more.

''I shouldn't have done that—''

''I shouldn't have let it happen,'' she said simultaneously.

''I'm your superior, for God's sake.'' Turning away, he

faced the window and stared down at the street below. "I know better than to—"

"We made a mistake," Erin interjected. "We'll deal with it like adults."

His expression was hard when he turned back to her. "Will we?"

"Yes." She was still breathless, could still feel the pressure of his mouth on hers, the need crawling inside her.

"I was out of line," he said. "You were vulnerable—"

"I'm *not* vulnerable."

Lowering his head, Nick cursed. "This can't happen again."

"It won't," she assured him, but her mind was still floundering. "I was shaken up. Let's not make this any more complicated than it needs to be."

He shot her a stony look that told her he wasn't buying it. Then, turning abruptly, he started for the door. "Go to bed, McNeal. I'll send Mrs. Thornsberry to stay with you tonight."

Erin wanted to argue, but she knew better. She didn't want Nick to come back. Not when her heart was still pounding and her lips tingled with the feel of his mouth against hers. Lowering herself to the sofa, she watched him walk out the door, wondering how in the world she was going to handle working for a man who made her lose control every time he touched her.

Nick had always prided himself on control. That's what made it so impossible to believe he'd just gone against every shred of intelligence he'd amassed over the last thirty-eight years, and kissed Erin McNeal. His deputy, for Pete's sake! A woman with a wild streak that ran right down the center of what was probably a very pretty back. What was the matter with him, reacting like an oversexed schoolboy, when he was grown man with a man's responsibilities?

But Nick knew that kiss wasn't the worst of it. He'd wanted her with the kind of urgency he hadn't felt for…too long to acknowledge. If she hadn't pulled away, he wouldn't have stopped. Not with one kiss. Not even with two. How the hell was he going to handle this?

"Damn you, Frank," he murmured.

Pausing at his truck, he risked a glance at the window of her second-floor apartment. The lights were still on. He was still aroused, and the frustration pounding in his groin annoyed him no end.

Gritting his teeth, he unlocked the truck door and slid inside. He'd have to be careful in the coming weeks. As much as he didn't want to admit it, maybe he was more vulnerable than he'd thought. Not emotionally, he assured himself, but physically. After all, a man's needs could be shoved aside for only so long. Nick needed female companionship. Stephanie would eventually get used to the idea of having a woman around. Maybe a woman would help fill the void in both their lives.

What Nick *didn't* need was Erin McNeal. Just because she made him hot around the collar didn't mean she was right for him. She was exactly the kind of woman he wouldn't bring into Stephanie's life. His little girl had already been hurt once by a reckless adult. He'd rip out his own heart before he'd let that happen again.

It struck him then that Erin was the first woman he'd kissed since Rita's death. That it hadn't been a chaste kiss disturbed him and made him realize he'd taken a step into yet uncharted territory.

Unexpectedly, the old, familiar pain stirred deep in his chest, the wound so newly healed that it still bled when probed. Nick rode the waves of pain, surprised by their force after three long years. The grief still cut him on occasion. Rita's death had taken something vital out of him, bits and pieces that could never be replaced. Nick had vowed the day he buried her that he would never again put himself through the agony of loving someone.

Shoving thoughts of Rita ruthlessly aside, he muttered an oath, his voice sounding low and rough in the silence of his truck. Erin McNeal was off-limits. Not only to protect himself, but to protect Stephanie. After what had happened today, Nick knew with the utter certainty of a man who'd already experienced hell that Erin would hurt them both if he allowed it. No matter how much he wanted her, no matter how much he liked the way she looked, or respected her as a police officer, he could never allow himself to care.

Slamming the truck into gear, he pulled onto the street and started for home. No, he assured himself, he didn't care about Erin. She didn't need him looking out for her. If she wanted to self-destruct, that was her business.

Hopefully, he would be able to talk Mrs. Thornsberry into sitting with her tonight. Nick knew it was a cop-out, but he wasn't up to it—even if Erin was one of his deputies. The fact of the matter was he wasn't the only one who hadn't been prepared for that kiss. He'd seen the shock on Erin's face as well. Another reason stacked on top of a dozen others to keep his distance. The more successful he was at avoiding her, he decided, the better off they'd both be in the long run.

Chapter 6

Erin didn't want to think about the kiss. She didn't want to deal with the reality that in the instant Nick's mouth had been pressed against hers the world had melted away and nothing existed except the moment between them. The ramifications of that line of thinking were too dangerous—even for a risk taker like herself. To acknowledge that he'd been on her mind every waking hour since was to admit she was susceptible to him. That she'd wanted him to kiss her. That she wanted him to kiss her again.

She refused to believe any of those things.

Erin figured she was getting pretty good at denial.

As she left the town limits and drove toward his house, she told herself the only reason she was going to Stephanie's party was for the little girl's sake. She might be a difficult child, but considering the hand she'd been dealt—namely the death of her mother and a devastating spinal injury—Erin couldn't blame her. She couldn't ignore her birthday. Steph needed every ounce of kindness the adults around her could give.

Erin knew it would only make things worse if she alienated herself from Nick. He might have the wrong idea about her, and they might have different philosophies on police work and law enforcement in general. They'd definitely made a mistake with the embrace and that fateful kiss. But he was still her boss, and this job was too important to blow because of something as silly as a kiss. Come hell or high water, she was going to make it work.

Just because she'd barely seen him in the last week didn't mean that encounter had affected their professional relationship. It didn't mean he was avoiding her. Or that she couldn't look him in the eye. They were adults, she told herself for the hundredth time. They could handle this. Dammit, *she* could handle it, even if he couldn't.

Shoving thoughts of Nick aside, she looked down at the wrapped package on the passenger seat beside her and smiled. It had taken her most of the day yesterday—her day off—and a trip to Chicago, but she'd finally found the perfect gift for Stephanie. A veil of satisfaction settled over her; she couldn't wait to see that little girl smile.

Five minutes later, she pulled into the driveway and parked next to Nick's Suburban. Though it was early evening, she'd expected to see kids playing on the swing set or shooting baskets in the hoop by the garage. But the yard was deserted. Bandito grazed contentedly near the fence, swatting flies with a tail that was a little too long, a little too tangled. There were no laughing children. No games of hide-and-seek. No adults lounging in lawn chairs. Beside Nick's Suburban and Mrs. Thornsberry's old Buick, the only other car there was Hector's.

Lifting the package, she got out of the cruiser and made her way to the front door. She told herself she wasn't nervous about seeing Nick. She wasn't here to see him, though the fact that she would was inevitable. Still, the thought of facing him after the kiss they'd shared made her palms sweat.

She told herself it was silly to get nervous over a friendly embrace that had gotten out of hand. This was a kid's birthday party, for goodness sake. Erin was on her dinner hour and only had about forty-five minutes before she had to get back to her shift. Enough time, she mused, to give Stephanie her gift and grab that piece of cake Mrs. Thornsberry had promised. And maybe even show Nick she wasn't avoiding him—since that kiss obviously hadn't meant a thing to either of them.

Wiping her damp palms on her uniform slacks, Erin rang the bell. Her heart stopped dead in her chest when the man in question opened the door. She'd never seen Nick out of uniform, and the sight of him made her feel light-headed. It didn't surprise her that he looked even better in faded jeans. The black Polo shirt he wore made his eyes look darker. She wondered if he was one of those people whose eyes changed with their moods.

For several long seconds she stood silently, praying he didn't see the color she felt rising in her cheeks. "Hi," she said, hefting the package. "I wanted to bring this by."

"McNeal," he acknowledged finally, eyeing the package. "How's the head?"

"Still pretty hard."

He didn't smile, but Erin saw the flash of amusement in his dark eyes. "Good thing, I guess, all things considered."

The silence built for a moment. He made no move to invite her inside. Feeling awkward, she looked down at her boots.

"You were scheduled to work tonight," he said.

She'd tried to convince herself his decision to schedule her for work didn't have anything to do with the fact that he didn't want to see her. Of course, she wasn't at all concerned about that. Just because Hector's car was in the driveway didn't mean she should be invited to the party, too, did it?

"I'm on my dinner hour," she said quickly. "I've only

got a few minutes.'' Not knowing what else to say or do, she shoved the package at him. ''I wanted to make sure Stephanie got this.''

He took the box. ''Uh...thanks. I'll make sure she gets it.''

''Great.''

Erin told herself she wasn't disappointed that he wasn't going to invite her inside. That she hadn't wanted to see Stephanie's eyes light up. Or see Nick smile. She'd only known them a little over a week. It wasn't like she was a friend he would invite to his daughter's birthday party. Still, the sinking sensation in the pit of her stomach was acute.

''Oh, Erin!''

She jumped at the sound of Mrs. Thornsberry's voice, and watched the woman approach. ''I'm so glad you came. I had to fight off Hector to save you a piece of cake. I hope you like German chocolate.''

Nick frowned. ''She's on duty, Em.''

''For heaven's sake, there aren't any rules against police officers indulging in birthday cake while on duty.'' Mrs. Thornsberry smiled sweetly at Erin. ''There's a big piece with your name on it in the kitchen.''

Erin returned the smile, torn between not wanting to irritate Nick and appeasing the nanny. She'd wanted to give Stephanie the gift herself, but he seemed adamantly opposed to her staying. ''Thanks, Mrs. Thornsberry, but—''

''Nick, where are your manners?'' the older woman scolded. ''Aren't you going to invite her in?''

Nick shot the woman a dark look.

''For goodness sakes, she's got time for a piece of cake.'' Giving him an annoyed glance over her shoulder, Mrs. Thornsberry headed for the living room.

Erin's discomfort grew. Nick obviously wasn't happy to see her. It was clear he didn't want her there. Glancing back at her cruiser, she took a step back. ''I've got to get back—''

"It's all right." He opened the door wider and stepped aside. "Come on in."

"I didn't mean to intrude."

His gaze locked with hers. Erin felt stripped bare by the power behind it. She'd never had a difficult time with eye contact, but Nick's gaze was so intense she couldn't hold it.

"I figured we probably couldn't avoid each other much longer," he said in a low voice.

She looked anywhere but into those dark, dangerous eyes of his. "I wasn't—"

"Avoidance probably isn't a good strategy, anyway, considering we work together."

Heat suffused her cheeks. Something warm and jumpy fluttered in her chest when images of the kiss came to her unbidden. The feel of his mouth against hers. The way he'd wrapped her in his arms. The hardness of his body as he pulled her close.

She wanted to say something flippant, maybe just to prove to him that blasted kiss hadn't affected her in the least, but the power of speech seemed to have left her. She stepped past him, and every nerve ending in her body went on alert when the tangy essence of his aftershave curled around her brain. The memory of the kiss sharpened, expanded, until it filled her with a longing she wanted desperately to deny.

Nick motioned toward the hall. "I appreciate you bringing a gift. It wasn't necessary, but I'm sure Steph will like it."

Feeling breathless and off-kilter, Erin started down the hall, wishing she'd heeded her own common sense and brought the gift by when Nick wasn't home.

They reached the living room a moment later. Hector nodded a greeting from his place on the sofa. Mrs. Thornsberry looked on from the kitchen doorway. Steph sat in her wheelchair in the center of the room, surrounded by crumpled wrapping paper and assorted gifts.

"Hi, Steph," Erin said. "Happy birthday."

"Thanks."

Her heart melted when the little girl smiled. Such a pretty smile. Too bad she didn't do it more often.

"Dad got me a new easel for sketching," she said. "Want to see my new pad?"

"Sure." Erin took the pad from her, feeling inept, since she didn't know a thing about sketching, and opened it to feel the texture of the paper. "Very nice. What do you sketch?"

"Sometimes I sketch Bandito. Sometimes my mom, but I'm not very good at faces, so I mostly just make stuff up. I'm pretty good at evening gowns and dresses, too."

"Ah, a budding clothes designer," Erin said.

Pride jumped into the little girl's eyes, and her grin widened. "My dad says I'm going to give Liz Claiborne a run for her money."

"I don't doubt it." Erin handed her the sketch pad. "Maybe you could show me your drawings sometime."

"'Kay."

Mrs. Thornsberry took Erin's gift from Nick and set it on Stephanie's lap. The little girl picked up the box and shook it. "Sure is big."

Leaning against the wall with his arms folded, Nick smiled at his daughter, the first genuine smile Erin had seen since she'd walked in.

"Have at it, honeybunch." His gaze met Erin's, the smile he'd given his daughter still flirting with his mouth.

He had one of the nicest smiles she'd ever seen. Too bad he didn't use it more often. Disconcerted that she'd noticed something she shouldn't have, she looked away.

Stephanie stripped the paper from the box. Erin watched, anticipation building in her chest. The little girl's hands stilled. The crackle of wrapping paper stopped abruptly.

Dead silence fell over the room. Stephanie stared at the bright orange basketball, blinking as if someone had just played a cruel joke on her.

"It's a basketball," she said dully.

Erin's stomach went into a slow roll. Praying her carefully chosen gift didn't turn into a negative experience for the girl, she stepped forward. "I saw the hoop above the garage door outside and thought you might like to start playing again."

The little girl stared at Erin, her blue eyes wide with the kind of hurt Erin knew too well. She'd seen that look before; she'd felt it in her own heart a hundred times in the last several months. She knew intimately the harsh realities of shock and pain and betrayal. Her heart cramped in her chest when those bottomless blue eyes filled with tears.

"I can't play basketball anymore," Stephanie said in a small voice. "My legs…"

"Oh, honey, you can," Erin said gently. "You can take lessons if you want to. Disabled people play basketball and win marathons and do all sorts of fun things."

"I want to, but I can't." Stephanie looked at her father. "Why did she get this for me? I can't play anymore."

Erin's breath jammed in her throat. The pain struck with such force that she couldn't breathe. All she could do was press her hand to her breast and pray the little girl would understand. The last thing she wanted to do was hurt this child who had already been hurt so brutally.

"Oh, my," Mrs. Thornsberry said. "Steph, honey, I'm sure Erin didn't mean—"

"I can't play!" the girl cried. "I don't want it."

"But you *can* play, Steph," Erin said. "Honey, I'll teach you—"

"That's enough." Nick's voice cracked through the air like cold steel being snapped in half.

The words jerked Erin's gaze to his. His jaws were

clamped tight, his hands clenched at his sides. He glared at her, his eyes as hard and infinitely cold as glacial ice.

She stared, vaguely aware that the room had become as quiet as a tomb. Hector gaped at her as if she'd just pulled out her pistol and shot the chandelier off the ceiling. Mrs. Thornsberry made a show of gathering gift wrap off the floor.

Erin looked at Stephanie. "I'm sorry," she said helplessly.

Spinning the wheelchair, uttering a single, heart-wrenching cry, Stephanie fled from the room.

Mrs. Thornsberry and Nick started after her simultaneously, but the older woman stopped him. "Let me handle this one, Nick."

He halted, uncertainty etched into his features as he watched her disappear down the hall.

Erin felt physically ill. She hadn't even considered the possibility that the basketball would upset Stephanie. How could she have been so insensitive? Why had she expected that little girl to understand something no one had ever bothered to explain?

Erin's gaze swept to Nick's. She nearly winced at the anger she saw burning there. "I didn't mean to upset her," she said. "I didn't think—"

"That's your problem, McNeal," he snapped. "You don't think before you act."

Erin stepped back, hurt that she'd been so terribly misunderstood, angered that her judgment had been called into question once again by a man whose opinion was becoming increasingly important to her.

Erin didn't lose control of her emotions easily or break down in front of people at the drop of a hat. She'd learned the futility of tears at a very young age. But as she stood there taking in Nick's angry expression, thinking of how badly she'd hurt that little girl, tears threatened her dignity.

"I've got to get back to work." Turning abruptly, she started for the door.

"Wait a minute."

Erin didn't stop. She didn't trust her emotions not to betray her, and he was the last man on earth she wanted to break down in front of.

Letting herself out through the front door, she sucked in a breath of cool night air, thankful to be out of the house. When she reached the grass, she broke into a run.

The front door slammed behind her. Nick, she thought, and quickened her pace. When was she ever going to learn not to push the envelope in everything she did?

Blinded by the tears building behind her eyes, she stopped at her cruiser and fumbled for her keys.

"I'd like a word with you, McNeal."

She looked over her shoulder to see him crossing the lawn. Terrific. Here she was about to lose it, and he wanted a word with her. She had to hand it to him—the guy had great timing.

"I've got to get back to work," she said.

"It'll wait."

For an instant she was tempted to ignore him, and get in the car and drive away. Of course, she didn't. Erin had never been one to run away from her problems. So why did she feel the quiver of the fight-or-flight instinct every time Nick got near her?

She didn't turn to face him when he came up behind her and stopped. "You want to tell me what that was all about?" he demanded.

"I'm sorry," she said.

"Why don't you turn around and look at me?"

Unduly humiliated, she swiped at the tears with her sleeve. "I said I was sorry, Nick. What else do you want?"

"I'm just trying to understand you. I don't have a clue why you bought Steph that ball. Why don't you help me out?"

Slowly, Erin turned. Raising her chin, she met his gaze. "I gave her that basketball because I want her to know she's strong and capable and doesn't have to stop living just because she's in a wheelchair."

"She can barely stand, McNeal. How on earth is she supposed to play basketball?"

"It's called wheelchair basketball, Nick. Don't tell me you've never heard of it."

"She's not ready for that."

"How do you know?"

"Because I'm her father," he said. "I know what she's been through. I know what she can handle."

"She's ready, Nick. She'll eventually do it whether you're ready to accept it or not. She can do a lot of things you don't seem to be ready to accept. Once she realizes it, you'd better learn to deal with it, because she's not going to stop." The words came out in a rush. Harsh. Damning. So true her chest ached with the need to prove to him she was right.

His eyes narrowed. "You don't know what you're talking about."

"I spent two months coaching disabled children. Wheelchair basketball. Therapeutic horseback riding. Marathon racing. The kids love it. They *love* it! I've seen their faces light up. Their confidence bounce back. Their outlook on life improve dramatically." Shaken by her own words and the emotion barreling through her, Erin broke off. She'd said too much, she knew, but once the words had started flowing, she hadn't been able to stop.

Nick stared at her. "Stephanie is still adjusting. She's...fragile. Not only physically, but emotionally. I won't risk her getting hurt again."

"At what cost to her?"

His face darkened. "You're crossing a line you don't want to cross, McNeal."

"I'm good at crossing lines, Chief. That's what I do best. For future reference, you should keep that in mind."

"You're reckless not only with your physical safety but with that smart mouth of yours."

"You asked, Chief. I'm telling you what I think. You're smothering that child—"

"She needs to be protected."

"She needs to live her life to the fullest extent, risks be damned."

"Recklessness is what put her in that chair to begin with!" Nick moved toward her, his jaw set. "I won't let it happen again, so back off!"

His words and the anger behind them stopped her cold. Erin stood there trembling, breathing hard, wondering what Pandora's box of pain she'd opened inside him.

As if realizing he was clinging to control by little more than a thread, Nick turned away abruptly. Walking to the front of the car, he put his hands on the hood and lowered his head.

For several long minutes the only sound came from the chirping of crickets. Erin leaned against the car door, shaken, aware that her heart was beating too fast. She wanted to tell him about the weeks she'd spent doing volunteer work at the Quest Foundation, an agency that specialized in helping disabled children adjust. But he was so angry she wasn't sure it would make any difference.

Shoving away from the car, he straightened. Erin heard him sigh, then he approached her. "I'm sorry," he said.

"It's all right. This is none of my business—"

"I lost my temper. It's not the first time, and it's definitely not all right." He bit out an oath, then gave her a canny look. "Stephanie is everything to me, McNeal. Everything. I love her more than life. She's been through hell in the last three years. I don't want her hurt again. I'll do whatever it takes to keep that from happening."

His eyes were the color of midnight, and so tortured Erin

wanted to reach out and touch him, just to let him know he wasn't alone, even if she knew he wouldn't believe it.

"I know you only want what's best for her," she said.

"That includes keeping her safe."

"Nick, I didn't mean to overstep. I'm just..."

"Impulsive?" One side of his mouth hiked into a half smile.

"It's not the first time I've been accused of that." Erin let out the breath she'd been holding, relieved that he'd purposefully quelled the tension between them. "How did she end up in the wheelchair?"

Nick waited so long before answering that for a moment Erin thought he wouldn't answer at all. When he did, his voice was so low she had to lean forward to hear him.

"A car accident three years ago. My wife was killed. Stephanie received a spinal injury. She spent two weeks in intensive care."

He looked out across the lawn, into the darkness. Even in profile, Erin saw the tight clench of his jaw and the raw emotion in the depths of his eyes. Her heart went out to him as she watched him struggle for words.

"Two weeks later, I had to look into those innocent eyes of hers and tell her she might not ever walk again. That was one of the hardest things I've ever had to do." His laugh held no humor. "All she was worried about was whether or not she'd be able to take care of Bandito. That from a little girl who lived for basketball and horse shows, and who'd just lost her mother. Her courage humbles me."

"I'm sorry, Nick. I know that must have been tough." The words didn't seem adequate.

"Yeah, McNeal, me, too. She's a terrific kid."

"I know." Erin longed to reach out to him. To touch that strong jaw. Run her fingers over his shoulders until they were no longer rigid. To relax the clenching of his fists by taking his hands in hers. But she didn't do any of those things because she knew that wasn't what he needed.

His eyes met hers. Even under the cover of darkness, she felt exposed beneath that heady gaze. She wanted to tell him that disabled children could ride horses with the help of special equipment and adult spotters, but something told her now wasn't the time. His emotions were too close to the surface, and she knew he didn't want them prodded.

Neither of them spoke for several minutes. Erin gave him that time, knowing he needed it, not sure how she would react if the strong man she'd come to respect broke down. She wasn't sure she could trust herself to do the right thing if he did. The urge to touch him was too powerful, and at the moment she was feeling downright weak.

"Is there a possibility she could walk at some point in the future?" she asked.

"She's had two operations already. Her neurosurgeon seems optimistic."

"What about pain?"

"Thank God it's minor and can be controlled with anti-inflammatory drugs, for the most part," he said. "She has some feeling and a little strength in her left leg. But in the last six months, she's developed a rare post-traumatic condition called syringomyelia."

"One of the kids I worked with up in Chicago had the same condition. It's where a tumor forms at an injury site or surgical site, right?"

His gaze sharpened, and Erin knew he hadn't expected her to be familiar with the condition. "Most people haven't even heard of it."

"There's an operation—"

"Laminectomy and duraplasty." Nick grimaced. "The procedure's untested. Risky."

"What kind of risks?"

His mouth curved into that half smile again. "Ah, McNeal, you're getting really predictable."

"Best case scenario," she pressed.

"Best case, Stephanie would regain feeling in her legs

and be able to start physical therapy immediately. Worst case scenario is that the formation of scar tissue or further spinal cord damage could cause further paralysis. It could significantly lower her quality of life, possibly even her life expectancy. If we leave it be, she might eventually regain enough feeling to use a walker one day.''

Erin absorbed the words, wondering what she would do if faced with the same devastating dilemma. ''You're willing to settle for that?''

''I nearly lost her once.'' Nick looked across the driveway to where Bandito grazed next to the fence. ''I won't risk losing her again.''

Nick wasn't sure why he'd opened up to Erin. Maybe because he sensed she somehow understood, when most people couldn't. Maybe it was the fact that she, too, was no stranger to tragedy. Maybe that kinship was what kept bringing them together.

It had been a long time since he'd spoken to anyone about the accident that had turned his life—and his daughter's life—upside down. He didn't like to talk about the dark months that followed, preferring to keep that era of his life buried. He'd spent months grieving. The kind of black grief that came with the loss of a soul mate. Grief he'd kept bottled because he couldn't stand the thought of the poison inside him leaching out and affecting Stephanie.

Shoving thoughts of the past aside, Nick gazed at Erin. She leaned against the car, staring out across the lawn toward the pasture, where he could hear Bandito nipping the grass.

''I'm sorry I came down on you so hard,'' he said. ''That was uncalled for.''

''You know, Chief, I'm starting to get used to you yelling at me.''

She elbowed him lightly, and he knew she was trying to

dispel the high emotion of just a few minutes earlier. For that, he found himself unduly grateful.

"I didn't know you had worked with disabled kids," he said after a moment. "That's commendable."

"The Quest Foundation works with all types of disabled children. Head injuries. Spinal injuries. Down's syndrome. Muscular dystrophy. A few months after the shooting, I volunteered and spent a couple of months coaching wheelchair basketball. Teenagers mostly. A couple of times I went out to the equestrian center and spotted young riders. To say the experience was eye-opening would be an understatement."

"I'll bet."

"Nick, those kids loved the horses! I guess it's the same concept as bringing dogs into cancer wards and retirement homes. Like dogs, horses have an incredibly positive effect on kids."

"You coached wheelchair basketball and yet the sight of Steph's wheelchair still affected you when you first saw her."

"It wasn't the wheelchair."

"What was it, then?"

Her teeth scraped over her lower lip. "Seeing the wheelchair made me…remember. The shooting. And Danny."

"Flashbacks?"

Blowing out a sigh, she nodded.

"Ah, McNeal." Lowering his head, he pinched the bridge of his nose. "Post-traumatic stress?" he asked after a moment.

"Survivor's guilt is what the department psychiatrist called it. I had nightmares, sleeplessness. A lot of guilt that just wouldn't leave me alone."

"That's why you volunteered."

She smiled, but there was no humor in it. "After living through something like that, I needed to give something back. The psychiatrist recommended this agency."

"Did it help?"

"It got me through some tough months. For a while, I even made a difference. I made some of those kids smile. You know, Chief, I can be quite a clown when I put my mind to it."

The thought elicited a smile from him. "I'll bet."

"But it didn't take long for me to realize I couldn't hack it. It just sucked too much energy out of me, and brought on too many flashbacks of the shooting. I know that sounds selfish, but after a while I just couldn't do it anymore. Those beautiful children who'd been hurt so terribly, facing so much difficulty..."

"You weren't selfish. Human, maybe. But the bottom line is you did it. You made a difference. That's what's important."

Hearing a sigh shudder out of her, Nick studied her silhouette. His throat constricted when he saw the glimmer of tears on her cheeks. Had he caused that?

Ignoring the swirl of panic in his gut, he stepped away from the car and turned to her. Putting his finger under her chin, he forced her gaze to his. "What's with the tears, McNeal?"

"I'm sure you'll have a hard time believing this, but I never cry."

"I'm sorry I seem to be so good at making you." The urge to comfort was surprisingly strong, his resistance damnably weak. He was standing so close he could smell the familiar scent of her hair mingling with the sweetness of her breath. The light from a three-quarter moon illuminated her features just enough to let him see the caution in her eyes and the shape of her mouth. Sweet mercy, he wanted to kiss her.

Nick brushed his thumb over her cheek, catching a tear. He knew touching her was a mistake. Just as he knew holding her now would be a mistake that would lead to certain disaster. Everything inside him screamed for him to turn around and walk away. If he got involved with her in any way, she would wreak havoc on his life. But there was no way he could stand back and watch her cry while he did nothing.

Something powerful and fundamental stirred low in his gut. He didn't even bother to fight it. He didn't dare name it. He was tired of fighting when it came to this woman, tired of resisting what was quickly getting the best of him. She'd stripped him bare tonight, and he'd allowed it. What was one comforting embrace? One kiss between friends?

Nick figured he was getting pretty good at rationalizing.

"Come here," he whispered.

Her startled gaze met his. "You know what happened the last time we tried this."

"Yeah, and if I remember correctly, it was pretty damn good."

He didn't wait for her. Stepping closer, he cupped her face with his hands. He felt softness and tears. Smelled the enticing scent he'd dreamed about too many times in the last few days.

Shock registered on her face, but he didn't care. She wasn't the only one he'd shocked. He was most certainly shocking himself, but he wasn't going to let that stop him, either.

Backing her against the car, Nick drew her mouth to his with slow deliberation. She didn't close her eyes, and he saw them widen, heard her quick intake of breath, felt his own catch in his throat.

One moment she was as rigid as a board, the next like melted honey in his arms. Nick felt her go fluid as he coaxed her lips into submission. He opened his mouth and used his tongue, daring her to accept him. With a small sound deep in her throat, she parted her lips and welcomed him in.

Something hot and urgent broke open inside him, unleashing a part of him he'd kept bottled up for so long.

Need and lust and something else he didn't want to name
sprang free.

He deepened the kiss, using his tongue, tasting the far-
thest reaches of her mouth. Her body felt lush and soft
against his. Frustration burned in his groin as he pressed
against her, but the contact only made him want more.

He heard a sound, realized he'd growled low in his
throat. She shifted closer and another jab of lust arrowed
through him. His hands slipped from her face, grazing her
shoulders, stopping at her breasts. Her gasp ended in a
groan when he cupped her through her uniform shirt. She
arched into him, and Nick's control teetered. His fingers
went to the buttons. He fumbled, cursing silently when he
realized his hands were trembling. One button sprang free.
His overzealous fingers popped the next two. Then his
hands were inside her shirt, seeking flesh, touching lace and
softness and woman.

Her breasts were firm and round and high. Nick cupped
her through her bra, marveling at her softness. He brushed
his thumbs over the hardened peaks of her nipples. She
shivered. He wanted to feel her flesh, warm and supple
beneath his hands. He wanted to put his mouth on her.

Two more buttons went by the wayside. He struggled to
find her bra clasp. Not in front. He slipped his arms around
her. No rear closure. Frustration and a tinge of embarrassment pounded through him. "What kind of bra is this?"
he whispered.

"Uh, athletic..."

Nick didn't hear the rest of her response. Tugging the
bra up over her breasts, he leaned forward and took her
nipple into his mouth. Erin cried out, arching, giving him
full access. Her response splintered the remainder of his
restraint. Caution shattered. He knew he was out of control,
but she was so exquisite, so responsive, he gladly relinquished it, refusing to think of the consequences, of what
he might be risking.

He didn't remember closing his eyes. All his brain registered was that she was against him, and he was hard and pulsing and so ready he thought he might end it all right then and there. The realization stunned him, thrilled him. For the first time in years, he felt alive. Whole. On fire and burning out of control—

"Chief?"

The voice reached him as if through a fog. An instant later, recognition exploded in his brain. Stephanie's nanny, for Pete's sake! Nick scrambled back. Erin turned away in an attempt to conceal her state of undress. Shaken, dangerously aroused and more embarrassed than he'd been since the time in his teens when he got caught making out in the back seat of his mother's car, he faced Mrs. Thornsberry.

Chapter 7

"**W**hat is it, Em?" Nick winced at the sound of his voice. Hoarse, breathless, it sounded as if he'd swallowed a chunk of concrete.

The older woman stood twenty feet away, her hands on her hips, looking at him as if he'd just landed his spaceship at the end of the driveway. "I didn't mean to interrupt," she said primly.

Nick didn't move. He couldn't get any closer, not without her noticing his state of arousal. "You didn't interrupt anything," he said.

"Uh-huh."

Uncomfortable, he shifted his weight from one foot to the other. "McNeal and I were just talking."

"I figured it was something like that." Mrs. Thornsberry clucked her tongue. "Steph asked for you."

Concern and a hefty jab of guilt stabbed through him. His daughter had been upset. She needed him. And here he was making out with one of his deputies in the driveway.

"Is she all right?" he asked quickly.

''She's fine. She's waiting for you out by the garage.''

''By the garage?'' It was nearly her bedtime. What was she doing out by the garage?

''Good night, Nick,'' the nanny said.

Feeling like a kid who'd just ticked off his mom and would have hell to pay in the coming days, he watched her walk away.

''I've got to go.''

Nick turned at the sound of Erin's voice. She stood next to her cruiser, her eyes dark and cautious in the moonlight, her lips glistening. He could still feel the pressure of her mouth against his, recall the sweet smell of her breath, the scent of her hair. The memory sent another rush of blood to his groin.

What had he done? Why did he keep making the same mistake over and over when it came to this woman? She wasn't right for him. She wasn't right for Steph. Erin was wild and impulsive and would end up breaking both their hearts. So why couldn't he keep his hands off her?

''Uh...'' Nick resisted the urge to rearrange himself. He was still painfully aroused, his body screaming for release. He was going to have to start dating. Take up running. Cold showers. Maybe he'd just shoot himself in the foot. Anything but get involved with Erin McNeal.

''Steph asked for me,'' he said. ''I've got to go.''

Without speaking, Erin opened the car door and slipped inside. Nick approached, not sure what he was going to say, knowing he couldn't let what had just happened between them go without explanation. ''McNeal.''

She slammed the car door, then lowered the window. ''Tell Steph I'm sorry about the basketball, will you, Nick?''

''Sure.'' He leaned down. ''Erin...''

''You don't have to say it.'' She started the engine.

Nick figured he didn't have a choice but to say what needed to be said. ''This can't happen again.''

"I know. I shouldn't have come here tonight."

He grimaced. "Probably not."

Her flinch was barely perceptible, but Nick saw it, and he hated that she was paying the price for his own lack of control.

"I'm turning the remainder of your training over to Hector," he said. "I think we should steer clear of each other for a while. This isn't fair to either of us." He wasn't exactly sure what "this" was, but knew it was something they shouldn't be partaking in, no matter how good she felt in his arms.

"Of course. I agree." She said the words a little too quickly and with a little too much enthusiasm.

Nick didn't want to debate the issue. His body sure didn't agree, but he let the statement stand. Straightening, he stepped away from the car. Without looking at him, she put the car in gear and drove away.

He watched the taillights disappear, aware that his heart was beating too fast, that his palms were wet with sweat. He refused to believe anything had happened between them that didn't have to do with hormones or three years of celibacy. Nothing happened, he told himself. Not a damn thing.

Starting toward the house, he shut out the annoying little voice in the back of his mind that called him a liar.

He strode toward the front door, intent on spending a few minutes with Steph before bedtime, but the unmistakable sound of a basketball against concrete stopped him. Curious, he skirted the sidewalk and peered around the side of the house, where a spotlight illuminated the portion of the driveway he'd concreted back when she'd first started playing basketball. Stephanie sat in her wheelchair, the bright orange basketball Erin had bought her poised in her hands, her determined gaze glued to the rusty hoop above the garage door. Concentration scrunched her features as she judged the distance between ball and hoop. An instant later, she leaned forward, thrust the ball upward and let it roll off her fingertips in a perfect arc. Nick held his breath. The ball bounced off the rim.

"Oh shoot!" she said, as the ball hit the concrete.

The sight of his little girl shooting baskets shouldn't have moved him so profoundly. But as he watched her push her wheelchair forward to catch the ball, then lean forward and prepare for another shot, his heart convulsed in his chest. The ensuing jab of pain took his breath.

She needs to live her life to the fullest, risks be damned.

Erin's words rang uncomfortably in his ears. She was wrong, Nick assured himself. Stephanie needed protecting. If he'd been there for her the night of the accident she wouldn't be in that wheelchair.

Needing a moment to rein in his emotions, he leaned against the side of the house, telling himself he wasn't over-protective. Steph *needed* someone to look after her. Someone to keep her safe. Someone to keep her from getting hurt again.

After a moment, Nick approached his daughter. He smiled, but his face felt plastic and he feared she would see straight through him. His little girl had become increasingly perceptive in the last couple of years.

She looked at him from beneath her lashes and grinned. "I missed my shot."

Nick swallowed, terrified the emotion crowding his throat would overtake him. "I saw that."

"I'm sorry I was so mean to Erin."

"Erin's fine. She understands and told me it's okay if you don't want the basketball. She'll get you something else."

Stephanie lifted the ball to him. "I never noticed this when she first gave it to me. Check it out, Dad."

Nick looked down at the orange globe. Pain broke apart and scattered deep in his chest at the sight of his daughter's name scrawled in sweeping black handwriting above the autograph of a popular Chicago Bulls player.

"Well, I'll be," he muttered.

"Pretty cool, huh? How'd Erin know he's my favorite player?"

Nick didn't know what to say. Not to his daughter. Certainly not to Erin, who must have driven more than two hundred miles, plus somehow wrangled a personalized autograph.

Stephanie looked down at the ball in her hands. "I was thinking about what she said."

"What's that?"

"About...you know, wheelchair basketball. I saw these guys playing on TV, but I didn't think I could ever do it."

"You can do anything you want, honeybunch."

"Well, I thought maybe I could, you know, take some lessons or something. I used to be a pretty good player."

"You sure that's a good idea?"

"My back doesn't hurt that much, if that's what you're worried about. Maybe we could ask Dr. Brooks."

Nick cleared his throat, hoping his voice wouldn't break and reveal the pain in his heart. "It's past your bedtime, honeybunch."

She cocked her head. The movement made her look like she was six again and challenging his authority, as she had so many times over the years. "Will you at least think about it?"

He stared at her, shaken and so full of love for this child that he ached with the need to hold her and keep her safe. Another part of him wanted desperately to make her happy—to let her play basketball and do all the things a little girl should be able to do. For the first time since the accident, he wondered if one was at odds with the other. He wondered if Erin McNeal was right.

"I'll think about it as long as you promise not to become a professional basketball player," he said after a moment.

"I couldn't handle you being on the road for long stretches."

She turned thoughtful. "You think professional players miss their dads when they're on the road?"

"You would." Grinning, Nick leaned forward and tugged gently on her ear. "But I'd miss you more."

Wheeling the chair back, Stephanie bounced the ball toward him. "So, I *can* take lessons?"

Nick caught the ball, but couldn't bring himself to bounce it back to her. "I'll think about it, sweetheart, all right?"

"Promise me you'll think hard about it, Dad, okay?"

"I promise."

Erin sat at her desk and stared out the front window of the police station, trying not to think about Nick—and failing miserably. Frowning, she looked down at the blur of forms and reports spread out in front of her, and typed a line of information into her computer. Unable to drum up the least bit of enthusiasm for her work, she resumed her vigil of watching the cars as they drove down Commerce Street. She'd been hard at it since seven that morning—two hours ago—and only sixteen cars had passed. Logan Falls, she thought. Life in the fast lane.

What in the world was she going to do about Nick?

Hector's philosophy on training new officers differed dramatically from Nick's. While the chief had started her out with making rounds, Hector preferred to pawn off his paperwork on her, while he did his rounds alone. Erin wasn't happy about the desk work. On the other hand, she didn't feel much like company today.

She wanted to blame Nick for her sour mood but knew she had no one to blame but herself—and that blasted kiss. How was it she could build an illustrious career in a police department the size of Chicago's, yet in her first week in Logan Falls she'd managed to alienate her counterpart, tick

off her boss and generally screw up at every turn? What
had she been thinking, letting Nick kiss her like that? What
on earth had she been doing kissing him back?

She wanted to believe the kiss was a result of high emotion in the wake of Stephanie's reaction to the basketball.
Or Nick's anger. Or her own guilt over having upset the
little girl. But Erin knew better, and she wasn't going to
start lying to herself now. She'd wanted Nick to kiss her,
wanted that hard, uncompromising mouth against hers—
consequences be damned. No amount of denial was going
to change any of it, or the fact that her pulse kicked every
time she thought about doing it again.

Her cheeks heated at the memory of their encounter in
his driveway, but she quickly shooed it away. She couldn't
change what was already done. It had been two days since
the kiss, and she hadn't seen him since. She told herself
that was best. She didn't need a man like Nick messing
with her head and teasing her body with promises that
would do nothing but make them both miserable in the long
run.

He'd told her it was her recklessness he couldn't tolerate.
Erin knew it had more to do with the fact that she was a
career cop who wasn't afraid to put herself on the line.
Well, she'd had her fill of men who couldn't handle her
being a police officer. Warren Prentice was a prime example, and it still disturbed her deeply that six years ago
she'd been naive enough to nearly throw it all away in the
name of love.

Love? Whoa. Where had that crazy notion come from?
Erin certainly wasn't naive enough to believe in the fallacy
of love—or risk her career over it. Things were better if
she avoided Nick, she assured herself. Simpler. A hell of a
lot safer. She'd do her time in Logan Falls. Get back on
her feet. Hopefully, in six months, Frank would reinstate
her, and she could move back to Chicago where she be-
longed.

She started when the bell on the front door jingled. Expecting Hector, she felt a jolt of surprise when Stephanie opened the door and rolled inside. Not sure how to react in light of the fiasco at her birthday party, Erin looked down at the form in front of her and typed another line of information into the computer.

"Hi."

Erin looked up and felt her mood soften as she watched the little girl struggle to get her wheelchair through the door. "Hi, Steph," she said. "Everything okay?"

"Yeah." The answer lacked the enthusiasm one would expect from a nine-year-old. "Is my dad around?"

Concerned, Erin shoved away from the computer and watched her approach. "You're not sick, are you?"

No, I'm just desperately sad and lonely and need someone to talk to. Erin saw the words in the little girl's eyes as clearly as if she'd spoken them. Compassion and an odd sense of understanding squeezed Erin's heart. How many times had she felt that same sadness growing up without her mother? She wondered if Nick saw the same sadness when he looked into his daughter's eyes. She wondered if it tore him apart, because there wasn't anything he could do to fix it.

"I was hoping my dad was here so he'd take me home," Stephanie said.

"Nick's at the courthouse today. Hector said he'd be there most of the day. I can call him for you if you want."

Stephanie looked at her backpack. "Can you take me home?"

Nick had forewarned her that Stephanie skipped school occasionally, and had instructed both of his deputies to call the principal and take his daughter home to Mrs. Thornsberry if she showed up at the station when he wasn't around.

"Sure I can." Erin figured it was the least she could do, since she'd upset Stephanie so terribly the night of the party. "Now I have an excuse not to finish this paperwork."

It took Erin nearly ten minutes to help Stephanie out of her wheelchair and get her strapped in the cruiser. By the time she stowed the chair in the trunk and climbed behind the wheel, she'd broken into a sweat. For the first time, she realized fully the weight of Nick's responsibility when it came to his daughter. She knew he shouldered that responsibility without complaint—but she also realized fully the love and devotion that was required to care for a physically challenged child.

Pulling onto Commerce Street, Erin steered the cruiser toward Nick's house.

"I guess you think I acted like a brat about the basketball," Stephanie said after a moment.

The statement startled Erin. Not knowing exactly how to respond, she glanced away from her driving and studied the girl. "That was my fault, honey. I should have realized the basketball might upset you."

"It doesn't. I mean, it did at first, but not anymore. After I got used to the idea, I started thinking it might be fun to, you know, play."

"It's okay for you not to like it, Steph. I'll take it back and get you something else—"

"But I do like it," she insisted. "I just...when you first gave it to me, I started thinking that I won't ever be able to walk again, and it made me feel sad. But after I thought about it awhile, I started thinking maybe I could take some lessons or something."

"You want to take wheelchair basketball lessons?" Erin asked cautiously.

"Maybe. I mean, you said kids in wheelchairs could take lessons. Didn't you say that, Erin?"

She thought of Nick and wondered how she should handle this. "How did your dad feel about lessons?"

''He worries too much, but he's always like that. Mom used to call him a worrywart. But he promised he'd think about it.''

Erin blinked, surprised that Nick had told Stephanie he would consider letting her take lessons. He'd seemed dead set against it. The thought that he might have softened his stance sent a ribbon of warmth through her heart. ''So…you had a pretty good birthday, after all?''

''Pretty good.'' Sighing, Stephanie looked out the window. ''My dad's pretty cool. He let me stay up past my bedtime for once. He even got me a green parakeet. I named her Bertha. And Mrs. Thornsberry made that really yummy cake. She's like my grandmother, or something. I just wish…'' The little girl's voice trailed off.

Erin gave her a moment, then pressed. ''You wish what, honey?''

''I wish my mom could have been there. I mean, she'd probably be sad that I'm in a wheelchair, but she always made me feel better. She was pretty, and she laughed a lot. She made my dad laugh, too. He hardly ever laughs anymore.''

The words sent a pang through Erin. The mention of Nick's wife sent another, more complex, pang right through her. ''Your dad told me about your mom. I'm sorry.'' Remembering her own childhood, and the death of her mother, she ached for the little girl.

''I miss her sometimes.''

''I know what you mean,'' Erin said easily.

''You do?''

''I lost my mom when I was six.''

Stephanie turned wide blue eyes on her. ''You mean your mom died, too?''

Erin nodded. ''She had cancer.''

''That must have been really hard, since you were only six. Did you cry?''

''I cried a bunch. I missed her so much.''

"I used to cry all the time, but I don't anymore. I even saw my dad cry once. He thought I didn't see him, but I did. It was kind of weird. I told Mrs. T. about it, and she said everyone cries when they're sad. I never told my dad I saw him, though. I figured he'd be embarrassed or something."

Erin smiled despite the fact that she felt the warmth of tears in her eyes. She wondered how a nine-year-old could be so perceptive.

"Is that why you skip school, honey? Because you're sad?"

"I don't know." Steph's eyes skittered toward the window, then down to her sneakers. "Sometimes I get mad. I mean, not at my dad or Mrs. T. or anything. I just get mad because I miss my mom and I can't do stuff, like play basketball and ride Bandito."

Erin wasn't sure how to tell an innocent nine-year-old child that life wasn't always fair. "It's okay to be mad, Steph, but skipping school isn't such a good idea."

"I know."

"But you know what?"

The little girl looked over at her. "What?"

"It helps to talk about it. And I think your dad and Mrs. T. are pretty good listeners."

"So are you."

Feeling her own emotions rise, Erin glanced in the rear-view mirror and swallowed hard.

"Does that yucky feeling that makes you want to cry ever go away?" Stephanie asked.

"It gets easier," Erin said carefully. "Pretty soon when you think of your mom, you'll just smile and think about how much fun she was to be with, and it won't hurt so much to think about her."

"She *was* pretty fun. She used to braid my hair. Once she even braided Bandito's tail. He looked pretty funny."

Erin looked away from her driving and grinned "See?" she said. "You're smiling already."

They rode in silence for several minutes, then Erin turned the cruiser into the driveway. In the adjacent pasture, the Appaloosa raised his head and watched them. "Hey, there's Bandito," she said.

Stephanie waved to the horse and blew him a kiss through the open window. "He's so pretty. I showed him at the county fair when I was in 4-H. I won first place in western pleasure class. We rode in the trail class, too, but he's never been good at backing. I could show you my ribbons if you want."

"I'd love to see them. In fact, I'd love to see Bandito, too."

The little girl's face brightened. "Really?"

"Sure." Erin stopped the cruiser.

"So, you really *do* like horses? The other day I thought you were just, you know, trying to be nice."

"I like horses a lot. And I *am* really nice." At Stephanie's smile, she added, "Once you get to know me."

"Do you really think I could ride him sometime, Erin? I mean, with my legs the way they are? You talked about it the other day, and I've sort of been wondering."

Caution demanded Erin tread carefully when it came to this child. She didn't want to give her false hopes. The little girl had had too many disappointments in recent years to build her up for another letdown. Nick seemed to be dead set against her taking on any activity that could be even remotely dangerous. On the other hand, Erin knew for a fact Stephanie could at least sit atop her horse; Erin had seen severely handicapped children ride horses with the help of adult spotters in the weeks she'd volunteered at the Quest Foundation. She'd personally spotted one such teenage boy afflicted with syringomyelia. Stephanie wasn't severely handicapped. Surely Nick wouldn't deny her that small joy in the name of safety. He had, after all, softened his stance on the basketball. Why would he object to her sitting atop Bandito?

"Do you want to give it a shot?" Erin asked, praying she hadn't just committed herself to something that would once again put her and Nick at odds.

Stephanie's grin was all the answer she needed.

"Oh, honey, I don't know." Mrs. Thornsberry worried her pearl necklace with nervous fingers.

"Oh, please, please, *please!*" said Stephanie, using her arms to rock her wheelchair back and forth on the kitchen floor. "Bandito is so lonely, Mrs. T., and Erin said she'd spot me."

"Spot you?" the older woman asked. "What's that?"

"Uh...walk alongside the horse to make sure she doesn't fall off," Erin clarified from her place at the kitchen door.

"Oh." Mrs. Thornsberry shot Erin a stern look. "You've done this before?"

"I volunteered at the Quest Foundation in Chicago for a couple of months. They've got a renowned equestrian program."

Recognition flared in the older woman's eyes. "I know of it. Very reputable organization."

Erin nodded. "Volunteers go through an intensive training program."

Mrs. Thornsberry still didn't look convinced.

"On my first day," Erin continued, "I watched a fourteen-year-old paraplegic ride for the first time. I'll never forget the look on his face when they lifted him onto that horse. It was one of the most moving experiences of my life."

"C'mon, Erin, come see my ribbons," Stephanie interjected. "I have a trophy, too."

Mrs. Thornsberry dried her hands on a dish towel and looked down at Stephanie. "Honey, why don't you go get your boots while Erin and I have a little talk."

Erin took a deep breath, certain that "talk" was synonymous with lecture. She'd overstepped again. Not the first time since she'd set foot in Logan Falls.

"You're not going to talk Erin out of spotting me, are you, Mrs. T?" Steph asked.

"Scoot." Mrs. Thornsberry pushed the wheelchair toward the door. "Dig your riding boots out of your closet, and I'll help you put them on. If your feet are swelled, you can wear your sneakers."

"Really? Okay!"

When the little girl was out of earshot, the older woman turned to Erin. "It's been a long time since I've seen her so excited."

"I hope I haven't gotten her hopes up for no reason," Erin said. "I don't want her to be disappointed."

"You mean if Nick doesn't approve?"

She met the older woman's gaze steadily. "He seems dead set against any activity that could be perceived as dangerous."

"Nick's a good man, Erin. He can be uncompromising, particularly when it comes to Stephanie. But he's devoted. I've never seen a more committed, loving father than Nick. His entire life centers around that girl."

"That's never come into question—"

"Of course it hasn't."

"But he's also a little…" Erin let her voice trail off, not sure how to put into words what she felt in her heart without sounding harsh, or appearing judgmental. She didn't have children; didn't know the first thing about raising them, either. Still, she'd had some experiences in her life that made her unable to ignore what she knew to be true.

"Overprotective?" Mrs. Thornsberry's gaze turned knowing.

Erin nodded. "There are a lot of things Stephanie can still do that Nick refuses to consider. I think that's where some of her frustration comes in."

"You mean her skipping school?"

"I think she's crying out for something she's not getting."

"Nick is a *good* father," Mrs. Thornsberry said fiercely. Busying her hands by adjusting her apron, she turned to the counter. "Rita's death was hard on this family. Stephanie nearly died that first night. Good heavens, Nick spent so much time at the hospital with her that first terrible week, he practically didn't have time to grieve. But Rita's death changed him. And not all the changes I've seen in him were good."

"What changes?"

"He's always been a very private man. He's not vocal about his feelings—well, unless he's angry. He isn't good at reaching out. After Rita's death, he just...shut down."

"You mean emotionally?"

"That's exactly what I mean. He was crazy about Rita. But she drove him nuts." As if immersed in memories, Mrs. Thornsberry smiled. "Rita was a free spirit. A daredevil, if you will. She never listened to anyone. Never followed the rules. She liked loud music. Liked to drive fast with the top down on her convertible. She was into skydiving—at night, of all times. Scuba diving—dove with sharks down in Florida a few years back. Good heavens, she even went bungee jumping once. She'd do anything that was fast or dangerous or both. Drove Nick crazy."

Erin had an idea where the conversation was heading, and her heart did a long, slow roll under her ribs. "What happened?"

"Rita was out with Stephanie one night. Rita and Nick had quarreled earlier. He never told me that, but I heard them. As usual, Rita was driving too fast. She lost control of her car at the Logan Creek bridge. The car flipped and went down the embankment. The top was down on the convertible, so it offered no protection. I'd been working for them for a couple of years at the time. I'd just put in a casserole for dinner when the deputy called Nick." Mrs. Thornsberry removed her bifocals and made a show of cleaning the lens with her apron. "Lord have mercy, what that man must have gone through." The older woman shook her head. "He hasn't been the same since."

Erin remembered Nick's account of the accident, and realized he'd left out most of the details. For the first time, his overprotective nature toward his daughter made perfect sense. "That's the accident that put Stephanie in the wheelchair?"

Mrs. Thornsberry nodded. "He'd warned Rita about driving too fast, but she wouldn't listen."

"That must have been terrible for him."

"This family has seen more than its share of tragedy. I suspect Nick is so protective around Steph because he's afraid of losing her, the way he lost Rita. I keep telling myself he'll come around and stop being so...so vigilant. But it's been three years. He hasn't moved on. Not with Stephanie." The older woman looked at Erin. "Not with his own life."

Erin knew immediately they were no longer talking about Stephanie, or Nick's overprotective nature, but the fact that she and Nick had been caught in the throes of a passionate kiss the night of Stephanie's birthday party. The memory made her cheeks flame.

"There hasn't been anyone for him since the accident," Mrs. Thornsberry said. "That's a long time for a man to be alone."

"We're not involved," Erin said quickly.

"He's been...preoccupied since you came along. Nick isn't frivolous when it comes to women."

Translated, Mrs. Thornsberry was telling her that Nick didn't kiss just any woman out in his driveway. Erin didn't know what to say, didn't want this woman getting the wrong idea about her and Nick. There wasn't anything between them. Just that blasted, earth-shattering, mind-numbing kiss.

The older woman smiled wisely. "I've seen the way he looks at you."

"Like he wants to throttle me." Erin forced a laugh, determined to keep the conversation from going in a direction that would put into words a problem that had become increasingly difficult to deal with.

"You've shaken him up, Erin. You're strong willed and don't let him bully you. Until you came into his life, I didn't realize how badly he needed that."

Despite her efforts to keep the conversation light, Erin's heart beat hard and fast in her chest. "I'm not the right woman for the job," she whispered a little desperately.

"That, my dear, remains to be seen."

"I can't get my boots on!" Stephanie rolled her wheelchair into the kitchen, her face filled with disappointment, her sneakers on her lap. "My feet are swelled," she announced.

"Your dad will have to rub them for you tonight." Mrs. Thornsberry clucked her tongue. "For now, you can wear your sneakers." Kneeling in front of the little girl, she shot Erin a look over her shoulder. "Put that other sneaker on for her, will you, Erin? Bandito is waiting."

"Up and at 'em!" Erin lifted the little girl up onto an ever-patient Bandito's back.

"I can't get my leg over," said Stephanie.

"Yes, you can." Erin ducked under Bandito's neck and tugged the child's leg into place. "Sheesh, how much do you weigh?" she teased. "A ton?"

"No!"

"Feels like it."

"Hey, I'm on!"

The joy in Stephanie's voice struck a chord in Erin. The change in the little girl was dramatic. Her cornflower-blue eyes were alight with happiness, her lips pulled into a grin. Erin had never seen her so excited, and felt her own excitement build in her chest like a rainbow in the wake of a spring storm.

Stepping back, she studied girl and horse carefully. "You're going to have to hold on to the horn," Erin said. "Don't let go no matter what."

Biting her lip in concentration, Stephanie wrapped both hands around the leather horn. "'Kay."

Five minutes later, Erin led Bandito down the aisle toward the barn door, with Stephanie astride. The little girl's right foot dangled uselessly, but she gripped the horn with white-knuckled determination. Satisfied, Erin said, "Looks like we're set. Let's take Bandito into the round pen."

"I don't like not being able to use my legs. Bandito knows leg commands."

"You two will just have to compensate." Standing on the left side of the horse, Erin led him toward the pen a dozen yards away. "Horses are smart, Steph. Bandito can be retrained, can learn new ways to receive his commands."

On reaching the pen, Erin opened the gate. She looked up at Stephanie and found the little girl grinning from ear to ear.

"He remembers me," she whispered. "I can tell."

"Of course he does," Erin said. "Horses don't forget someone they love just because they haven't seen them for a while."

She led the horse around the pen, watching the animal, but barely taking her eyes from Stephanie. The September sun beat down on Erin's dark blue uniform, and she broke into a sweat. It was warm for fall in the Midwest, but she was so caught up in the magic on Stephanie's face, she barely noticed the heat. It was the perfect day for a little girl to ride her horse.

"I want to trot," Steph said.

"No way."

"I won't fall off."

"That's what people say right before they fall off."

Stephanie giggled. "Okay, at least walk him a little faster. He needs the exercise."

"I'm the one who's getting all the exercise," Erin grumbled good-naturedly, but she was thinking of Nick. "No trotting, kiddo."

"Okay, maybe we'll save that for next time."

Erin brushed a drop of sweat from her temple, hoping with all her heart there was going to be a next time.

"This is great!"

"Easy for you to say," she said. "Bandito and I are doing all the work."

Grinning despite the fact that she was breathing hard, and getting her clean uniform all sweaty, Erin continued around the pen. Dust coated her boots and the bottom of her pants. Her hair slowly unraveled from its knot at her nape, but she didn't care. She was having too much fun watching Stephanie—and feeling the heady rush of satisfaction that came with the knowledge that she'd made a difference in this sweet child's life.

At the far end of the ring, Erin finally paused.

"What's wrong?" asked Stephanie.

"I'm getting a stitch in my side." She was about to ask Stephanie if she wanted something to drink when movement at the end of the driveway drew her gaze. Erin's heart plummeted when she spotted Nick's Suburban speeding down the driveway, a rooster tail of dust in its wake.

Chapter 8

Nick's heart stopped dead in his chest when he saw Stephanie in the round pen astride Bandito, with Erin walking alongside. He couldn't believe his eyes. The horse was walking fast enough to seriously injure Stephanie if she lost her balance and fell.

How could Erin act so irresponsibly?

He brought the truck to a skidding halt in front of the barn, out of sight from the pen. Throwing open the door, he hit the ground running. By the time he entered the barn, he was breathless not only from the short run, but from the burgeoning anger that had his pulse racing like hot mercury through his veins.

Nick had always prided himself on control. A father at the age of twenty-nine, he'd trained himself to keep his emotions in check, keep a constant grip on his temper. But as he watched Erin lead the horse through the rear door of the barn with his little girl astride, his temper ignited.

"What do you think you're doing?" he asked.

Erin stopped, her gaze wary and level on Nick. "I was—"

"Don't be mad, Dad."

Stephanie's words struck him like a stinging lash. Nick looked at his daughter and felt the fist of emotion lodged in his chest tighten even more. "I'm not angry with you, Steph."

"Don't be mad at Erin, either," she said. "She didn't do anything wrong. Riding Bandito was my idea."

Shaking with the remnants of fear and a powerful anger he hadn't been prepared for, Nick approached the horse slowly and reached for Stephanie. "Come here." He dragged her into his arms. Her little-girl scent surrounded him like a soft cloud. "Are you okay?" he asked.

"Dad, I'm okay. Geez, we were just walking."

He closed his eyes against the ensuing burst of emotion. He wouldn't let this innocent child be hurt. Not again. Certainly not by a reckless adult.

"You smell like Bandito," he said.

Stephanie grinned. "I like the way he smells."

Not wanting her to notice his state of mind, he forced a smile. "Go inside and ask Mrs. T. to fix a pot of coffee for me, would you, honeybunch?"

The little girl eyed him suspiciously. "You're going to yell at Erin, aren't you?"

He heard the woman in question behind him, putting Bandito into his stall, but Nick didn't look at her. He wasn't sure what it would do to him if he did. He was angry and wanted to stay that way. "Erin and I are going to have a talk."

"About what?"

"About boundaries and responsibility." Carrying Stephanie over to the wheelchair, he settled her in the seat. "Tell Em I'll be inside in a few minutes."

Stephanie looked past him toward Erin. Nick didn't miss the quick, uncertain smile, or the spark of newfound respect in his little girl's eyes. It had been a long time since Steph had smiled at anyone but him and Mrs. T—and she didn't do it nearly often enough to suit him. He wondered how Erin McNeal had managed to reach her in such a short period of time.

"I gotta go," Stephanie said to Erin "Sorry you got all sweaty and dirty."

Erin looked down at her uniform. "Hey, a little dust never hurt anyone."

Ignoring Erin as best he could, Nick helped his daughter maneuver the wheelchair around, then watched her disappear through the door. Aware that his heart rate was dangerously high, he closed the door behind him and turned to face Erin.

In keeping with her tough-guy image, she raised her chin. "This isn't as...premeditated as it looks."

He started toward her. "Really?"

She stepped back. "Stephanie came to the station asking for you. She skipped school and needed a ride home. You were at the courthouse, so I drove her home. One thing led to another and—"

"One thing led to another?" Nick barely recognized his own voice. "That's a lame excuse, don't you think?"

"It's the truth."

"Just who do you think you are, walking into my home and endangering my daughter like that?"

"She wasn't in any danger."

Nick ground his teeth at her denial. "That horse weighs a thousand pounds. He hasn't been ridden in over three years. Don't tell me she wasn't in any danger."

"Bandito is well trained and even better behaved." Erin took another step back. "Stephanie wanted to ride, Nick. She begged me to take her riding."

"So you suggested she hop up on his back and go for a spin? And that's not irresponsible?"

"It's compassionate. She loves that horse—"

"She's a nine-year-old kid with a serious spinal condition. She isn't qualified to make the decision as to whether or not she can ride a horse. Neither are you."

"She did great. Nick, she laughed, for God's sake. She *laughed!* The instant she got on that horse, she came alive."

"I'm aware of her wants, McNeal. I don't need you pointing them out to me."

"Are you sure about that?"

Nick tried to bank his boiling temper, but she was pushing him too hard. "You don't know anything about her. You sure as hell don't know anything about me."

"Maybe I know more than you think."

"What's that supposed to mean?"

"I know about the accident, Nick. I know what happened to your wife. I know why. I think that explains a lot about you."

He paused two feet away from her. If he got any closer, he wasn't sure what he would do. Kiss her, maybe; he was too angry to be rational. He didn't have a rational bone in his body when it came to this woman.

"This doesn't have anything to do with Rita," he said.

"Maybe this has more to do with her than you realize."

"This is about you and your recklessness and the havoc that kind of recklessness wreaks on people's lives. Stephanie and I have been through it once, and I don't plan to let you or anyone else put us through that same hell again."

"Life is full of risks," she said softly. "You can't stop living because you're afraid of getting hurt."

"Don't get living and living dangerously confused, McNeal. Not everyone has your taste for adrenaline."

"This isn't about me. It's about you and the fact that you're holding on too tight—"

"This is about you risking my daughter's safety because you need some kind of personal absolution."

"Maybe I'm just a convenient scapegoat because you can't face your own fears."

Nick's control snapped with an almost audible click. Anger and fear and another emotion he didn't want to name burst free, like shrapnel exploding from a bomb. He reached Erin in a single, swift stride. Her eyes widened, but he didn't stop. Grasping her arms, he moved her backward. "You have a real gift for saying the wrong thing at the wrong time."

She gasped when her back met the wall. "You're out of control."

Nick knew he'd lost the battle for emotional distance—if he'd ever had that to begin with when it came to this woman. He'd somehow gotten tangled up with her, physically, emotionally, and the only way he knew how to save himself was to drive her away once and for all.

"Damn right I am," he said, and lowered his mouth to hers.

Erin hadn't expected Nick to kiss her gently. She'd expected urgency and heat and the fire she'd seen in his eyes.

What she got was nothing like what she'd expected.

His kiss spoke of desire. The raw sensuality of it overwhelmed her. He tasted of restraint and frustration harnessed by a tattered veil of discipline that was quickly disintegrating. The combination took her breath away and tested every ounce of control she possessed. A well of unleashed emotions rushed through her like a river bursting its banks. She rode with the current, letting it push her, tumble her, until she barely knew up from down, until she no longer cared.

His hands slipped from her biceps, down her arms, igniting every nerve ending along the way. His fingers entwined with hers. All the while his mouth undermined her judgment, tore down her defenses until she stood silent and still and accepted him with every fiber of her being. When he slipped his tongue into her mouth, she welcomed him. Vaguely, she was aware of him sliding her hands upward, until he pinned her to the wall, her hands stretched above her head, his body snug against hers. She felt the weight of him, the hard shaft of his arousal like steel against her belly. Blood pooled in erogenous zones she never knew existed.

Nick tore his mouth from hers. He was breathing hard, his breath warm and sweet against her cheek. He gazed at her through heavy-lidded eyes. "Let's have it out, McNeal," he whispered. "Right here. Right now. You know I want you. Let's cut to the chase and get this out of our systems once and for all."

Without waiting for a reply, he kissed her. Hard. Hungrily. With an unrelenting intensity that left her dizzy from a troubling mix of confusion and lust. She shouldn't be kissing him back. She knew better than to play with fire. And at the moment, Nick Ryan was like a powder keg about to explode. Erin knew she would be the one to get burned. He didn't care about her. He was angry with her.

So what was he doing kissing her? What was *she* doing letting him?

Her intellect told her to pull away. To stop the insanity before things went too far. But her body refused the command and proceeded to betray her. Vaguely, she was aware of his hands sliding down, skimming her shoulders, pausing at her breasts. The contact brought a moan to her lips. Her nipples beaded. Her breasts swelled against his hands, straining against the confines of her bra. The ache between her legs turned liquid and soft.

"What do you say, McNeal?" he whispered. "There's a loft a few feet away. I don't think we can ignore this much longer."

Anticipation coiled deep inside her. When his fingers went to the button of her slacks she didn't stop him. A gasp escaped her when his hand pressed flat against her belly.

She wanted to protest, but his kiss battered her senses. Too much stimuli coming too quickly for her brain to process. She couldn't think. Couldn't breathe. She didn't seem to need either of those things as long as he didn't stop touching her.

A mewling sound broke from her lips when his finger slipped inside her. The contact shocked her. His boldness stole her breath. Her body arched involuntarily. She cried out, but his kiss swallowed the sound. Control fluttered away, taking the last of her wisdom, the last of her dignity. Her body clenched, released. The madness built like a storm, promising a violent end. She opened to him. Felt the burn of his fingers against her most intimate place. He stroked her, driving her higher, closer to the edge, beyond the point of no return.

"Don't fight it, McNeal," Nick whispered darkly. "Don't fight me."

The meaning behind his words shocked her. She'd never known need could be so powerful. She wanted Nick more than she'd ever wanted anything in her life. More than she thought herself capable. But even as he kissed her like she'd never been kissed before, and caressed her body with hands that were driving her slowly insane, his anger stood between them as tangibly as a block of ice. She couldn't let him touch her out of anger.

Putting her hands against his chest, she twisted away from him. "I can't do this." She stumbled back, flushed, embarrassed, her body trembling. "Not like this."

Nick let her go, his eyes dark and menacing, his nostrils flaring with each breath. "Why not?"

Erin turned away from him, unable to face him, struggling to control her breathing. "You're angry."

"That didn't seem to bother you a moment ago."

"I don't want this to happen out of anger."

"What exactly do you think is going to happen?"

She stared straight ahead, starkly aware of him behind

her, appalled that she'd stepped right into his trap. "Nothing," she said. "Nothing's going to happen."

"You sure about that?"

Erin knew what he was trying to do. Push her away so he wouldn't have to face the fact that there was more going on between them than either of them was willing to admit. Emotions and issues that didn't have anything to do with matters of the flesh.

Humiliation that she'd lost control burned through her. She didn't give her body on a whim. She hadn't taken a lover since her disastrous breakup with Warren years ago. Until she met Nick, she hadn't even missed the physical aspect of a relationship.

Taking a deep breath, she turned to face him.

He gazed levelly at her. "I'm sorry," he said. "I shouldn't have done that. I shouldn't have said those things." His jaw flexed. "I shouldn't have touched you."

No man had ever gazed at her the way Nick Ryan did. She wondered how he could look intense and coldly distant at the same time. Erin couldn't keep her eyes from making a quick sweep of him, taking in the rise and fall of his wide chest. The rigid set of his shoulders. The fact that he was still blatantly aroused.

"I have to go," she whispered in a strangled voice.

Never taking her eyes from his, she backed toward the front door. He watched her with predatory intensity, his expression inscrutable.

"Stay away from Stephanie," he said in a quietly dangerous voice. "She likes you, Erin, but she's vulnerable. I don't want her hurt."

"I'd never hurt her," she said.

"I know you wouldn't. Not purposefully. But she's fragile, and I don't want her heartbroken when you decide to go back to Chicago."

Erin steeled herself against the words. She told herself they didn't hurt. That she didn't care. She was a cop; relationships weren't her thing. Still, she felt his words like the jab of a bayonet right through her solar plexus. Dignity forgotten, she turned and fled the barn without looking back.

Erin promised herself she wasn't going to cry. Not again, for goodness sake. It seemed crying was getting to be a habit since she'd moved to Logan Falls and taken up residence on Nick Ryan's hit list. The problem, she decided as she got into her cruiser and slammed the door, was that she'd started breaking her own rules. The ones she'd been living with and doing just fine by since the day Warren had broken her heart and proved to her that most men didn't have the self-assurance to handle a relationship with a woman in a dangerous profession.

Only she knew Nick Ryan wasn't like most men.

As she pulled out of the driveway, she made the mistake of looking in her rearview mirror and catching a glimpse of Stephanie sitting on the front porch, waving her back. The little girl looked so forlorn sitting there with her horse-show trophy in her lap that Erin's throat locked up. A hundred yards away, Nick stood at the barn door, his arms crossed at his chest, watching her pull away.

Erin's heart ached for both of them. Stephanie because she wanted so desperately to lead a more active, normal life, and Nick because he couldn't bear the thought of his child taking any kind of risk. A heartbreaking situation. The only question that remained was which one of them would end up losing the most, and how much it would cost them.

Stay away from Stephanie.

Nick's words rang in Erin's ears, and another wave of pain sliced under her rib cage. For the first time, she realized just how involved her heart had become. The thought elicited an uncharacteristic jab of panic. When was she ever going to learn that police work and relationships didn't mix? Not relationships with men. Certainly not with their children.

It was obvious Nick didn't want to get any closer to her. Well, at least not emotionally. A physical relationship with a man unable to risk his heart for fear of losing it was something she wanted no part of, no matter how attracted she was to him. Not that she wanted his heart in the first place, she reminded herself firmly.

Stephanie, on the other hand, had already snagged Erin's heart. Not a good thing, considering Nick had all but forbidden her to see her. She knew if her feelings for the little girl got any deeper, she herself was going to get hurt. Best not to get involved. Nick didn't want her in either of their lives. He wasn't ready to care for anyone. Stephanie certainly didn't need any more hurt in her life. Maybe Nick was right. Maybe Erin should just go back to Chicago and forget both of them.

And cows had wings.

Not ready to return to the station and risk running into Hector with a kiss-bruised mouth and red-rimmed eyes, Erin turned onto County Line Road and headed away from town. Shrouded with trees from the greenbelt that ran along Logan Creek, the route was virtually deserted. With a little luck, she'd have a few minutes to pull herself together.

She was so caught up in her thoughts that she didn't see the black Lincoln behind her until it was nearly on top of her. Not opposed to handing out a speeding ticket, she eased up on the gas pedal and reached for her emergency strobes switch.

"Okay, speed racer—"

Her words were cut off abruptly as the Lincoln's bumper slammed into the rear of her cruiser. The impact jolted her. Erin gripped the wheel, surprise burning in her gut. She turned her head to get a look at the driver, but like the sedan that had hit her at the school crossing, the windows were darkly tinted. Glancing in the rearview mirror, she checked for a license number to call in, but there was no plate.

Recalling lessons from driving courses she'd taken over the years, she put her foot on the brake. Probably a drunk, she told herself, checking her speedometer and slowing. Never taking her eyes from the car, she reached for her radio mike to call Hector for backup.

Another more forceful jolt knocked the mike from her hand. She looked up in time to see the Lincoln veer to the left and try to pull alongside her. She leaned forward and snagged the mike off the floor. Instinct had her pressing down on the cruiser's accelerator.

"This is McNeal. I've got a code one. County Line Road just west of the Logan Creek bridge."

The Lincoln was nearly alongside her now. She looked over. Her stomach did a slow, sickening somersault when she spotted a shotgun muzzle sticking out the open passenger-side window.

"Code eight! Hector, this is Erin! He's got a damn shotgun! He's trying—"

Her windshield exploded. Glass pelted her. Erin didn't have time to scream. She jerked the wheel to the left, hoping to bump the Lincoln and send it off the road. In the side mirror, she caught a glimpse of the hood. Engine whining, the Lincoln drew up fast on her left. She looked down at the speedometer. Only fifty miles an hour. It seemed like they were going a hundred.

A second shotgun blast rang out. Erin ducked instinctively. Her hand went to her revolver, jerked it from her holster. Glancing in the rearview mirror, she saw that the Lincoln had fallen back.

The cruiser hit a bump and lurched wildly. Realizing she'd veered onto the shoulder, she stomped on the brakes, but it was too late. The Logan Creek bridge loomed before her. The car pitched. Erin saw tall grass. A green kaleidoscope of trees rushed toward her. Oh, God, the car was going to roll. Bracing against the seat back, she screamed, praying the men in the Lincoln didn't decide to brave the ravine and finish the job they'd started.

Chapter 9

Nick should have realized Stephanie would be angry with him. He couldn't expect her to understand why he'd sent Erin away, that he was only interested in protecting his little girl, and saving them both from another run through hell.

The truth be told, Nick wasn't even sure if *he* understood all the intricacies behind his inability to deal with Erin. The one thing he knew for certain was that his instincts were telling him she was a threat. To Stephanie. Maybe even to himself. He wasn't sure which scared him more.

Nick hadn't wanted to acknowledge the similarity between Rita and Erin. But the truth was indisputable; the parallels were now clear. Rita had been a risk taker. Spontaneous. Careless. Daring. Once upon a time he'd loved her for it. But she'd dared fate one too many times. The pain he'd endured after her death had soured his taste for risk, especially when it came to matters of the heart. In the last three years he'd paid the price for loving her a thousand times over.

Was he headed in the same direction with Erin by caring

for her? What about Stephanie? She had lost her mother, her ability to walk—and the precious happiness known only by children. Had he put his little girl's heart at risk by allowing her to get close to another risk taker?

He wanted that happiness back for his child. Wanted it back for her so badly he felt it with every cell of his body. As much as he was attracted to Erin—as much as he'd begun to care for her—she was exactly what they didn't need. A relationship with the gutsy lady cop from Chicago would be nothing short of disaster. He couldn't let himself get any closer. God in heaven, he couldn't let his heart get involved.

Nick nearly laughed at the absurdity of the situation. No, he assured himself, he wouldn't fall for Erin McNeal. Yes, he was...attracted to her. What red-blooded American male wouldn't be? She was sexy as hell. But the bottom line was that he refused to put himself or his daughter through any more heartbreak no matter how much he liked the way Erin kissed.

He could handle his urges. Given some time, he'd find a nice woman he could care for, and eventually bring her home to Stephanie. A woman who knew how to cook and didn't spend her time wrestling suspects and playing with guns. Nick could keep his distance from Erin, he told himself. He possessed the control. He certainly possessed the will.

In his dreams, maybe.

He stood on the front porch and stared at the driveway where her cruiser had disappeared just ten minutes earlier. Guilt tugged at him for the way he'd treated her. What had he been thinking, putting his hands on her like that? That wasn't his style. She hadn't deserved to be humiliated. She hadn't deserved to be pawed at like some kind of sex object. She was no more ready for that kind of relationship than he was. What in the world had prompted him to act so out of character?

Lust, he figured. The hell of it was he hadn't cared at the time. He'd wanted her, had used his own anger as an excuse to cross an indelible line. He'd been so out of control, he hadn't been able to walk back to the house for a while, not without Mrs. Thornsberry noticing the state Erin had left him in.

Nick had too much respect for Erin, and women in general, to treat her with such blatant disregard. In the back of his mind, he'd known what he was trying to accomplish. He'd intended to drive her away permanently with his crude advances. Only his plan had blown up in his face the moment he'd felt the warmth of her flesh beneath his fingertips. When she'd looked at him with those bottomless green eyes, his plan had collapsed beneath the weight of his own desperate need to touch her. He'd ended up losing control and forgetting everything the moment he'd taken that first, sweet taste of her mouth.

"Nick?"

He turned, arching a brow at Mrs. Thornsberry's tone. "What is it, Em?"

The nanny pushed open the screen door and shoved his cell phone at him. "It's Hector. Erin's been in an accident."

A plume of dust clouded the air as Nick raced the Suburban down the driveway. He reached for the radio mike. "Hector, did she give her location?"

"County Line Road is all I heard, Chief. Called in a code one, then an eight. It sounded urgent. Said there was a shotgun—"

Nick cursed at the last word, vaguely aware that he'd flipped on the emergency lights and floored the accelerator. "Where on County Line Road?"

"Logan Creek bridge. You want me to meet you out there?"

The mention of the Logan Creek bridge gave Nick pause, but only for a moment. "Get an ambulance—"

"Parke County Rescue is en route."

"I'll see you in a few minutes." Nick racked the mike. An odd sense of déjà vu engulfed him as he turned onto County Line Road. It had been nearly three years since his wife's accident, but he remembered every agonizing detail with a clarity that made his heart race. Shaken by the force of the emotions surging through him, he gripped the steering wheel and willed his pulse to slow. He wouldn't think of Rita now. He wouldn't think of that terrible day. Or the black months that followed.

He wasn't involved with Erin McNeal, didn't care about her. If she'd gotten herself hurt—or worse—he wouldn't feel it all the way to his soul, the way he had when Rita had died. McNeal was his deputy, nothing more. A troubled cop who'd needed a chance to get back on her feet after a tragic shooting. He'd lent a hand. He liked the way she looked, and had behaved badly. But that was where it ended. He refused to analyze his feelings for her any more deeply than that.

He wouldn't tempt fate by caring for a woman who didn't hesitate to put herself on the line. Nor would he risk his daughter's young heart. No matter how attracted he was to Erin, he wouldn't get involved with her. He wouldn't let her hurt him. He wouldn't let her touch him emotionally. He was immune, dammit. Had been since the night Rita had quietly died in his arms. Never again would he lay his heart out on the chopping block so that fate could slash it at will.

His heart thrummed like a jackhammer when he spotted skid marks near the bridge. Fear gripped him with clawlike fingers as he brought the Suburban to a screeching halt. Throwing open the door, he hit the ground running.

"McNeal!"

The car wasn't anywhere in sight, but the pungent smell

of burning rubber filled the air. He stopped at the bridge, dizzy with fear, sick with remembrance. His gaze followed the skid marks to the edge of the asphalt, where they tore into the shoulder. The car had barely missed the steel girders, cutting a path through the weeds, then plummeting down the embankment.

He stumbled to the edge of the road. His heart rolled when he spotted the overturned cruiser a few feet from the muddy creek bank. A second later he was moving, scrambling down the steep incline. "Erin!" He heard her name as if the voice had come from someone else.

His pulse raged as he sprinted toward the vehicle. "McNeal! Answer me, dammit!"

Dropping to his knees outside the driver's side door, Nick leaned forward, peered inside, and his heart simply stopped. Erin's lifeless form hung suspended, held in place by her safety belt. Her face was deathly pale, her eyes open and staring. Nick's first thought was that she was dead.

"McNeal!" Panic knifed through him. Without thinking, he reached for her. Her flesh was cold to the touch. She didn't stir. "Erin! Honey, can you hear me?"

Her answer came in the form of an elongated groan. She blinked at Nick. "Oh, Nick. I think I screwed up."

The sound of her voice nearly undid him. His emotions rose dangerously to the surface. Relief. Thankfulness. A hundred others he didn't want to name. For a moment he couldn't speak, could do nothing but sit back and thank God she was alive.

"Do you hurt anywhere?" he managed to ask after a moment.

She shifted, her brows knitting. "That's a really dumb question at this point, Chief."

He stared at her, choking back emotions that were trying to strangle him. He was losing it, and she was cracking jokes. "Where do you hurt?" he croaked. "Your neck? Your back?"

"Everywhere except the soles of my feet."

A tension-breaking laugh squeezed from his throat. "You scared the dickens out of me."

Closing her eyes, she smiled faintly. "Me, too."

"I smell gas. Honey, I've got to get you out of the car. Can you move?"

Both of her hands opened and closed. "Yeah."

"What about your legs?"

Her face screwed up with the effort, but Nick saw her ankles flex. "I can move. Let's do it. I don't want to take a chance on becoming a s'more."

Praying he wouldn't cause additional damage in the event that she had a spinal or neck injury, Nick crawled halfway through the window, then reached up to release her safety belt. "I'm going to unsnap your belt. Just relax and fall against me, okay?"

She nodded.

Holding her in place with one arm, he released the belt and felt her sag against him. "Feel okay?"

"Doesn't even hurt."

Nick closed his eyes as another wave of emotion pushed through him. "I'm going to set you down and pull you out of the car. Don't move. Just let me take care of you, okay?"

He should have known she wouldn't obey. By the time he'd backed out of the overturned car, Erin was crawling on all fours. "Nick—"

"I told you to lie still," he growled.

"There was another vehicle. A Lincoln. There was a gun—"

The hairs on the back of his neck stood on end. "Whoever it was, they're gone." Rising, he looked over his shoulder and thumbed off the strap of his holster. "I'll ask you about the car in a moment, okay? Right now I want you to lie down. I've got a cervical collar and blanket in my truck—"

When she started to stand, he merely swept her into his arms. "When are you going to learn to follow orders?"

"Maybe my next life." She looked toward the road. "The other car. Are you sure it's gone?"

"There was nobody here when I drove up. Hector's on his way. An ambulance is en route—"

"They tried to kill me, Nick. Shot out the windshield. I couldn't see. The bridge came out of nowhere...."

"Shh." The need to protect her made him grind his teeth. "I'm armed. No one's going to hurt you."

She felt delicate cradled in his arms. Even through the stench of gasoline, her tantalizing scent floated around his brain. He resisted the urge to put his face against hers and close his eyes just to feel her warmth, just to make sure she was really there.

Grunting with the effort, he ascended the ravine with her in his arms, then settled her onto the grass. A sound from the ravine arrested Nick's attention. They both looked over in time to see fire engulf the cruiser.

"Oh, my God," Erin said hoarsely. "You saved my life."

Nick didn't want her gratitude. He didn't like the way she was looking up at him with those large, green eyes of hers. The combination was messing with his head and making him want to hold her tight and never let go.

"For having just flipped your cruiser, you sure are talking a lot," he growled.

"You're not going to fire me for wrecking it, are you?"

"Depends on how badly the town council rakes me over the coals. I'll let you know."

When she started to sit up, he gently pressed her back into the grass. "Easy, McNeal. Do me a favor and just lie still for a couple of minutes, okay?"

She didn't fight him.

"I'm going to get that collar and blanket. Don't move." He loped to the rear of the truck and threw open the door.

Rummaging quickly through the emergency case, he removed what he needed, then rushed back to her. Dropping to his knees, he fastened the cervical collar around her neck, then snapped open the blanket and covered her from chin to the tips of her toes. Even through the flannel he could see that she was trembling. A cut stood out stark and red on her left temple. Nick hated seeing her pretty skin marred.

"This will help keep you from going into shock," he said.

"I know the drill, Chief. But I'm okay. Honest."

Before he realized he was going to touch her, he raised his hand and pressed his fingers to her cheek. She flinched, but her flesh felt like velvet. Warm. Supple.

She watched him cautiously, her eyes darkening to the color of a forest at dusk. Her hair was spread out beneath her like shiny scraps of silk. Despite the cut on her temple and the smudge of dirt on her chin, he thought he'd never seen a woman look so thoroughly beautiful.

Leaning forward, he pressed a kiss to her forehead. "I'm glad you're all right, McNeal."

She smiled up at him. "Thanks for saving my neck."

"Well, you've got a really nice neck." He tried to smile at her, but failed. "I'm sorry for the things I said to you back at the house. I'm sorry for the way I touched you."

"Nick, it's okay—"

"No, it's not. I had no right."

"I'm a big girl. I knew what I was doing."

"You were upset when you left my house. I did that to you. I don't know what I would have done if you'd been..." Before he could finish, a choking wave of emotion hit him. He straightened, but suddenly he couldn't speak. His throat locked up. His insides turned to jelly. The shakes hit him with the violence of an earthquake. As the first shivers went through his body, he knew just how deep his feelings for this maddening, recalcitrant woman had become.

"Nick?"

He stared at her, aware of the softness of her flesh beneath his fingertips. The slight tremble of her slim body beneath the blanket. She'd come so close to death.... His control hovered just beyond his reach. A jab of panic made him pull his hand away from her. His tremors deepened. His stomach clenched. He didn't want her to see him like this.

Without answering, he rose and walked toward the Suburban. His chest was so tight he could barely breathe. His legs felt wobbly. On reaching the truck, he put both hands against the hood and leaned forward. He felt nauseous, as if someone had kicked him in the gut.

"Nick."

He didn't answer. Didn't turn around to look at her. Didn't even have the strength to tell her to stay away. He just stood there breathing hard, sweating, fighting the panic and whatever else gripped him so tightly that he couldn't move without falling into a heap at her feet.

"Hey," she said gently, "are you okay?"

He jumped when she came up behind him and put her hand on his shoulder. He wanted to tell her to get back under the blanket. To lie down because she could be in shock and not even realize it. That she could have a spinal injury or a head injury and have yet to feel the pain.

Instead, he leaned against the truck, shaking, unable to face her because he didn't want her to see the truth his expression held. "Stay away," he said in a low voice.

"What's wrong?"

"For crying out loud, McNeal, you shouldn't be up and walking around."

"I need to know if you're all right," she whispered.

"I'm fine."

"You're shaking—"

"Forget it."

The wail of a siren in the distance broke the tension that had risen between them. The sound sent a flutter of relief through Nick. He told himself it was because he wanted her to get checked out as soon as possible. But he knew part of the reason he didn't want to be alone with her was because he didn't want her to prod the wound that had just been reopened.

Knowing he couldn't avoid the inevitable, clamping his jaws to keep his expression neutral, he slowly turned to her. His knees went weak at the sight of her tears. They shook him to his foundation, sent the last of his resistance out the window. With an oath, he crossed the distance between them. He didn't remember reaching for her. He didn't remember enveloping her in his arms. All he knew was that the feel of her against him was so right it brought tears to his own eyes, and made him want to protect her from the world, even if she didn't want it that way.

"Why are you crying?" he asked, pressing his face against her hair and breathing in her scent. "You're safe. You're with me. Everything's going to be fine."

"What about you?"

"I'm fine." He swallowed, fighting for control, hating it that the accident had scraped him raw and left him bleeding.

"You don't look fine to me."

"One catastrophe at a time, McNeal, all right?" Pulling back slightly, he looked into her eyes, trying not to tumble into their green depths. "You weren't crying or anything after you left my place, were you?"

"Nick, this wasn't your fault," she said firmly.

He wasn't sure he believed her, but he let it slide. He didn't want to take on any guilt. He had enough emotions to deal with just knowing how differently things could have turned out. "What happened?" he asked after a moment.

Her eyes were luminous and incredibly large in the pale

frame of her face. When she opened her mouth to speak, her lips trembled. "I think it was a professional hit."

Nick paced the emergency room hall, high-grade anxiety pumping through him with each beat of his heart.

I think it was a professional hit.

Erin's words rang like a death knell in his ears. He wished he was surprised, but he wasn't. Not after the incident at the school. A hundred unanswered questions tumbled through his mind. Simultaneously, the need to protect her rose inside him in a violent tide that threatened his viselike grip on control.

Who wanted Erin McNeal dead?

"Chief Ryan?"

Nick spun at the on-call doctor's voice. "How is she?"

The doctor came through the double doors of the emergency room and stopped next to Nick. "She's very lucky. A few bruises and cuts. CAT scan looks good. X rays are normal. We're waiting for blood tests, but I think she's good to go home. You can talk to her now."

A spiral of relief tunneled through him. "Thanks, Doc."

Turning, Nick shoved through the emergency room doors. He scanned the room, his gaze drawn to the woman lying on the gurney in the corner. Something warm loosened in his chest when her gaze met his. Then her mouth curved in a tentative smile, and despite his worry and the questions buzzing around inside his head, he couldn't keep from smiling back.

Never taking his gaze from hers, he approached the gurney. "Has anyone ever called you a trouble magnet, McNeal?"

Her smile widened to a grin. "What do you think?"

"If I wasn't so glad you're all right, I'd probably chew you out just for the hell of it."

"You actually smiled a little when you saw me. I think that's a good sign." Surprising him, she raised her hand

and pressed it to his cheek. "I didn't realize you worried so much."

Nick winced at the contact, knowing she was referring to his emotional reaction back at the accident scene, but he didn't step back. Every pleasure center in his body focused on that small, warm contact.

"You have a really nice smile, Chief. You should try it more often."

Low-level shock rippled through him, mingling with the pleasure of her touch, and went straight to a place he knew better than to acknowledge now. Only then did he notice her slightly dilated pupils and realized the doctor had probably given her something for pain. Just what he needed: a sexy, vulnerable deputy he was attracted to beyond reason in need of protection. Terrific. "You're high as a kite," he grumbled.

"I may be...medicated, but I can plainly see that you have a nice smile." Sighing, she relaxed back into the pillow. "And you smell really, really good."

Not knowing what to say to that, feeling the back of his neck heat—and another part of his anatomy follow suit— he grasped her hand and lowered it to the gurney. "We need to talk," he said. "Think you can answer some questions?"

Her gaze skittered away. "All right."

Compassion stirred in his chest when he realized she wasn't quite ready to relive the incident. He wished he didn't have to put her through it, but he couldn't let it go. He figured neither of them had a choice in the matter.

"I need to know what happened," he said. "I also need a description of the car so I can notify the highway patrol."

"Sure." He watched her force her cop's mask into place. "Black Lincoln. Four-door. Maybe a 2000 model. Illinois plates. There's a big dent on the right front quarter panel."

"Dent?" His interest piqued. "The car *hit* your cruiser?"

She nodded. "The bumper, and the rear quarter panel."

"I'll see if I can get someone out here from the state lab to lift some paint. That might help us nail down the make and model." He grimaced. "What about the driver?"

"I only saw the passenger."

"Can you give me a description?"

"Caucasian male with dark hair. Maybe forty years old. I didn't get a good look. I mean, he had this shotgun aimed right at my head...." Her voice trembled with the last word.

Nick looked away, giving her a moment to regroup. He didn't like the way this was shaping up. Who would be trying to hurt this woman? Someone from her past? An acquaintance? A crazy? Or was there something more ominous in the works?

He looked down at her, felt another stir of compassion. She wasn't crying. He knew she wouldn't cry now. Not Erin McNeal the cop. But even that didn't diminish the vulnerability he saw. She was pale. Shaking. But she never let on that she was scared. Not for one second, and his respect for her—which was already sky-high—kicked up another notch.

"You're doing fine, Erin."

"Hey, it was just a little wreck. Of course I'm fine." She said the words with a little too much enthusiasm.

Nick sighed, not bothering to point out the "little wreck," as she'd put it, could have cost her her life.

"The doc isn't going to keep me here, is he, Nick?"

"You got something against hospitals, McNeal?"

"Only when I'm in them. Do you think you could take me home now?" she asked. "If I get poked one more time I'm afraid I'm going to have to draw my weapon and start shooting doctors."

He forced a smile at her attempted humor, wondering if the repercussions of what had happened had penetrated the fog of shock and medication. "I'll take you home," he said. "We can talk there."

Even through the haze of medication, every muscle in Erin's body ached with a vengeance by the time they reached her apartment.

Nick opened the door, then motioned toward the sofa. "Sit down," he said. "I'll get you a blanket, then I'm going to make some coffee."

Without protest, she limped to the sofa and eased onto a cushion. Hugging a throw pillow to her chest, she pulled her legs under her, and tried not to think about how close she'd come to getting seriously hurt—or worse.

The incident had done more than shake her physically. Her confidence had taken another direct hit. She didn't like feeling so...helpless. She certainly didn't like feeling threatened. The instant she'd seen that shotgun pointed in her direction, Erin had been bombarded with a hefty dose of both.

The clatter of dishes in the kitchen drew her attention to Nick, and she sighed. As much as she didn't want to admit it, she was glad he was there. He represented solidity in a wild, unpredictable sea of too much emotion and not enough fact—elements Erin could do without in her present state.

From her perch on the sofa, she watched him stride from the kitchen to her bedroom. Erin tried not to notice the controlled grace with which he moved, or the underlying restlessness that surrounded him like a dark aura. He seemed thoughtful tonight. Edgy. Unsettled. She wondered if any of those things had to do with the way he'd reacted at the accident scene. Nick wasn't the kind of man to let something like a car wreck shake him. She wanted to think he'd been shaken up because he'd been worried about her, but the more logical side of her knew that wasn't the case. He'd been thinking of Rita, she realized. Erin knew firsthand the face of grief, and saw clearly the mark it had left on this man's heart.

He returned a moment later with the comforter from her bed and draped it over her. "Is your head clear enough for you to answer some questions?" he asked. "The coffee is going to be a few minutes."

She nodded, knowing it was silly to think she could delay talking about what had happened. She was a cop. She was going to have to face the fact that someone had tried to kill her. Then she was going to have to do something about it.

"I need to know everything." He dropped into the love seat across from her and looked at her expectantly. "Details. Descriptions. Possible motives."

Erin told him about the black Lincoln, the passenger with the shotgun, and how her cruiser had been run off the road. Nick listened intently, making an occasional notation in his notepad, his dark eyes watchful and razor sharp.

When she finished, he went to the kitchen for their coffee, then took his place across from her again. "That's not the kind of crime we normally see here in Logan Falls."

"I know."

"That's happened twice since you've been in town. First, the dark sedan tries to run you down at the school crossing, and now this. Both of them had Illinois plates. What do you make of it?"

"I'm not sure," she said, bringing the cup to her lips and sipping. "Seems a little coincidental, doesn't it?"

"Makes me wonder why someone is trying to kill you."

The words jolted her, even though they'd been expected. "I was a police officer for nine years. I worked narcotics for a year. Maybe I ticked someone off. Maybe someone I put away got out of prison. I don't know."

Nick didn't look happy about the scenario. Rising, he strode to the kitchen and snatched up the phone. She watched him as he called in a description of the vehicle and put out an all points bulletin with the highway patrol.

Erin couldn't quite believe this man had so many facets. One moment he was hard and uncompromising, the next exquisitely gentle. The same man who chewed her out on a regular basis could also kiss her senseless, and take her self-control apart bit by bit with those long, magical fingers of his.

He still wore his uniform, and she found her eyes drawn to the wide span of his shoulders, his muscular forearms, the way his torso tapered to narrow hips and runner's legs. The top button of his shirt was open, revealing a layer of fine, black hair. She wondered what it would be like to part that shirt and run her fingers along that pelt of hair to the hard muscles of his abdomen. She wondered if he would resist her. If he would pull her into his arms and kiss her until she was intoxicated with pleasure. She stared, fascinated, appalled that she was openly fantasizing about a man she could never have a relationship with.

Hanging up the phone, he walked back to the living room and took the love seat across from her. "Is there anything you haven't told me?" he asked. "A convict recently released from prison? A personal vendetta? Anything like that?"

"Not that I know of."

"What about the shooting you were involved in six months ago?"

She should have anticipated the question, but it jarred her with unexpected force. The warehouse. Danny. The mistake she would never live down. Oh, how she wanted to put all that behind her. "I've already considered the possibility of a connection," she said. "It doesn't pan out. What happened that night doesn't warrant any kind of...vendetta."

"Most shootings don't make a lot of sense, when it comes right down to it." Leaning forward, Nick set his cup on the coffee table between them and hit her with a narrow-eyed look. "I need to know exactly what happened that night, Erin."

She gripped her mug and concentrated on the warmth radiating into her icy fingers. "Like I told you before, I botched a bust and got myself shot. Danny got hit. I hit one of the perps—"

"Who?"

"We never identified him. He was gone by the time backup arrived."

"How do you know for sure you hit him?"

"There was quite a bit of blood at the scene, but no suspect and no body."

Interest flared in his expression. "Why didn't you tell me?"

"I know what you're thinking, Nick, but none of what happened that night is relevant to what happened today. It happened months ago, in another city, and we have nothing that ties the two incidents together."

"No ties we can see. You know as well as I do that we can't rule out a connection." His jaw flexed. "Is there anything else you haven't told me?"

Erin knew she'd made him angry for not being up front from the beginning, but she didn't like dredging up what had happened that night. She wanted to put it to rest, wanted to put it behind her so badly she could barely bring herself to think about it, let alone discuss it.

"Tell me the whole story. Now. No holds barred."

She flinched at the steel in his voice. "I've already told you what happened."

"You left out a few crucial details, McNeal. Now spill the rest of it."

"It's...complicated."

"I've got all night."

She'd thought she was prepared. But the swirl of shame in the pit of her stomach told her how much it was going to hurt to see the condemnation in Nick's eyes when she told him the truth. She didn't want to believe his opinion had become so important to her. But it had. And she knew then what the truth would cost her. His respect, she realized. The tentative friendship they'd formed. Whatever it was that had been burgeoning between them since the moment she'd walked in the door of the police department and he'd leveled her with those dark, dangerous eyes of his. Until now, she hadn't even realized how precious those things had become—and the realization thoroughly stunned her.

"Danny and I got an anonymous tip that there was going to be a drug buy in a warehouse down on the South Side. A few pounds of black tar heroin. Some cash. It was routine stuff. We were both pretty sure of ourselves back then. Cocky. A little too fond of the rush." The laugh that squeezed from her throat held no humor. "We went in alone. No Drug Enforcement Agency. No backup. We wanted all the credit."

The memory crystallized. The anticipation. The exhilaration. Then the crushing blow of disaster. "Danny went in first—two, maybe three minutes before me. I waited until the last minute, then radioed for backup. I went in through the rear. We should have waited. We should have..." Her words trailed off as the weight of their mistakes pressed down on her. "Things went awry from the start. By the time I got inside, two men already had Danny down on the floor. They were well dressed. Armed to the hilt. Calm." Her voice sounded strangely foreign in the dead silence of her apartment. "They were going to kill him," she said. "Execution style. A cop, for God's sake. Just like that."

A shiver swept the length of her, and she realized with some surprise that her teeth were chattering. She hadn't expected the retelling of that night to be quite so difficult. Not after all this time. But it took every ounce of strength she possessed to continue.

"I couldn't let them kill my partner." Her eyes met Nick's. For the life of her, she couldn't guess what was going on in the depths of that cool, emotionless gaze. In light of what she was about to tell him, she wasn't sure she wanted to know. "I was outnumbered. Outgunned. But I *wanted that bust.* I didn't care about the risks. I didn't consider the possibility that someone might get hurt." In her mind's eye, she saw clearly the terror on Danny's face. She recalled her own terror with such stark clarity that she could feel her heart beating out of control, her breath coming shallow and fast, the oxygen stalling in her lungs. "I drew my weapon and ordered the men to drop their guns and get on the ground."

Nick stared at her, his expression intense. "What happened next?"

"There were only supposed to be two of them. That's what Danny's snitch had told him. He'd been reliable in the past. I didn't see the man on the catwalk until it was too late." The horror of that moment crept over her like an avalanche, cold and smothering. "He came out of nowhere. I looked up at the catwalk, and…like I told you before, he was just a kid. Sixteen, maybe seventeen years old. He smiled at me. That freaked me out." Leaning forward, Erin put her face in her hands, trying to shut out the images, the blood, the guilt. "He had a gun, Nick. I should have stopped him, but I couldn't. I couldn't bring myself to shoot that kid. All my training—none of it mattered because I didn't have the courage to stop him. I just stood there like a stupid rookie while he raised his pistol and shot me down."

Across from her Nick cursed.

"I fired as I went down—and hit him, evidently—but by the time I got my senses back, one of the other two men had already shot Danny in the back."

"You're certain you shot the suspect?" he asked.

"Yes. I saw him fall from the catwalk."

She closed her eyes against the wave of emotion. She hated the thought of telling him the rest of it. In a small corner of her mind she wondered how he was going to react when he found out she'd traded her own life for her partner's.

"I could have stopped it. Had I reacted like a cop, I could have prevented both of us from getting hit."

"Hindsight is twenty—"

"Danny got shot because I didn't have the guts to do the right thing."

"You were under fire," he said. "If you weren't scared at a moment like that, you wouldn't be human."

"I wanted the bust so badly I didn't use good judgment. When the chips fell and things went awry, I panicked. I shot the kid, but only when it came down to saving my own neck. I didn't do the same for Danny. I didn't back up my partner. My God, that's unforgivable...." Her voice broke.

The ensuing quiet bore down on her with the weight of the world. Shame slashed her with the efficiency of a switchblade as the echo of the words she hated to the depth of her soul resounded inside her head.

I didn't back up my partner.

Steeling herself against the condemnation she expected to see in Nick's expression, Erin risked a look at him. To her utter surprise the only thing she saw was understanding.

"You did your best, McNeal. That's all any of us can do. You hesitated because the suspect was a kid. That's a tough call."

"A kid with a gun isn't any less dangerous than an adult."

"True, but the use of deadly force is never an easy decision for a cop, especially if there's a kid involved and you have a split second to decide whether or not to end his life."

Swallowing the lump in her throat, Erin looked down at

her hands, pressed them hard against the pillow to keep them from shaking. "You make it sound as if it's all right."

"Maybe it's not all right," he said. "You had two choices and neither of them were easy. That's hard to accept, but we have to, because we don't have a say in the matter, Erin."

"Danny's paralyzed," she said. "He'll never work as a police officer again, not on the street. I can't help but ask myself, did I do that to him? I see that same question in his eyes every time I see him. He doesn't say it. He's too good a man to lay blame. But I see it. I see it in his wife's eyes. I see it in his children's eyes. And I feel it in my own heart every time I think about what happened that night." She raised her shimmering gaze to his. "So, tell me, Nick, did life go on for Danny?"

Chapter 10

Nick was no stranger to guilt, or the hell it could bring down on someone's life. He considered himself an expert on the subject. After all, he'd lived with his own twisted version for three long years. He knew firsthand the way guilt battered the mind and ravaged the spirit, much the same way cancer invaded, then ate away at the body.

That Erin McNeal suffered the same debilitating affliction over an event that hadn't been under her control disturbed him deeply. That he'd been so hard on her early on—and dead set against hiring her for a job she was clearly qualified for—sent a different kind of guilt tumbling through the wall he'd sworn he wouldn't let anyone penetrate.

"Did you try to ID the suspect you shot?" he asked.

"The hospital check didn't pan out—none of the area emergency rooms had reported a gunshot wound. The lab typed the blood. DNA tests were run, but there wasn't a match in the national database."

He nodded, realizing the Chicago PD had reached a dead

end at that point. He and Erin had, too. If there was a connection between the warehouse shooting and the incident out at the Logan Creek bridge today, they weren't going to find it anytime soon.

Damn, he hated dead ends.

"You know what happened to Danny wasn't your fault, don't you?" he asked.

A smile whispered across her features, as soft and fleeting as a summer breeze. "So I've been told."

"But you don't believe it."

Her gaze faltered, and she looked down at her hands, stilled them. "The last time I went to see Danny, he wouldn't talk to me. He wouldn't even look me in the eye."

Nick wanted to go to her, but he resisted the urge. Touching her was dangerous business under the best of circumstances. To touch her now would surely lead to disaster. He wanted to comfort her, but at the moment he wasn't sure he'd have the strength to pull away. Not when her intoxicating scent filled the small space around them, and he could still vividly remember the feel of her in his arms. The softness of her flesh. The taste of her mouth. He knew better than to pour gasoline on red-hot embers.

"Danny didn't expect you to take a bullet for him," he growled. "No cop expects that."

"He expected me to back him up. Let's face it, Nick, for a cop, I committed the ultimate sin."

"And you're going to make damn sure you pay for it, aren't you, McNeal? You punish yourself with guilt. You take crazy risks. Have you ever bothered to think of the people you'll hurt if something happens to you?"

Her mouth tightened. "Don't try your tough-love routine on me, okay, Chief?"

"You did your best. That's all any cop can do."

"Tell Danny that. Tell his wife. Better yet, tell his kids that when they ask their dad to play ball with them and Danny has to tell them he'll never get up out of that chair—"

"Stop it," he said harshly.

Across from him, Erin stared at him, her hands gripping the pillow. "He hates me," she choked out.

"He hates what happened to him," Nick said. "That doesn't mean he hates you. That doesn't mean he blames you."

"Frank pulled me—"

"Frank pulled you off the street to keep you safe. He knew you needed some time to recover. He *didn't* pull you because you were a bad cop."

He watched her emotional dam fracture with all the restraint he'd come to expect from Erin. Tears welled and overflowed, but she didn't utter a sound. She blinked rapidly. Her throat quivered with a forced swallow. Why couldn't she just let it out and be done with it? Why did she always have to be so tough?

Compassion tightened his own throat at her show of strength. But that sense of compassion was spiked with the dreaded awareness that at some point he'd come to care for her. The knowledge swirled in his head like a stray bullet, cutting him, penetrating a part of him he'd sworn to never again lay open to a woman. How could he let that happen now? How could he let himself care for Erin McNeal? A woman who would do nothing but put him through the wringer with her impulsive behavior and recklessness. A woman who'd already touched his daughter's heart.

A woman who'd gotten dangerously close to his own.

The realization stunned him. Terrified him. Threatened every emotional wall he'd so diligently built around himself.

A sudden need for space sent him to his feet. Without looking at her, he strode to the other side of the room. He needed distance. Dammit, why did it have to be this woman who could topple his defenses without even trying, and make him want her so badly he shook with the need to touch her? Why did it have to be Erin McNeal who was everything that would ultimately destroy him if he got any closer?

Raking a hand through his hair, he stared unseeing into the kitchen, not sure what to do next. He knew if he turned around and looked into her eyes, he would go to her. He would wrap his arms around her trembling shoulders and simply hold her until the tremors stopped. Only he wouldn't stop with just holding her this time. He wouldn't stop with just a kiss. He wanted all of her, and he wasn't sure how much longer his control would last.

Nick figured he was getting pretty good at playing with fire.

"Nick?"

Ignoring the alarm blaring in the back of his mind, he slowly turned. His heart knotted in his chest when her gaze met his. In that instant, he saw too much, too clearly. Her beauty took his breath. Her vulnerability called out to his instinctive need to protect. At the same time, her strength demanded his respect.

The combination completely undid him.

And in the soft depths of her gaze, he saw his own fate.

She hadn't moved from her place on the sofa. He started toward her before he even realized he'd made the decision to hold her. Her expression turned wary, but she didn't move, didn't break eye contact.

Dropping to his knees in front of her, he reached for her. Her welcoming sigh shredded the last of his control. Wrapping his arms around her trembling shoulders, he pulled her to him. Her scent infused his brain, taunting his weaker side, intoxicating the rest him. Vaguely, he was aware of her arms going around him. His name on her lips. And then she was against him. Warm. Soft. Driving him slowly to insanity.

"It hurts, Nick, knowing I'm responsible for what happened to Danny. It won't stop hurting."

"It's okay to hurt, McNeal. Go ahead and let go of it. Let it out."

"I'm trying, but it just keeps getting all tangled up inside me."

"I'll help you untangle it." Pulling back slightly, he gazed into her soft eyes and felt an unwanted emotion shift and then free fall. "First we've got to figure out who's trying to hurt you. Then we'll deal with what's going on inside that head of yours. One disaster at a time. All right?"

She choked out a laugh. "You're the only person I've ever talked to who understands."

"We probably know some of the same demons," he said.

"I guess it's a small world when it comes to demons, isn't it?"

"Sometimes." Her eyes were so clear he thought he could see all the way to her soul. But he also saw questions lurking there, and pulled back just in time to keep himself from falling headlong into that incredible gaze, afraid he might not ever surface. Afraid he might not ever want to.

"The accident this afternoon," she began. "It made you remember, didn't it?"

For a split second, he considered denying it. Mostly because he didn't want to discuss it, didn't like dealing with that painful old wound. But she was right, and they both knew it. His demons had been there this afternoon. Taunting him. Torturing him. Making him remember until he ached with the memory of another car accident that had forever changed his life.

"There are some things you never stop remembering," he said. "Even when you want to. Even after you're healed."

"Are you healed?"

He figured he was about as healed as a man could get after living through the hell of losing a mate. The grief was no longer like a raging beast cut loose inside him. At some point in the last months, the pain had softened to a dull ache that came and went like a capricious illness. Still, he didn't like having that ache probed, certainly not by a woman who threatened to tear the newly formed scar wide open.

Without answering, he rose and eased onto the sofa beside her. As if it were the most natural reaction in the world, Erin leaned against him and laid her head on his shoulder.

"I know what happened today must have been rough for you. I'm sorry."

"It's not like you had a choice in the matter, McNeal."

"Do you want to talk about it?"

He'd known she would eventually ask. He wasn't sure how he felt about that, talking about his dead wife to a woman he was attracted to beyond his good judgment and miles beyond his common sense. A woman whose recklessness stood between them as tangibly as a brick wall.

"Rita's accident happened not far from where you went off the road this afternoon," he began. "Seeing your cruiser down by that creek shook me up."

"Oh, Nick, that must have been terrible for you."

"I'm all right, McNeal. I've been all right for a long time."

"How did it happen?"

Nick took a deep, fortifying breath. "Rita liked to have fun. Only her idea of a good time was pretty extreme. Hell, I had to rappel down into a cave once when she got into a tight spot and couldn't get out." The fact that he could think of her and smile surprised him. It also surprised him that at some point in the last months, he'd lost the ability to conjure up her face the way he used to. He wondered what that meant in terms of healing. He wondered what that meant in terms of his relationship with Erin.

"I can't tell you how many times we fought about her

driving too fast,'' he continued. ''Because of Stephanie, mostly. Because I worried. It was almost as if Rita liked to gamble with fate. Always made me wonder how much value she put on what we had. Our marriage. Our daughter.'' He shot Erin a hard look. ''Rita was irresponsible as hell. Headstrong to a fault. It took a toll on our marriage, but I loved her anyway.

''As a cop, I knew the stats. And I knew her card would come up one day. But Rita was invincible—or so she thought. Always said she wanted to stay twenty-nine forever. On her thirtieth birthday, I bought her a car. Not just any car, but a convertible. It was small. Fast. And made for speed. It was exactly what she wanted. It was exactly what she didn't need.''

Nick had expected the punch of grief to be brutal. To his surprise, it wasn't. At some point, the pain had softened to a melancholy ache that was no longer savage in its intensity.

''Two weeks later, we had a fight. I don't even remember what it was about. Something unimportant, more than likely. But we were both angry. She took Steph and went for a drive.'' Nick broke off, aware that his heart rate was up. Sweat dampened the back of his neck. He wasn't sure why he was recounting the details of that afternoon, but now that he'd opened the floodgates, he couldn't stop the flow.

''I was the first to reach her.''

''Oh, Nick.''

He jolted when Erin took his hand, and he drew strength from her. ''Rita was pinned inside. Unconscious. I knew right away she was in a bad way. Steph was in the back seat, crying. I remember thanking God they were alive. I thought—'' His voice broke as the emotions burst through the barriers he'd erected and fortified.

Vaguely, he was aware of Erin squeezing his hand. The contact was warm. Reassuring. It had been a long time since he'd let anyone reassure him. He wasn't certain why her touch at that moment meant so much to him, but it did. He accepted it, absorbed her strength, trying not to think of the meaning behind his ability to do so.

"I managed to get Steph calmed down, but by the time I got to Rita..." His voice trailed off, but he took another deep breath and continued. "She never regained consciousness. She died in my arms."

Erin's vision blurred as the tears built in her eyes. Mrs. Thornberry hadn't told her that Nick had been the one to buy Rita the convertible. She hadn't realized he'd been shouldering so much guilt, and she felt his pain as if it were her own. The sheer power of it struck her like a fist, taking her breath away.

Nick stared straight ahead, his jaw set. She couldn't stand to see him that way. Hurting. Isolated. Blaming himself for something that wasn't his fault.

She didn't plan to reach for him. She knew that wasn't what either of them wanted. But on a deeper level, she knew that was exactly what they needed.

Turning to him, she pressed the backs of her fingers to his jaw. "That must have been devastating, Nick. I'm so sorry."

"It was tough for both Stephanie and me. But we've moved on. We're doing all right."

"Do you still love Rita?"

"Part of me will always love her. We had a lot of good years together. But when I close my eyes, I don't see her face anymore like I used to. I don't smell her perfume when I enter a room. I don't wake up in the night thinking she's lying beside me."

Erin couldn't imagine the pain of losing a soul mate. She'd always thought she'd loved Warren all those years ago. Only now, faced with this man's grief, did she realize they hadn't even come close.

It was clear to her Nick still loved his wife deeply and needed more time before he was ready to move into another relationship. Erin wasn't sure why that knowledge disturbed her so much. A relationship was the last thing she needed in her own life. It was the last thing Nick needed, too. Neither of them were ready. The realization should have relieved her, but it didn't.

"This might sound odd in light of everything you've gone through, Nick, but I think you're actually a very lucky man."

"How's that?"

"A lot of people go through life never knowing what love is. Somehow, I think that's the ultimate failure."

"Or maybe the ultimate failure is watching that love slip away when there's not a damn thing you can do about it."

"When it comes to matters of the heart, most times control doesn't enter the picture," she pointed out.

He cocked his head, his eyes darkening as his gaze raked over her. "If you want to keep your sanity, you keep your control no matter what."

Erin sensed they were no longer talking in generalities, but about the spark that threatened to burst into flames every time he looked at her, every time he spoke her name, every time he touched her.

"Maybe control isn't everything it's cracked up to be," she whispered.

Nick looked alarmed for an instant, then his mouth curved in an amused half smile. "I think those painkillers gave you a loose tongue, McNeal."

Embarrassment washed over her. She wasn't sure why she'd said it, but she didn't think it was the medication. Maybe because she wanted to deal with whatever was happening between them. Tonight seemed to be the night for clearing the air. The problem was she didn't think either of them were thinking about clearing the air at the moment. There were too many emotions. Too many ghosts. Too many sensations coming all at once, and she was as overloaded as a circuit breaker in an electrical storm.

"The doctor gave me a mild muscle relaxant, and for your information my head's as clear as a bell," she said.

"Well, *that's* a relief. I wouldn't want to take advantage of you if you were mentally incapacitated."

The words sent a nervous laugh tumbling out of her when she realized that was *exactly* how she felt every time she was with him. Mentally incapacitated—and bound and determined to make a mistake that would cost her greatly.

"Your eyes are dilated," he whispered.

"I don't think that's because of the muscle relaxers, either." Raising her hand, she touched his jaw with her fingertips.

He winced at the contact, his gaze darkening, intensifying. "Ah, McNeal, I should have known you liked to play with fire."

"Is that what I'm doing?" she asked.

"That's exactly what you're doing, and we're both loony to be even considering it. I don't think either of us needs to get burned." Intertwining their fingers, he slowly lowered her hand, then released her. "I'd better go before we both become pyromaniacs."

"Or risk spontaneous combustion," she whispered, but her words held no conviction. Maybe because the thought of that kind of heat intrigued her more than it should have. Maybe because she wasn't sure what she wanted. The only thing she knew for certain was that his touch was electric, and her body was conducting that electricity to every pleasure center in her brain.

Logic told her to get up and see him to the door. He was right. But they weren't just playing with fire; they were playing with a stick of dynamite with a short fuse that would leave them both in pieces if it exploded. Nothing but heartache would come from any of this.

But when his gaze met hers, she knew the race was done.

She had no idea who'd won or lost. Oddly, she no longer cared. The only thing that mattered now were the short, dangerous inches separating them, and who was going to bridge the gap.

Leaning closer, Nick drew her to him with slow, agonizing deliberation. Erin let herself be guided, anticipation and dread locked in mortal combat. His lips touched hers with devastating gentleness. A warning blasted in her brain even as the need twisted inside her. Then his mouth was warm and firm against hers as he coaxed her into submission.

He's in love with a memory.

The warning faded beneath the onslaught of pleasure. When he probed her mouth with his tongue, she opened, wanting more. Growling low in his throat, he went in deep, tasting her, devouring the last of her restraint.

Sensation assaulted every inch of her body. Erin felt lost. Afloat on a tiny raft in the midst of a raging sea. One more emotion, one more sensation, and she would be flung over the side, never to be found. But the dark, mysterious depths beckoned her, and she was helpless to resist, like a sea-weary sailor lured by a siren onto treacherous rocks that would send his ship to the bottom of the sea.

Nick cupped her face. Angling her head, he kissed her deeply, possessively. Erin reached for him, her arms encircling his neck. Her hand swept down the length of his back, feeling hard-as-steel muscle quivering with restraint.

"This isn't a very good idea," he murmured. "But you're so damn irresistible."

His voice barely reached her through the roar of blood in her ears. Before her befuddled brain could register a reply, his mouth swooped down again. He kissed her with ruthless skill until she was shaking and weak with desire. Never taking his mouth from hers, he lifted her, easing her more fully onto the sofa. Erin leaned back into the pillows, her every sense honed as he came down on top of her.

A gasp escaped her when he lay full length against her. Bracing himself with his arms to keep his weight from crushing her, he deepened the kiss, ravaging her mouth. She opened to him, her tongue warring with his. Lust rippled low in her belly when she felt his hardness against her hip. Heat spiked lower, burning her until she thought she could no longer bear it. Instinct took over. She opened her legs. He moved in, arching against her. Her body reacted with dizzying intensity. Her control fled. She felt intoxicated, as if she were high on some powerful drug she would never get enough of.

A thousand reasons why she shouldn't make love to this man stormed her brain. He was everything she didn't want. Too strong. Too protective. He couldn't handle her being a cop. He only wanted sex, not a real, lasting relationship. But for Pete's sake, *she* wanted sex. Anything to staunch the fire that threatened to burn out of control.

Erin knew better than to give in to desire, but the need in her heart and the heat in her body destroyed the voice of reason. She relinquished control, felt it tumble away, and gave her body over to the flames.

Chapter 11

Nick had forgotten just how powerful lust could be. And he knew what he was feeling for Erin McNeal was only lust. Simple, uncomplicated, no-strings-attached lust. He was a red-blooded American male who'd been celibate for too long. Of course he wanted her. She was attractive. They were both just tired of fighting it. That was all this was about.

If that was the case, a little voice asked, why did all the other emotions banging around inside him scare the living daylights out of him? Why did he lose sleep thinking about her? Worrying about her? Caring about her, for God's sake? Why did the knowledge that he couldn't keep her safe terrify him so?

Shoving the thoughts ruthlessly aside, he deepened the kiss, exploring the wet silkiness of her mouth. She felt incredibly good beneath him. Pliant. Warm. So soft he ached with the need to feel her bare flesh beneath his hands. The need sent his fingers to the buttons of her uniform shirt.

His hands shook so badly he couldn't manage them. Frustration poured through him.

"Let me," she whispered, and began working the buttons.

Her shirt parted, and a lacy white bra came into view. He cupped her breasts, found them small and utterly exquisite.

"You're beautiful," he murmured, and brushed his thumb over the hardened peaks of her nipples.

Erin cried out, her body bucking beneath him. Nick clenched his jaw, struggling to keep a grip on control. He wanted to take his time with her. He wasn't a fast lover. Had never been that way. But nothing was the same with this woman. She drove him too close to the edge, too quickly. He wasn't even undressed yet and already felt on the verge of ending what promised to be one of the most erotic experiences of his life.

Lifting the edge of her bra, he eased it up and over her breasts. Urgency burned him. Nick broke the kiss. He wanted to taste her. Wanted her flesh in his mouth. Her body writhing beneath him.

She nearly came up off the sofa when his mouth closed around her nipple. She arched and cried out his name. He suckled, but the intimate contact wasn't enough. He wanted more. Wanted to be inside her. Needed her more than the very air he breathed.

Breaking contact, he trailed kisses up her throat to her mouth. He kissed her deeply, losing himself in her sweetness, telling himself this was part of the ritual, and that it didn't have to mean anything to either of them.

With shaking hands he fumbled with her belt, managed to get it open. He groaned when he felt her own hands around him, driving him wild. Need cut through him like shears through gossamer fabric. He kissed her temple, her cheek, her neck. He lowered her zipper, found her belly flat and firm beneath his palm. She tensed when his fingers found her curls, but he didn't stop. He kissed her, his tongue entering her mouth the same moment his finger slipped inside her. Hot, wet silk surrounded him.

Erin cried out, her body going rigid beneath him. He stroked her, barely hearing her call his name over the roar of blood through his veins.

This wasn't just sex.

The thought blindsided him.

Pulling back just enough to see her face, he looked down at her, felt something vital shift in his gut. Simultaneously, panic swirled low and deep in his chest.

She gazed back at him, her cheeks flushed, her eyes soft with desire. Perspiration dampened her forehead. Her mouth was kiss bruised and wet. Good Lord, he *wanted* her, more than anything.

Nick closed his eyes, stunned by the depth of feelings raging through him. He didn't want just a single night of lovemaking, he realized. He wanted a lot more than merely her body. He wanted all of her. Heart. Soul. Her very spirit. God help him, he *cared* for her.

The swirl of panic grew into a tornado.

He'd broken his own cardinal rule. A rule that had been nonnegotiable for three long years. A rule he'd embraced and lived by since loving and losing his wife.

Erin McNeal was exactly the kind of woman he didn't need. She would finish the job of turning his life upside down. She would rip out his heart and not even realize what she'd done. She would hurt Stephanie—his sweet, innocent child who'd already been hurt so terribly.

The old pain surfaced, like a slick of oil spreading over water. The need to protect his heart—and his daughter's—warred with something more complex. The combination made him feel sick and cold and as old as the world.

Gently, he pulled away from Erin and rose. His groin throbbed with the need to be inside her. Frustration clawed at him. His heart ached with the realization of what he'd allowed to happen. How could he have let himself care about this woman?

Aware of the rush of blood through his veins, the dizziness swirling in his head, Nick stood with his back to her and willed his head to clear. He couldn't look at her. Not when he was painfully aroused and holding on to control by a thread.

"Nick?"

He set his jaw against the urge to turn around and go to her. He wouldn't do that to himself. He wouldn't do that to Stephanie. "Stay away from me, McNeal."

He heard her rise behind him. He winced when her hand settled on his shoulder. "What's wrong?" she asked.

Slowly, he turned to her. The sight of her gutted him. Her eyes were soft with desire, cautious with uncertainty. Her uniform shirt was unbuttoned, and he saw her bra and the swell of encased flesh. Her mouth was red and swollen from his kisses. Her scent surrounded him like a sweet elixir.

He wanted her. He wanted her so badly he was almost willing to put himself through the agony she would surely bring him. Almost.

He wasn't strong enough to survive another loss.

Steeling himself against the sight of her, he said, "I've got to go."

"Nick…"

Spurred by the knowledge that if she touched him again, he wouldn't have the strength to walk away, he started for the door. "Effective immediately, you're on administrative leave."

"Administrative *leave?*" she echoed incredulously. "Wait a minute!"

He didn't stop. "In the interim, one of my deputies or I will take turns watching your apartment."

"Watching my apartment?"

"Someone has declared open season on you, or have you forgotten about that?"

"No, but—"

"You'll still receive full pay. I'll notify you when you can come back to work."

"I don't accept those terms!"

He prayed she wouldn't come after him. He wasn't sure what he would do if she touched him. Pull her against him and kiss her until they were both senseless, probably. Or maybe ease her down to the floor and make wild, passionate love to her until neither of them could move.

Quickening his pace, he flung open the door. The urge to glance back at her was strong, but he didn't do it. He didn't want to see the hurt in her eyes. He didn't want to know he was the one who'd put it there. He stepped into the hall. She called out his name. He slammed the door behind him.

"Chief?"

Nick jerked at the sound of Hector's voice. He looked up from the paperwork on his desk to see his deputy standing in the doorway of his office, staring at him as if he'd shaved his head and put a ring in his nose.

"Didn't you hear your line buzzing?" Hector asked.

Nick frowned at the phone on his desk, noticing the blinking light. It wasn't the first time in the twenty-four hours since he'd last seen Erin that he'd zoned out. "Who is it?" he growled.

"Frank Rossi returning your call."

Waiting until Hector retreated into the main reception area, Nick punched the line. "It's about time you called, Frank. I was starting to think you were avoiding me."

"Now, why would I do that, partner?" the other man asked.

"Maybe it has something to do with Erin McNeal."

"My favorite niece," Frank said easily. "Good cop, too. How's she working out?"

"Just fine, if I didn't mind my deputies getting run off the road and shot at. Any idea what that might be about?"

Tense silence buzzed through one hundred miles of fiber-optic cable.

"I figured you might be able to fill me in, since you didn't bother when you sent her down here," Nick snapped. "Who's after her, Frank?"

A curse broke the silence, then Frank sighed. "Is she all right?"

"She's fine. I put her on admin leave. I'm still waiting for an answer."

"I don't have all the answers, Nick."

"Since you obviously know more than I do, let's start with what you *do* have."

Frank sighed. "You're aware of the shooting she was involved in six months back? The perp she took out in that warehouse the night Danny Perrine was shot?"

"What about it?"

"We had DNA pulled from the blood at the scene. It was a long shot, but we sent it out anyway, hoping for a lucky break. Preliminary results came back, but when we punched the info into the national database we didn't get a match."

The hairs on the back of Nick's neck stood on end. "So, you didn't ID the thug she shot. What does that have to do with someone putting McNeal on their hit list?"

"Erin and Danny Perrine were operating on a tip that night in the warehouse, Nick. There was supposed to be a heroin buy. A couple of pounds. Some cash. In the scope of things, it should have been small time."

Nick wasn't sure he even wanted to hear what Frank was going to say next. He didn't like mysteries when it came to police shootings. He sure as hell didn't like the way this one was shaping up. "Who was the thug?"

"Does the name Damon DiCarlo ring a bell?"

Nick barely heard the last part of the sentence over the pounding of his pulse. "If he's any relation to Vic DiCarlo, I'd say we have a hell of a problem on our hands."

"Damon is his son."

It was Nick's turn to curse. Vic DiCarlo was Chicago's version of John Gotti. Ruthless. Powerful. With a reputation for violence that left even veteran cops nauseous. "You kept me in the dark, you son of a bitch."

"Save it, Nick. I'm not finished."

"Why didn't I know about this?"

"You didn't know because I didn't know. Regardless, I thought Erin would be safe down there."

Cold realization crept over Nick like freezing rain down the back of his neck. "Erin shot Vic DiCarlo's son."

"That's what we suspect."

"Why did it take the Chicago PD six months to figure it out, for crying out loud?"

"Damon DiCarlo doesn't have a record," Frank said. "He's never even been arrested. So his DNA wasn't in the database. We had to get a warrant and search his apartment. We finally got something from a hairbrush. To extract DNA, we had to find a hair with a damn root attached. That took some time. After the lab typed it, we had to match it with the blood we found at the scene. That's no easy feat."

"Have you picked him up?"

"We would have picked him up weeks ago and found some other way to collect his DNA, but Damon DiCarlo is missing. The feds have had surveillance teams out looking for weeks, but no one has been able to locate him."

"How long has he been missing?"

"Six months."

Nick cursed again. "What about the old man?"

"He's in Sicily where we can't touch him—"

"He's not in Sicily, Frank."

The other man hesitated. "Intelligence tells us he is."

"I'll bet he's in the States. Maybe even here in Logan Falls. He's after Erin, damn you."

"That's not possible."

Nick ground his teeth. "You put Erin and my entire town at risk."

"The Chicago PD doesn't operate on hunches, Nick. I suspected DiCarlo was involved, but I couldn't act until I had proof."

"What about Erin? Did she know?"

"She suspected. It was Danny Perrine's snitch who tipped them off. Erin didn't have any proof."

Anger lashed through Nick like a bullwhip. He'd deal with Erin and her not confiding in him later. Right now, he needed facts. All of them. "Tell me what I need to know, Frank."

"From all appearances, Damon was running heroin," Frank said. "He'd been using since high school. Vic was of the old school. Like most of his Mafia cronies, he didn't approve of drugs—particularly heroin. He probably didn't even know Damon was running his own little show. I suspect Erin shot Damon in the warehouse that night, injuring him or possibly even killing him. Vic DiCarlo found out about it and covered for his son. He didn't want his son's reputation within the Mafia family tarnished, so he picked him up and took him to a doctor. If his son died that night, he may have gone to Italy simply to bury him. We were going to pick up McNeal as soon as we knew the whole story."

"You're too late," Nick said tonelessly. "We've had two incidents here already—"

"If DiCarlo wanted her dead, she'd already be buried."

A wave of fear washed over Nick, mingling with the anger, burgeoning into something volatile and dangerous. He looked down, found his free hand clenched into a fist so tight his knuckles hurt. "I want McNeal protected."

"I can have a U.S. Marshal down there first thing in the morning. We'll transport her to a safe house out of state—"

"Make it two marshals, and they'd damn well better be here before morning." Fear stabbed through the anger like an ice pick through slush when he realized Erin wasn't the only one who was vulnerable. His entire family was at risk. Stephanie. Mrs. Thornsberry. "I want my family protected, too."

"DiCarlo isn't after you or your family, Nick."

"Unlike you, Frank, I'm not willing to take that chance. Just do it. Two marshals for Erin, and two for my family." Without waiting for a reply, Nick slammed down the phone.

He couldn't believe it had come to this—the sludge from Chicago's underworld leaching all the way down to Logan Falls. Why the hell hadn't Erin confided in him?

The urge to go to her was overwhelming. He had to know she was safe. He had to keep her that way until the marshals arrived. But the need to protect Erin was tempered with the terrifying knowledge that he hadn't been able to keep Rita safe. He hadn't been able to keep Stephanie safe.

Nick stood abruptly, aware that his heart was beating out of control. How was he going to protect her and his family against a Mafia kingpin who had his own private army at his beck and call? Striding to the door, he swung it open and stepped in to the outer office.

Hector looked up from his desk, his brows drawing together. "What's wrong, Chief?"

"I want you to get the cruiser and follow me to my house." Crossing the room, Nick unlocked the gun cabinet and removed the department shotgun, which hadn't been touched since last year, when he'd cleaned it up for the Boy Scout tour. "Take this along, with extra ammunition for your sidearm. Wear your vest."

"My *vest?*" The other man jumped to his feet, his eyes as big as saucers. "Holy cow, Chief, what's going on?"

"Precautionary measures. I just spoke with Chicago PD. Vic DiCarlo might be paying McNeal a visit for something that happened back in Chicago a few months back."

"Vic DiCarlo?" Hector's mouth dropped open. "*The* Vic DiCarlo?"

The name sent an icy finger of dread scraping up Nick's spine. "We're going to drive over to my house, then you're going to escort Steph and Mrs. Thornsberry to that physical rehab center in Indianapolis."

"Indianapolis? You mean, like, right now?"

"I mean like five minutes ago," Nick said sharply. "No one's looking for them, Hector. This is only precautionary. But I'd feel better if they weren't here in Logan Falls."

"Yessir! I'm on it, Chief."

"You'll be secure at the rehab center. Em has the address. Two U.S. Marshals will meet you there in a few hours. I'm going to stay here and make sure McNeal gets to a safe house."

Looking excited and uncertain at once, Hector strode to the coat tree and grabbed his hat. "I'll take good care of them, Chief. I'll guard them with my life."

Nick stood in the center of the room feeling gut-punched, praying that wouldn't be necessary.

Erin landed a punishing blow to the punching bag, the force of it vibrating up her arm all the way to her shoulder. She'd long since worked up a sweat. Her temper was beginning to calm, but her muscles felt like overcooked noodles. The bruises she'd received in the car accident weren't helping matters, but she couldn't stop now. Boxing, she'd learned, was the secret of the universe when it came to relieving stress.

Of course, it didn't surprise her that Nick Ryan had shot that theory to pieces.

She hadn't seen or spoken to him since the scene at her apartment the day before. Just as well, she told herself for the dozenth time. He'd had no right to put her on administrative leave. Other than to avoid her, he hadn't had a solid reason for pulling her off the street. He sure didn't have a reason for posting one of his deputies outside her apartment like some kind of bodyguard.

But she knew it was the bit about him avoiding her that bothered her most. It hurt, she realized. Not only because he'd pushed her away just when they'd formed a sort of tentative friendship, but more importantly because of all the other emotions swirling around in that foolish heart of hers. She cared for him—a lot more than was wise or prudent or all those other virtues she'd never gotten the hang of. She cared for him a lot more than a woman like her should, knowing what she did about men like Nick.

The thought made her want to laugh—or cry. She'd fallen headlong for a man who couldn't handle her being a cop. A too strong, too proud, overprotective man who would never tolerate her love of law enforcement. Who would never understand her. Who would always try to control her under the guise of keeping her safe.

A man just like Warren, who'd yanked her young heart out of her chest and torn it into little pieces right before her eyes. Six years ago, she'd stood there like a fool, feeling every rip, and finding herself willing to give up everything just so he would love her. No matter how much it hurt, she wouldn't make the same mistake with Nick.

A harsh laugh escaped her as she stilled the bag and centered up for her next blow. Why did everything always have to get so complicated, anyway?

Dancing to the left, she jabbed with her right arm and connected solidly with the bag. *Thwack!* The sound of her glove against vinyl echoed through the bedroom, giving her a small, greedy dose of satisfaction. So what if he didn't want her? Erin could handle that. The man was still in love with a memory, for God's sake. They were both better off without the complications a relationship would bring. She didn't need him or his uncompromising attitude.

Thwack!

Just because he was the only man who'd ever kissed her senseless didn't mean her feelings for him went any deeper than hormones.

Thwack! Thwack!

Just because her heart felt as if it were being ripped from her chest every time she thought of spending the rest of her life without him didn't mean she was in love with him, did it?

Love? Good Lord, who said anything about love?

"You ought to keep your door locked, McNeal. There seems to be a few shady characters running around Logan Falls lately."

Erin spun at the sound of Nick's voice. Her legs went weak as his presence registered. The blood drained from her head at the sight of him. She'd seen plenty of cops in her time, but she'd never seen a man look as good in a blue uniform as Nick. Of course, he didn't look happy to see her. Like that came as a surprise. He was never happy to see her—unless he was going to fire her or otherwise do his best to make her miserable.

She stared at him, aware of her pulse jumping, her heart climbing into her esophagus. His eyes raked her like cut onyx. His mouth was set into a grim line. She wondered how long he'd been standing there, watching her.

Intent on playing it cool, she turned away and threw another jab at the bag. *Thwack!* "What are you doing here?"

"We need to talk."

Thwack! "About what?"

"About Vic DiCarlo."

Everything inside her froze into a solid ball of ice. Reaching out, she stilled the bag with her gloves, then turned to Nick. For the first time, she saw the anger smoldering like hot coals in his eyes.

"Frank filled me in on your little secret," he said in a low, dangerous voice.

She didn't know what to say. "I know how this might look to you, but—"

"For crying out loud, don't play dumb, McNeal. It's insulting, and you don't do it very well." A humorless smile twisted his mouth. "You lied to me. You figured out DiCarlo wanted you dead the day the sedan hit you at the crosswalk, only you didn't see fit to discuss it with me, did you?"

"I didn't lie to you—"

"You shot DiCarlo's only son in the warehouse that night, McNeal. Did you think he was just going to let that slide?"

Erin felt the words like a punch. "I didn't know for certain who I shot in that warehouse."

"I don't believe you," he said. "I took a chance on you, and you lied to me. I took you on against my better judgment, and you made a fool of me." He laughed bitterly. "I didn't need much help, did I?"

His self-deprecating tone stirred her temper. "Back off, Nick."

"You suspected it was DiCarlo. You should have told me."

"Frank asked me to keep it under my hat until we had proof."

"Frank's an idiot for not having you in a safe house."

"You're overreacting," she said, but there was no conviction in her voice.

"The DNA came back, Erin. It's a match to Damon DiCarlo."

Suddenly, she felt sick to her stomach. "I'm sorry—"

"You might get off on adrenaline and the occasional game of risk, but I can do without it." He started toward her, his mouth set in a grim line. "You not only endangered yourself this time, but you endangered my town...and my family."

Erin had never seen him so angry. His jaws were clenched tight, his hands fisted at his sides. The sight of him, combined with the shocking knowledge that DiCarlo was behind the two attempts on her life, sent a wave of fear slicing through her.

"I wouldn't—"

"You brought my child into this." Nick reached her, eyes narrowed, nostrils flaring. "You put her in danger." He shoved the punching bag hard with the last word. The bag swung, catching Erin on the shoulder, hard enough to knock her off balance. Temper rising, she lashed out. Her glove glanced off Nick's jaw, sending him back a step.

Thwack!

Regret knotted her stomach the instant she hit him. In all the nine years she'd been a cop, she'd never struck anyone in anger. Not even when they'd deserved it. Yet here she was, taking her anger and fear and frustration out on a man who clearly didn't deserve it.

Anger flashed like black diamonds in his eyes.

"I'm sorry. I didn't mean to—" Erin barely saw the blur of his uniform as he rushed her.

In a classic wrestling move, he took her down on the mat. She landed flat on her back. Surprise rippled through her that she'd landed so gently. Anger followed when it dawned on her how easily he'd overpowered her. Those feelings turned quickly to something much more intense the instant he came down on top of her.

He straddled her, pinning her arms at her sides. "Don't ever hit me again," he growled.

Erin couldn't catch her breath. Too many emotions and sensations pummeled her all at the same time. He was too close. She was too weak to fight her feelings for him much longer. They were both too involved to do anything except make the situation infinitely worse.

"Let go of me," she said breathlessly.

"Not until you explain to me what the hell is going on."

"I can explain standing up."

"Like you did a moment ago, when you punched me?"

His left jaw was red. She stared at him, guilt tugging at her conscience. "I'm sorry."

"I've been beating my brains out for days trying to figure out who wants you dead, McNeal. All the while, you're holding out on me."

"What did you expect me to say, Nick? That I need a job, but by the way, there's an outside chance a well-known Mafia don is trying to kill me? I'm sure that would have gone over well."

Nick cursed.

"Frank thought I'd be safe in Logan Falls," she said.

"That was incredibly irresponsible of both of you!"

"I didn't intend to endanger your family." The repercussions of her own words settled over her like a dark cloud. "Oh, Nick... You don't think Stephanie... I wouldn't—"

"You didn't even consider the possibility, did you, McNeal?"

Erin felt the words like the blade of a knife slicing her clean through. "I wouldn't endanger her. Where is she?"

"I sent her out of town with Hector. She's safe."

Relief untwisted one of the dozen or so knots in Erin's gut. "I'm not going to let DiCarlo get away with any of this. I'm going to stop him."

Nick glared down at her, breathing hard, his face suffused with anger. "How are you going to do that? Wait until he comes knocking, then go after him with guns blazing, grenades exploding? Take him out with a little hand-to-hand? Or maybe you're going to put that black belt of yours to use and break his neck."

The burst of anger came so powerfully, so quickly, that for a moment Erin saw red. She bucked beneath him, trying to topple him, but he was too heavy, and her struggles were futile. "I'll take him out however I see fit."

Nick leaned closer. "I'm not going to let you do it."

"Why do you care?" she retorted.

"Call me a damn fool, but I don't want to see you hurt."

"You don't care about me," she snapped.

"That's where you're wrong," he growled. "It goes against everything I know about you, but I care. A lot more than I should, considering you have the common sense of a terrier pup who just had its bone stolen by a pit bull. I care a hell of a lot more than I want to. More than you want me to, in fact. But, dammit, I do. So don't think I'm going to let you walk into a dangerous situation alone, because it's not going to happen."

Nick couldn't believe he'd said those killing words. Not to Erin. But the moment he'd walked into her apartment and seen her in sweatpants and T-shirt, punching that bag, all bets were off. He hadn't even bothered to pretend he was still in control. Why should he? He hadn't been in control since the day she'd walked into his office and way-laid him with that big-city cop attitude and those pretty green eyes.

Now, as he stared down at her, his temper tangled with emotions he didn't want to deal with, and physical sensations more powerful than anything he'd ever known. Even knowing she was wrong for him—knowing fully she had no intention of changing her ways—he still wanted her. Wanted her so desperately he felt the need all the way to his marrow.

"You don't have the guts to care for me," she said.

She'd tried to make the words sound cavalier, but Nick knew his admission had surprised her. Hell, he'd surprised himself. This wasn't supposed to happen. They both knew it. So why hadn't he just kept his mouth shut?

"You're not making it easy," he growled. "I ought to walk away right now and let DiCarlo have you."

Erin snorted. "Like I need you to protect me."

"Oh, yeah, I forgot. You're *the* Erin McNeal. You can take on DiCarlo all by yourself. Just because most of his victims end up fitting in a coffee can after he's finished with them doesn't mean that would happen to you. Not Erin McNeal, female cop extraordinaire."

"Go to hell."

She tried to get up, but he kept her pinned. He wanted to shake her, anything to make her understand the danger she faced when it came to DiCarlo. "He wants you dead, McNeal. You shot his son. Maybe even killed him. What do you think he's going to do if he gets his hands on you?"

"He's not going to get his hands on me."

She'd spoken the words with conviction, but Nick didn't miss the shiver that rippled the length of her. He felt a swell of relief that she was finally beginning to understand the gravity of her situation.

"I'm taking you to a motel." Gritting his teeth against the ache that had taken up permanent residence in his groin, he hoisted himself off her and stood.

Propping herself on an elbow, she glared up at him. "I'll agree to go with you on one condition."

"Like you have a choice." He extended his hand, trying not to notice the way that T-shirt hugged her curves. "I'm not bargaining with you, McNeal."

"I'm not going to sit around and wait for DiCarlo to make his move."

If she hadn't been dead serious, he might have laughed. As it was, the determination in her voice put a brick of dread in the pit of his stomach. "You've got five minutes to pack a bag," he said. "If you're not ready to leave by then, I'll handcuff you and force you to come with me."

"You wouldn't dare."

"You know I will."

She reached for his hand, and he pulled her easily to her feet. "I want DiCarlo," she said.

"Evidently, the feelings are mutual."

"This is the perfect opportunity—"

"Pack, McNeal."

"Dammit, Nick, I owe it to Danny."

"Loyalty is an admirable trait, but it won't do you any good if you're dead." He looked at his watch. "You have four and a half minutes to pack a bag."

"If DiCarlo is so intent on finding me, why hasn't he made a move until now? It's been six months since the shooting."

"Frank said he's been in Sicily. As far as he knows, he was there burying his son."

"If, indeed, DiCarlo is behind this, his attempts to get at me were halfhearted at best. That's not his style."

"Maybe he wants you alive. He's not above a personal visit when it comes to revenge, especially when he gets to be the grim reaper."

Muttering an unladylike oath, Erin turned away and stalked to the opposite side of the room. Nick watched, steeling himself against the fierce need to protect her, and another need that demanded distance and objectivity.

"All right," she snapped. "I'll go with you. But only until we can come up with a plan. I'm not going to sit it out."

He considered telling her she could discuss that with the two U.S. Marshals who would be meeting her in a few hours to take her to a safe house, but decided she'd be easier to handle if she didn't know she was about to be pulled from the race.

"Okay, McNeal. You've made your point. Pack. You've got two minutes left."

As Nick watched her stalk toward her bedroom, he realized all he had to do now was figure out a way to keep his hands off her for the next few hours.

Chapter 12

Nick knew taking Erin to the Pioneer Motel wasn't the smartest thing he'd ever done. But mistakes seemed to be his specialty when it came to her. Considering the electric attraction that arced between them every time they were within earshot of each other, he was probably setting himself up for a night of frustration at best. But what else could he do? Walk away when it was now clear that someone was trying to hurt her? Nick had never been good at walking away—even when it was the smart thing to do. For the life of him he couldn't think of a safer place for her. He couldn't let her stay at her apartment. He couldn't take her to his house. So he'd opted for the Pioneer Motel—and a long, long night.

Located off the highway on the outskirts of town, the motel offered obscurity and the kind of anonymity that would buy them safety until the U.S. Marshals arrived. All he had to do was get through the next few hours without touching her. That shouldn't have been a problem, considering she was frothing at the mouth to get at DiCarlo.

"Nice place," she grumbled, tossing her overnight bag onto one of the double beds.

He locked the door behind them and flipped the dead bolt into place. "Welcome to Logan Falls's version of a five-star hotel."

Without looking at her, he inched a curtain aside and peered into the parking lot. Dusk had settled, but the sodium vapor lights hadn't yet come on. The parking lot was empty, except for a rumbling semi rig and an old station wagon. He should have been relieved there wasn't a Lincoln Continental with Illinois plates idling within plain sight. But he had been a cop long enough to know DiCarlo wouldn't be subtle when he decided to make his move.

Nick's unease had grown steadily stronger since he'd spoken to Frank just over an hour ago. Every time Nick thought of DiCarlo, and the man's reputation for violence, the hairs at his nape prickled. Every time he thought of DiCarlo getting his hands on Erin, that same uneasiness burgeoned into a cold fear that sat in his gut like a chunk of ice.

She was one of the most maddening, persistent people he'd ever met. How was it that the same woman who'd brought so much light and happiness into his daughter's life had brought so much tumult to his? She was impulsive. Headstrong. Courageous. Fallible. And more vulnerable than she would ever admit. How could he let himself care for a woman who planned to single-handedly bring down Chicago's most ruthless mafioso?

But, Lord, he didn't think he could stay away from her much longer. She appealed to him on a level that made him feel a little crazy—and in way over his head. Since the day she'd walked into his office and given him that cool once-over with those feline green eyes, Nick had been tied up in little knots. How was he supposed to deal with her when every time he looked at her all he could think of was how right it felt when he held her in his arms?

"Look at this."

Turning away from the window, he glanced at her and felt his mouth go dry. She sat cross-legged on the bed, her laptop opened in front of her. She'd changed into faded jeans and an old T-shirt before leaving her apartment, and the clothes clung to her in all the wrong places. Her hair was drawn back in a ponytail, revealing her slender neck and delicate jawline. He had the insane urge to go to her and run his tongue along her throat just to see if she tasted as good as she looked.

Gritting his teeth against the annoying rush of blood to his groin, Nick approached the bed. "What do you have there, McNeal, access to the Illinois Crime Lab Database?"

"Better." She shot him a superior smile. "A database still under development. It tracks the movement of known criminals, namely Mafia types. The big, mean dogs."

"Your favorite kind," he said dryly. "I'm not even going to ask how you got into that databank."

"You probably shouldn't." Her fingers danced over the keys. "Knowing you, you'd probably want to arrest me."

Scowling, Nick glanced down at the screen, where Vic DiCarlo's name blinked. "Our boy's been busy."

"A subsidiary of one of his corporations owns a Learjet. Modified fuel tanks for long hauls." She tapped a key, and the screen scrolled down. "A day after the warehouse shooting, his personal pilot filed a flight plan from New York to London. From there they flew to Sicily."

"Interesting destination."

"Family reunion, no doubt."

"Or a funeral."

Erin's finger quivered slightly when she hit another key. "Interesting perspective, Chief. But Sicily would also be a good place to rehab if you'd been shot."

"Just what do you plan to do with this information?" he asked.

"Use it to get DiCarlo off my back."

"What are you going to do, hit him over the head with your laptop?"

She looked up from the monitor and frowned. Her eyes were so clear and earnest that for a moment he thought he might do something stupid, like lean forward and kiss her until she forgot all about Vic DiCarlo.

"The computer says DiCarlo is in Sicily," he said instead.

"I think he's back in the States," she said. "He knows the feds are watching, so he did it secretly. No flight plan." She paused. "I think you and I should put our heads together and figure out a way to flush him out."

Anger unfurled in his gut, but Nick curbed it. It wouldn't do him any good to snap at her. He'd already tried that and it hadn't worked. Maybe he could shock her into believing the mob didn't mess around when it came to revenge.

"You shot his son, Erin. DiCarlo won't let it go. He's not going to forget about it."

"If DiCarlo wanted me dead, I wouldn't be here."

"Maybe he doesn't just want you dead. Maybe he wants to hurt you the way you hurt him. You know his reputation when it comes to cops. If he decides to make an example of you, there won't be enough of you left to bury." She started to speak, but Nick silenced her by raising his hand. "Do us both a favor and let the feds handle this."

Unfolding her legs, she rose quickly and crossed to the other side of the room. "I'm not going to walk away."

Nick reached down, punched the power button on her laptop and closed the case. "If I have any say in the matter, you will."

She glared at him. "Don't let your philosophy on female cops cloud your judgment, Chief."

"What the hell is that supposed to mean?"

"I mean that misplaced sense of honor of yours that cringes at the thought of me getting into a tight spot with DiCarlo. Admit it, Chief. For all your enlightenment, there's a part of you that thinks women and police work don't mix.''

A kick of anger surged through him. "Recklessness and police work is the mix that chafes me.''

She laughed sharply. "Right. That's why you nearly blew a gasket when I took down those two suspects during the Brass Rail robbery.''

"Your being female has nothing to do with it.''

"Hector would have gotten a pat on the back, a gold star and a free beer. He sure wouldn't have gotten assigned to the school crosswalk—''

"Hector wouldn't have risked his life on two small-time bums who would have been picked up by the highway patrol within the hour.''

"I'm not going to run away from DiCarlo just because the thought of me taking him down grates on your male sensibilities.''

Nick's temper uncoiled. He was across the room, his fingers closing around her arms, before he even realized he had moved. "You want to know what's wrong with that picture, McNeal?''

She stared at him, surprise and a hefty dose of anger suffusing her face. "Let go of me.''

"DiCarlo isn't some two-bit hood. He's cunning and he's ruthless. He's got an army of mindless goons just waiting for the chance to cap a cop. Call me a Neanderthal if that makes you feel better and helps you justify your need to make amends with your conscience, but I'm not going to stand by and let you get yourself cut up into little pieces in the name of decorum.''

The color drained from her face, but her expression remained fierce. "I'm a police officer, Nick. I go after the bad guys no matter how scary they are.''

"You're a powder keg, and you don't have the good sense to know when you're out of your league.''

"We're not going to agree on this.''

''Evidently.''

She took a step back, but Nick went with her. ''There's a difference between courage and taking needless risks just because you've got a score to settle with your conscience,'' he said.

''You can't handle my being a cop, and you've let that affect your actions when it comes to me.'' Erin's back bumped into the wall with a thud, stopping her backward progression.

''Maybe I can't handle it. But maybe you can't, either, McNeal. Maybe you're in this as deep as I am. Maybe we're both in so far over our heads that we don't know up from down.'' He stopped just short of touching her with his body. The restraint cost him, but he didn't let her know it. He desperately needed the upper hand, but knew with the certainty of a sailor watching his ship go down that he was about to lose that as well.

Never taking his eyes from hers, he reached for her hands and drew her to him. ''I care about what happens to you, Erin. I didn't want to. I didn't want a lot of things to happen when it came to you. But they have. I'm not going to let you go after DiCarlo.''

She was so close he could smell the warm, enticing scent of her, feel the heat coming off her, the electricity jumping from her body to his. Slowly, he eased her hands to his mouth and kissed her knuckles.

''Don't,'' she said breathlessly.

''Don't what? Worry about you? Don't care about you? Don't kiss you?''

He didn't miss her quick intake of breath. Her eyes widened when he took her fingertips into his mouth, and Nick knew then he wasn't the only one hanging on to control by a thread.

''Don't do something you're going to regret,'' she said.

''I already have.'' Reaching out, he trailed a finger down her throat, marveling at the silky feel of her flesh, wondering what it would be like to take the same track with his tongue.

She stared up at him, her cheeks suffused with color. "Funny, Nick, I never had you pegged as a risk taker."

"That's not the first time you've been wrong about me, is it?"

"I don't want to get in over my head."

"You already are." He smiled at her. "But you're not alone. But that's what risk is all about, isn't it?"

Her eyes darkened with the realization of what they both knew would happen next. "Why is it that getting any closer to you is the one risk that terrifies me?" she whispered.

"Maybe because we both know how good it's going to be. Maybe because we both know things won't ever be the same." He barely heard his own words over the drumming of his heart. Desire and a thousand other emotions he didn't want to deal with tangled inside him until he thought he would explode. He wanted her so badly he ached. He feared what it would do to him if he kissed her, if he totally lost his head and tried to seduce her.

Bracing his hands on either side of her, he leaned forward to kiss her. Just one kiss, he told himself, then they could sit down and discuss the problem like two adults. Cops, for Pete's sake. Nick would convince her to go with the nice U.S. Marshals. Erin would agree. The feds would bust DiCarlo. It would be over.

But the instant his lips touched hers, his tidy plans flew into disarray. The contact stunned him. The power of the kiss shook him to his foundation. The world shifted beneath his feet when she opened to him. He dug deep, plundering the velvet interior with his tongue. Marking her. Possessing her.

"I'm pretty new at this risk-taking stuff," he whispered. "Why don't you show me just how good it is?"

Her body went fluid against him, and Nick forgot about

control. He was tired of fighting what he'd wanted since the moment he'd laid eyes on her.

Moving against her, he kissed her hard. Her mouth. Her throat. He trailed kisses lower, his tongue lashing her flesh, tasting, savoring. He smelled the sweet, exotic scent of her perfume tempered with the heady aroma of sweat from her recent workout. The combination drugged him. Urgency heated his blood, burning him until he couldn't bear it.

Reaching around her, he slipped the band from her hair and watched it tumble like fine silk over her shoulders. "I love your hair," he said. "I want to see it, feel it. I want to get lost in it."

His hands trembled uncontrollably as he tugged her T-shirt over her head. She hadn't worn a bra, and her breasts were small and exquisite. Her waist was so narrow he could almost span it with his hands.

Awed by the beauty before him, he stepped back just to look at her, speechless and utterly humbled. "You're incredibly beautiful, McNeal."

Her nipples hardened to dark peaks. Nick drank in the sight of her, felt the desire cut him. Bending, he lowered his mouth to her and suckled.

Erin cried out, her body writhing against him. "This...is...too much," she whispered.

Cupping her face with his hands, Nick kissed her, then pulled back to look at her. "This isn't enough," he countered. "I want more. A lot more."

"Nick, this is crazy—"

"Insane," he agreed, and kissed the sensitive area just below her ear. "Do you want me to stop?"

"Uh...maybe we could just...slow down and think about it for a while."

"I can't seem to think straight when I'm kissing you, McNeal. What do you suggest we do about that?"

"Maybe we could wait until we're finished kissing."

He laughed, realizing that whatever bond had drawn him

to her had just tightened another notch. "We're going to finish it this time," he said.

She gazed at him, her green eyes sparking with uncertainty. "I'm afraid we're going to make things really complicated."

"They already are."

"Is that good or bad?"

"Catastrophic would be an understatement." Nick smiled anyway.

"I was afraid you were going to say that."

"I can't fight this any longer, Erin."

"Maybe we could stop fighting and just see what happens."

Never taking his eyes from hers, he slipped his fingers in the waistband of her jeans and worked them down until she was standing before him in nothing but her panties. Her legs were long and slender, with just the right amount of muscle definition. She was delicate and feminine and totally incongruous with anything cop.

He'd forgotten how beautiful a woman could be, and what that kind of beauty did to a man. His need for her was urgent and torturous, and for the first time in his life Nick refused to consider anything even remotely related to good judgment. He refused to consider the fact that he was about to venture beyond the point of no return.

Tentatively, she reached out and cupped him through his slacks. Setting his jaw, he moved against her, aware that the world had started to crumble beneath his feet. Fighting to slow his body, he stilled, trying to remember how he'd managed in the past. It had been so long since a woman had touched him. Since he'd even considered making love. He knew a moment of panic when he considered the possibility that it would all be over if he didn't slow things down.

Easing her hand to her side, he slipped his fingers beneath the waistband of her panties and eased them down her hips. His heart beat in an ever-increasing rhythm at the sight of her curls, dark against the pale flesh of her pelvis. He felt her hands at his zipper, but he didn't stop her this time. He didn't have that much control.

He kissed her languidly. Simultaneously, she tugged his slacks down his hips. Pulling away slightly, Nick fought off his shirt, then stepped out of his boxers. He kissed her neck, aware of his arousal nudging her belly, feeling every touch like a jolt of electricity.

Erin started toward the bed, but Nick swept her into his arms. Kissing her deeply, he crossed the room and lowered her to the mattress. She moved against him. The sensation of her flesh against his made him breathless and weak.

"It's been a long time for me," he murmured huskily.

"Me, too," she whispered. "Are you...okay with this?"

He knew what she was asking and suddenly it was important to him that she know he wasn't still mourning his wife. "You're the first since Rita," he said. "But I'm okay. I've had enough time, Erin. I don't feel like I'm cheating on her or anything."

Her smile dazzled him. "I'm glad, Nick. However this turns out, whatever happens between us after tonight, I want you to know I'm incredibly glad we've had this time together."

Her words elicited a smile—and a lot more emotion than he wanted to admit. He wanted to say more, but something made him hold back. He wasn't sure where this would lead. There were still too many issues standing between them. The only thing he knew for certain was that he cared for her, and he wanted to make love to her more than he wanted his next breath.

He touched her cheek, loving the softness of her flesh beneath his fingertips. He touched her eyelids. Her mouth. Her lips. He groaned when she suckled his fingertips. The sweet intimacy of it made his heart race. His restraint slipped another notch. He began to shake. Slowly, he withdrew his fingers from her mouth. Leaning forward, he kissed her lips, her neck. He drank in the taste of her, wanting all of her and more, knowing in some small corner of his mind that he would never get enough.

She gasped when he laved kisses over her breasts, then down her belly. She tensed when he reached her navel, but Nick didn't stop. One by one, his senses shut down until all he knew was the need raging through him.

"Let me kiss you here," he whispered, moving lower.

For a moment, he feared she would resist. Something broke free inside him when she opened to him. Her cry barely registered when his mouth found her. He savored her, knowing the moment was fleeting, telling himself that was the way he wanted it. Emotion blended with physical sensation, but he ruthlessly shoved it aside. He didn't want emotion. He wanted sex. His body craved release. Pure. Simple. Uncomplicated.

He didn't stop when she cried out his name. Her nails raked through his hair when she crested. Nick didn't relent, but took her to the precipice a second time, knowing that very soon he would go over the edge with her. He could only hope they would both survive the fall.

Erin had never dreamed lovemaking could be like this. Never dreamed her body and heart could be so intricately entwined—or so at odds. Never dreamed both could betray her so thoroughly.

"Nick..."

Fierce waves built low in her belly, shaking her from the inside out. He was making her lose control again. He was making her feel things she didn't want to feel. Physically. Emotionally.

"McNeal."

She opened her eyes to find him gazing down at her. The intensity of his gaze devastated her. She tried to hide what she knew in her heart to be true, what she felt in her body, but he'd somehow stripped her bare with those dark, knowing eyes, and looked into her soul, where all her secrets lay in a neat, endless row.

"That's never happened to me before," she whispered. "I mean, I've never...lost control like that."

"You've never..."

Embarrassment washed over her, but the need to tell him, to confess that she'd never before experienced her full sexuality, was stronger. She wanted him to know he'd just taken her to a beautiful, elusive place she'd never ventured. "I've...never... I mean, I've never..."

His eyes darkened with sudden understanding and he smiled. "Well, I'm honored to be the first."

Even through her embarrassment, she felt a smile emerge. "Don't let it go to your head."

"Ah, I already have."

"Why did you...I mean, why did you...make it happen for me that way?"

"It's been a long time for me. I think this is probably going to end...quickly. I didn't want it to be...one-sided."

His openness and his willingness to share something so very personal with her touched her deeply. "It hasn't been one-sided."

She could feel his rock-hard erection against her hip, and her own body clenched with anticipation. She knew getting involved with him was a mistake. She knew what it would cost her both personally and professionally. Her job. Possibly her career. She tried to convince herself those were the only things nagging at the back of her mind. But Erin knew her heart was at risk as well.

Nick Ryan was the kind of man she could fall in love with.

The thought terrified her. Thrilled her. Sent slow fingers of panic climbing up her spine.

So what if she admired and respected him? So what if she was attracted to him beyond reason? None of those things constituted love, did it? Toss in his inability to accept her being a cop, and she had a disaster on her hands.

As long as she didn't fall in love with him, she would be just fine. As long as she could walk away when this was over, she'd survive.

So why didn't that make her feel any better?

Her thoughts scattered when he kissed her. Shutting her eyes against the emotion closing in on her, she kissed him back with everything she was worth. She didn't want their relationship to get any more complicated than it already was. She'd already compromised a staunch personal rule by getting this close to him. She couldn't afford to let her feelings get tangled up, too.

"I've got to get inside you," he whispered. "Now."

Erin barely heard him for the pounding of blood in her ears. Her heart fluttered when he moved over her. Her entire body quaked when she opened to him.

"You're shaking," he said.

"This—what's happening—scares me, Nick."

"And to think I had you pegged as a risk taker." A tentative smile softened the hard lines of his mouth.

"Maybe this is a bigger risk than either of us bargained for."

"I'll never hurt you, Erin."

"I know." She knew he meant it. Just as she knew he couldn't keep that promise.

"Look at me," he said. "I want to see you when we become one."

His gaze burned into her. She couldn't move, couldn't breathe, couldn't look away. His eyes were dark with passion and shockingly beautiful.

He protected them both, and then every pleasure center in her body exploded when he entered her. There was an instant of discomfort as she adjusted to his size, then blistering heat, blinding sensation. She accepted him, rising to meet him. Slowly, he began to move within her. Pleasure screamed through her. She cried out his name. Once. Twice. Then her mind simply went blank. The powers of speech left her. She couldn't think for the sensations streaming through her. The waves built endlessly, crashing over her, through her, until she was tumbling out of control.

She had never imagined it could be like this between a man and a woman. Two human beings, joined together as one, sharing intimacies, trading hearts, maybe even their souls.

Nick moved her as no other man ever had. As no other man ever would again, she knew. He took her senses to the limit. Shattered all the barriers she'd so carefully erected. Broke her self-control. Claimed her heart.

And as she tumbled into another earth-shattering free fall, she knew her life had been changed forever.

Nick assured himself this was just sex. Mind-blowing, brain-numbing, body-jarring sex. The clenching in his chest every time he looked into the green depths of her gaze was nothing more than affection. Dammit, he didn't want it to be anything more.

He figured they both knew it was more than either of them had bargained for.

How on earth was he going to handle this?

Gritting his teeth against the pleasure building inside him, clenching his jaw against the crushing emotion in his chest, he took her to another climax. Erin cried out and shuddered beneath him. Sweat slicked their bodies, sealing him to her. She gazed up at him, pleasure glazing her eyes. She was incredibly responsive, so exquisite he didn't want it to end. But he couldn't stave off the inevitable.

Closing his eyes, he crushed his mouth to hers. She accepted him, and he went deeper, kissing her, filling her, touching the deepest, most intimate part of her. And he knew nothing would ever be the same.

Physically spent, emotionally shaken by the sheer power

of their lovemaking, he eased onto his side and pulled her
into his arms. She felt so good against him, he thought he
might just stay like this forever. He fully intended to make
love to her again—as soon as he could move. But he wasn't
sure when that would be, considering every muscle in his
body had turned to mush.

The wetness of tears on his shoulder sent a spike of concern through him. "McNeal?"

She tried to turn away, but Nick put his hand beneath
her chin, forcing her gaze to his. Alarm quivered through
him when he saw her tears. "Hey, honey, what's wrong?
I didn't hurt you, did I?"

"I'm fine." She blinked, and another tear rolled down
her cheek. "I never cry like this...."

"Honey, if I hurt you—"

"No, it's just..."

"Something I said?"

She shook her head.

Nick suppressed the swirl of panic in his gut. "Why are
you crying?"

"I don't know. I just...am."

Like *that* made any sense. "All right." It seemed like
the right thing to say, but he didn't have a clue what was
going on. "Look, Erin, if I said something, or hurt you in
any—"

She choked out a laugh and raised her eyes to his. "You
didn't hurt me, Nick."

He stared at her, not understanding.

"You made me *feel*. I mean, you really made me
feel...incredible. What we just shared...it was like magic.
Not just the physical part, but...all of it. It moved me.
That's never happened to me before."

A more powerful wave of panic surged through him.
This wasn't a conversation he wanted to have. Not when
his own emotions were so close to the surface he could feel
them tightening around his throat like a noose. Not when

she looked so fragile and sexy snuggled up against him, her cheeks flushed, her eyes teary.

She wiped at her tears. "I can't believe I'm...losing it like this just because we—"

"Had sex," he finished quickly.

"Right." She nodded vigorously. "We did. Have sex, I mean."

Silence reigned for a moment, then Nick felt the laugh in his chest break free. When Erin looked up at him and smiled, he laughed harder. Then she was laughing with him, a soft, musical sound that made him feel more alive than he'd felt in years. He laughed until tears streamed from his own eyes, and he felt giddy and weak.

When their laughter had dwindled to an occasional giggle, he cradled her against him and brushed his lips across her temple. "It blew my mind, too, McNeal," he said.

"I'm really glad I'm not the only one who noticed." She dazzled him with another smile. "I'd forgotten how powerful...sex can be."

"Maybe we're just out of practice."

"You know, Nick, we could probably spend the next couple of hours...you know...getting back into the swing of things."

He chuckled. Simultaneously, a wave of affection washed over him. Another more powerful emotion hit him in the gut like a fist. For a moment his throat was so tight he couldn't speak. Not because Erin was the first lover he'd taken since Rita, he realized with a start, but because of the way he felt about the woman he now held in his arms.

"What about you, McNeal?" he asked in a low voice.

"What about me?"

He smiled when she tensed. "Who was the jerk who convinced you a man who cares about you could never accept your being a cop?"

"What makes you think—"

"You, Erin. You've told me in a hundred different ways since I've known you."

For a moment he thought she wouldn't answer. He told himself it didn't matter that she preferred not to share her past with him. He certainly didn't have a claim on her. But he wanted to know what made her tick. Even more, he wanted to know what had made her so cautious.

She smiled, but to Nick it looked uncomfortable. "His name is Warren Prentice, upwardly mobile assistant district attorney extraordinaire."

"I remember the name from my days in Chicago," he said.

"I was a rookie. Fresh out of the academy. Warren prosecuted a case I made the bust on. We worked together and ended up getting...involved. He was older. Ambitious. Slick as oil. On his way to the top in a major way."

Nick did his best to ignore the jealously that nudged through him. "What happened?"

"I was naive and fell really, really hard for him. I never do anything halfway, Nick. It's always all or nothing, even mistakes. I fell for Warren for all the wrong reasons. We'd only known each other for two months when he asked me to marry him."

"You didn't—"

"No, I didn't marry him."

"What happened?"

"A few weeks after he proposed, I was in on another bust. Things got squirrelly. Not for me. I never even drew my weapon, but my partner did. No one got hurt, but the next time I saw Warren he very matter-of-factly told me I would be quitting the department if I wanted to be his wife."

"The old ultimatum."

"The worst part was that I was going to do it. As much as I loved being a police officer, I was going to throw it all away. I had my resignation typed out. I had an interview lined up for a corporate security job. I would have gone through with it if I hadn't realized that giving in to his fears meant sacrificing my dreams. In the end, I walked away.''

Nick's temper spiked at the thought of another man trying to control her like that, hurting her. A man she'd obviously loved at the time. ''I'm sorry, Erin. That must have been tough.''

''It was. I mean, it felt like the end of the world. I got really cautious after that. I haven't…been involved with anyone since Warren and—''

''Whoa.'' Nick turned to her so he could see her more fully. ''Let me get this straight. You haven't been…with anyone for six *years?*''

Her gaze faltered. ''He just left me…cold inside.''

''It was his loss,'' Nick said.

Erin's expression grew thoughtful. ''But you know, I think things worked out for the best. I could never give up who I am. Not for anyone.''

Her words disturbed him more than he wanted to admit. Not because he didn't admire her determination or her belief in herself—he prized both of those qualities—but because they provoked something inside him he'd just as soon not own up to.

''You don't have to give up who you are to love someone, Erin.'' His own words shocked him. Not because they weren't true or that he didn't believe them—he believed the statement fully and without question—but because he'd realized for the first time just how well he'd come to understand her.

''No, you don't have to give up who you are,'' she whispered. ''But you *do* have to be willing to take a certain amount of risk.''

Nick didn't want to think of the kind of risks she was referring to. Not when his heart was already on the chopping block and this woman all but had the cleaver in her hands. But God help him, he wanted her again. Wanted her

so badly he shook with it. Not just physically, he realized
with a start. He wanted more. He needed—

He squelched the thought before it could fully material-
ize. The repercussions of that line of thinking terrified him,
sent a jolt of panic up his spine.

His body had recovered. She'd managed to get his heart
rate up again. Well, he was a lot more comfortable having
sex than he was talking about whatever was exploding between them.

Without preamble, he reached for her and kissed her hard
on the mouth. She went rigid for an instant, then melted
against him. Need flashed through him, snapping his control. He plundered her lips. A sound escaped her when he
cupped her breasts, but he didn't stop. Couldn't stop even
if he wanted to. Because as surely as his heart had become
entangled with hers, he felt her slipping from his grasp. He
told himself it didn't matter. He and Stephanie were better
off without her. But not even the denial eased the clench
of panic in his chest.

Nick was through talking. He didn't want words or feelings or emotions. He didn't want to care for her; he simply
wasn't ready to take on a serious relationship. His logical
side told him to put a stop to this before either of them got
in any deeper. But his control failed him—not for the first
time when it came to Erin. And he knew with the utter
dread of a man on death row that it probably wouldn't be
the last.

Growling low in his throat, he kissed her harder. Desperation clawed at him. He moved over her. She opened to
him. Nick's heart hammered. His vision blurred.

"You don't fight fair, McNeal," he murmured.

"Neither do you."

He protected them and pushed inside her. The world
ceased to exist when her liquid heat wrapped around him.
Nick saw stars, swirling, exploding, arcing across his vision
like tiny meteors. Groaning, he moved within her, fighting

what he knew to be true, feeling the consequences of what he'd allowed to happen all the way to the pit of his stomach.

There was no future for them, he told himself. Just this moment of pleasure. Tomorrow he would send her back to Chicago with the two U.S. Marshals. Stephanie would be safe. His own heart would be safe.

And he'd never have to admit that he was falling hard and fast for Erin McNeal.

Nick wasn't sure what woke him. He lay in the darkness a moment, listening to the sound of distant thunder, aware that his heart was pounding. He didn't remember falling asleep. Didn't remember Erin curling against him...

She snuggled closer, and a wave of tenderness warmed him. Her face was smooth and innocent in the dim light slanting in through the window. The image of her with her head thrown back in ecstasy, her hair spread out on the pillow, came to him like an apparition. His body stirred with the memory. Heat. Urgency. A thousand other feelings and sensations he didn't want to deal with curled inside him, but he shoved them back, disturbed by their power.

Raising his head, he glanced at the alarm clock on the night table. Midnight. He reached for the phone and dialed Hector's cellular. Concern slithered through him when a recording told him the cell phone user had left the service area.

"Damn." Fighting a rise of alarm, Nick sat up and redialed. As he listened to the same recording a second time, alarm transformed into something icy and cold. From memory, he punched in the number of the physical rehab center in Indianapolis. A female clerk answered on the second ring.

"This is Nick Ryan. Has my daughter, Stephanie Ryan, or Emily Thornsberry checked in yet?"

Computer keys clicked at the other end of the line.

"We've got the reservation, Mr. Ryan, but they haven't checked in yet."

Cursing, Nick disconnected, his mind racing. Hector should have had them checked in by now. Where the hell were they? If they'd run into problems, why hadn't Hector called?

Nick jumped when his cell phone chirped, then he snatched the phone up and curtly uttered his name.

"Chief!"

The fear in his deputy's voice jolted him to red alert. "What's wrong?" he asked, wondering in a small corner of his mind why there was panic in his own voice.

"Two men...armed. They forced us off the road. Tied us up. Damn." Hector's voice broke.

Nick's nerves went taut. A dozen scenarios scrambled through his mind, none of them good. *"What happened?"*

"They got her, Nick."

Hector didn't need to say who for Nick to know. White-hot terror screamed through him. He didn't remember rising. He didn't remember crossing the room and stepping into his trousers. "Where's Stephanie?"

"They got her, Chief. Good Lord, they *took* her."

Chapter 13

Erin woke to panic. She felt it. Sensed it. Smelled it like gunpowder from a killing blast. Pulling the sheets up to cover herself, she sat bolt upright. "Nick?"

He stood amid the darkness on the opposite side of the room. In the sparse light slanting through the window, she could see he had on his slacks, no shirt, his cell phone pressed to his ear. A slow spiral of dread bored a hole right through her.

"When?" he snapped into the phone.

Erin rolled out of bed and began gathering her clothes. Good Lord, what was going on? Why was Nick on the phone? Why had he been shouting? She looked at her watch. It was just after midnight.

Nick cursed exorbitantly.

Even from across the room, Erin could hear him breathing. She stepped into her jeans, then tugged her T-shirt over her head. "Nick, what is it? What's happened?"

"Oh, no," he said into the darkness. "Oh, no. *No!*"

Erin flipped on the light. "Nick?"

Lowering the phone, he turned away from her and leaned against the dresser as if he suddenly no longer had the strength to support himself.

"What's going on?" she asked.

Her heart rolled over when he raised his head. His face was chalk-white. Sweat dampened his brow. She sensed danger, felt the violence coming off him in thick, choking waves.

She stepped back when his gaze met hers. In the depths of his eyes, she saw murder. Her heart began to pound.

"Steph and Mrs. T.," he said hoarsely. "They never made it to Indianapolis."

Confusion swirled for an instant—then the meaning behind his words struck her with the force of a freight train. "Oh, God. Oh, *no*." She felt gut punched. Taking another step back, she pressed her hand to her stomach. "Please tell me they're not—"

"Hector and Em are all right. The bastard has my little girl."

Erin didn't want to ask, but she had to know. "Di-Carlo?"

Without warning, he punched the dresser mirror. Glass shattered, spraying outward from the impact.

"Nick!"

"Why *her,* for God's sake?" he snarled.

"Nick—"

"If he hurts her, I'll kill him. I'll kill the son of a bitch with my bare hands."

"Stop it. Please."

"I've got to find her."

Erin saw blood on his knuckles, fought back a crushing wave of panic. "Calm down—"

"DiCarlo crossed the line," he said in a low, menacing voice.

She stared at him, wondering if he could hear the maniacal rhythm of her heart. "How did it happen?"

"A limo forced them off the road."

"We'll get her back."

"I should have realized it would come to this." His expression turned stricken and pale and as dangerous as a viper about to strike. "I should have been there for her. I wasn't. Just like I wasn't there for her the night of the accident."

The terror resonating in his voice ignited the same emotions inside Erin. She felt her control slipping, like sand through her fingers, no matter how tight her grasp. "This isn't your fault."

"I don't have time for this," he snapped.

Erin's stomach roiled and she felt nauseous. Oh, she hadn't meant to involve that sweet little girl!

"I've got to go to the station," he said.

"Let me come with you."

"Stay here," he ordered. "I don't need DiCarlo getting his hands on you, too." Without speaking, Nick bent and scooped up his uniform shirt. She watched, numb with pain, as he buttoned it with shaking, bleeding fingers.

He barely looked at her as he buckled his holster. "No one knows you're here. Don't open the door for anyone but me. Keep your sidearm close. You got that?"

Erin barely heard his words as cold realization crept over her. An instant later, the situation crystallized. DiCarlo didn't want Stephanie; he wanted Erin. The knowledge impacted her solidly, hitting a place that was raw and weak. She nearly crumpled with the blow.

Shaking, barely trusting her legs, Erin crossed the room. "DiCarlo doesn't want Stephanie, Nick. He wants me."

The rumble of thunder outside punctuated the thick silence that followed her words. Nick slipped his cell phone into his uniform pocket, then turned to her. Erin winced at the ice in his gaze. She couldn't believe that just a few short hours earlier he'd caressed her with such utter tenderness. Shared intimacies with her. Opened his heart. Stolen her own. Her heart shattered with the realization that he blamed her for Stephanie's kidnapping.

He hadn't said the words, but Erin saw the accusation in the depths of his eyes. She stared at him, willing herself to believe it wasn't her fault. But the truth made her sick with regret. Her heart broke with the knowledge that the man she loved blamed her for risking something as precious as his child.

"Don't do anything stupid," he warned.

"I'll stay." She couldn't, of course. She had to find Stephanie. Erin couldn't let that little girl pay for something she herself had done.

He crossed to her and kissed her then—a hard, emotionless kiss born of desperation and fear. But it moved her nonetheless. Moved her so profoundly that her throat locked up and she choked back a sob.

No longer trusting her legs, she backed toward the bed, then slowly sank to a sitting position. She had the sudden, irrational urge to tell him she loved him, fearing this moment would be her only chance, but she didn't.

"Watch yourself," he said. Then, without looking back, he opened the door and stepped into the night.

Erin slapped her badge down on the counter and shot the desk clerk her best don't-mess-with-me glare. "I'm a police officer. I'm commandeering a vehicle for a police emergency."

The desk clerk of the Pioneer Motel stared at her as if she'd just told him she was going to shoot off one of his fingers. "Wh-what do you mean?"

"I need a vehicle," she snapped. "Now!"

The young man jumped. "Uh...is a truck okay?"

"Fine. Give me the keys." She looked at the clock on the wall behind him. It was twelve-thirty. Outside, a crack of thunder vibrated the walls. How on earth was she going to find Stephanie?

The clerk unsnapped a key chain from his belt loop and handed it to her. "Should I call the police or something?"

"Chief Ryan has already been apprised of the situation."

The young man didn't look convinced. "When do I get my truck back?"

"You can pick it up at the station later this afternoon." She took the key. "Where's the vehicle?"

"Out back. Next to the Dumpster."

The pickup truck should have been *in* the Dumpster as far as Erin was concerned. She stalled it twice before getting out of the parking lot, and once on the way to her apartment. By the time she unlocked the door, her heart was raging with frustration. The minutes were ticking by, and she didn't have the slightest idea how to find Stephanie. Her police training told her to find Nick or call Frank in Chicago. The part of her that was crushed by guilt because she'd endangered a child's life wasn't thinking quite as logically. Erin knew DiCarlo wanted her, not Stephanie. It made perfect sense to offer up herself in exchange for the child.

The phone jangled as she closed the door behind her. Crossing the room, she snatched it up on the second ring. "McNeal," she said breathlessly.

Thick silence made the hairs at her nape stand on end.

"I've been calling your apartment every five minutes for the last half hour, Officer McNeal."

A sane person would have frozen in fear at the sound of Vic DiCarlo's voice. Erin wasn't feeling particularly sane.

Satisfaction rolled slowly through her that he'd done something so predictable. Thinking fast, she pressed the record button of her answering machine. "I've been busy," she said levelly. "You've got something I want."

"Ah, you don't disappoint me. I appreciate a woman who likes to get down to business quickly."

The cold ruthlessness in his voice made her break into a sweat. "Where's the little girl?" she asked curtly.

"I've been taking good care of her. I have a soft spot for children, you know."

Erin closed her eyes against the sudden rush of heat behind her lids. She tried not to imagine how frightened Stephanie must be. How helpless she must feel not being able to walk or run away from the bad man. Erin's police training told her to keep this impersonal. To keep her emotions out of the situation. But the part of her that was a woman and loved that child, the part of her that loved Nick, cried out with pain and fear and outrage. "If you hurt her, I'll kill you," she said.

"We both know I'm not interested in this child. I am, however, very interested in you."

She gripped the phone, her heart thundering. "What do you want?"

"I want you in exchange for the child, of course."

"I'm listening."

"There's a deserted grain elevator on Highway 59 about ten miles south of Logan Falls."

She looked at her watch. "I can be there in ten minutes."

"A word of warning, Officer McNeal. Come alone. If you call the police, if you contact anyone, including that police chief of yours, I won't hesitate to kill this child."

Bile rose in her throat, but she choked it down. Her hands shook so violently that for a moment she thought she would drop the phone. *Oh, God, please don't let him hurt her.* "I'll come alone," she said.

The line disconnected.

Nick paced the confines of the police station lobby like a caged beast. Terror and frustration rampaged through him. Something darker hovered just beneath the surface. The thought of his sweet, innocent child frightened and alone twisted like a knife in his gut. The thought of losing her—

He broke off the thought with ruthless precision. He wouldn't think of losing her. He wouldn't let that happen. He would die before letting her down again.

The phone shrilled. He snatched it up, cutting the ring short. "Ryan."

"It's Frank. I'm en route. Any news?"

"No." The quality of the connection told him Frank was on his cellular. Nick had called him on his way from the motel to the police station and briefed him on the situation.

"If I can hold it at eighty without getting stopped by the Indiana Highway Patrol, I should be there in an hour. Have you contacted the FBI?"

Nick glanced at his watch, realizing with a stark sense of despair it had only been five minutes since he'd hung up with the Chicago FBI office. "They're sending a team."

"What about Erin?"

Nick had sworn he wouldn't think about her. He didn't want to think about her. Didn't want to dig his emotional hole any deeper than it already was. But the simple utterance of her name was all it took to bring the image of her to the forefront of his mind. Make him remember the way she'd looked at him when they'd made love, when she'd been open and vulnerable beneath him, her eyes as soft as a Midwest sunset. He didn't like the feelings roiling in his chest. They were too close to something real and terrifying he didn't want to face. They made him realize he was in miles over his head and floundering helplessly to save himself.

God help him, he hadn't wanted to fall in love with her.

"She's at the Pioneer Motel." Nick's voice was hoarse.

"Good. Keep her there." The other man paused. "How are you holding up?"

"If DiCarlo hurts Steph, I'm going to kill him, Frank. I swear, I'll kill him."

"Easy, partner. Don't go there."

No false reassurances from Frank, Nick thought bitterly. But then, Frank was a cop. Cops were straight with each other, even in the face of tragedy. Both men knew what kind of man Vic DiCarlo was. Just as they knew what he was capable of.

The thought of a monster like DiCarlo getting his hands on his sweet child filled Nick with rage. The power of that rage stunned him, and for the first time in his life he wondered what he was capable of.

But he knew Frank was right. Letting his imagination run away with him would only make him crazy. He wouldn't do his daughter any good if he was a basket case. But he was so worried about her he could barely form a coherent thought. He needed to calm down. Think. Come up with a plan.

"Hang tight, partner," Frank said. "You've got my number. Call me if you hear from DiCarlo."

Nick disconnected, and looked around the room. He grappled for calm, ended up wanting to throw something. He wanted to break something with his bare hands. He wanted to hit something, anything to relieve the tension that had built up inside him like an overheated pressure cooker.

"What have you done with her, you bastard?" he said aloud.

For the first time in his law enforcement career, Nick was at a loss. He didn't know what to do or where to start. He didn't know how to get Stephanie back. He'd considered calling in his deputies, but instinct told him to wait. If DiCarlo got spooked, it was hard telling what he would do. But it nearly killed him that he couldn't do anything but wait.

Sinking into the chair behind his desk, he dropped his face into his hands and closed his eyes. His entire world had come apart in the last hours. First, he'd managed to get tangled up with a woman who would surely leave his life in tatters. Then his beloved child had been taken by a ruthless mafioso.

The urge to call Erin was strong, but Nick resisted it. He hadn't wanted to admit it, but the need to hear her voice was like a living thing inside him. She brought light into his darkness. Feeling into a heart that had numbed itself to emotion. Love into a soul that had been so battered it no longer knew the meaning of the word. He'd made love to her, then let her believe he blamed her for this. He couldn't imagine how much that had hurt her. Nick figured he was getting pretty good at blaming others for his own shortcomings.

The truth of the matter was none of this was Erin's fault. Not Stephanie's kidnapping. Not Rita's death or his daughter's spinal condition. Not his own fear of losing his heart.

The fact that Erin meant so much to him added a uniquely cruel twist to his terror. He knew what kind of woman she was. Independent to a fault. Cocky as hell. Too damn willing to put herself in the line of fire because she still believed in right and wrong, and because she still believed one good cop could make a difference.

The irony sent a harsh laugh from his throat. It was a bizarre sound in the stark silence of the office. He couldn't deny it any longer. He'd fallen in love with her. A cop! A woman with a taste for danger and a reckless streak that ran right down the center of her very pretty back.

At that moment, Nick would have sold his soul to hold her.

Suddenly the need to hear her voice overwhelmed him. He needed her. Erin didn't have to know he'd fallen in love with her. He didn't have to tell her. He wouldn't. As long as he had the strength to walk away when the time came, he'd be just fine.

Snatching up the phone, he dialed the Pioneer Motel.

A sleepy voice answered on the sixth ring.

"Room 135," Nick snapped.

"You mean the lady cop?"

His heart jolted. He hadn't identified either of them as cops when he'd checked in. "How do you know she's a cop?" he asked.

"She commandeered my truck, man. Said there was a police emergency of some kind."

Nick didn't hear the rest of the sentence. The terror inside him burgeoned into a monster, breaking free of the shackles of control. "This is Police Chief Nick Ryan. If she's still there, stop her—"

"Too late, man. She left ten minutes ago."

Nick should have realized she wouldn't sit this one out. Not when she felt responsible. Not when he hadn't bothered to tell her otherwise. Not when she already had two tons of guilt pressing down on her. "What kind of truck?" he asked.

"Blue Chevy, 1985." The clerk paused. "I *am* going to get my truck back, right?"

Nick disconnected, then stood abruptly, aware that he was breathing hard. Vaguely, he was aware of the roll of thunder outside. The patter of rain against the window.

She was going after DiCarlo.

Nick couldn't let her do it. Not alone. She didn't stand a chance against a man like DiCarlo. Nick couldn't let her get herself killed. Not the woman he'd come to love more than life itself.

He glanced at the wall clock. Twelve forty-five. Frank wouldn't arrive for another hour, the FBI sometime after that. If he could find the blue truck...

Not giving himself time to debate, Nick checked his sidearm, snatched up his truck keys and cell phone, and headed for the door.

Lightning split the sky, illuminating the entrance to the grain elevator fifty yards away. Erin slowed the truck and turned down the gravel drive. The monstrous building loomed like a dinosaur grazing amidst the endless rows of corn. Ten minutes earlier, a tornado warning had been issued by the National Weather Service for the counties west of Logan Falls.

Erin figured the situation couldn't get much worse.

She flinched at a deafening crash of thunder. Stopping the truck a few yards from the yawning mouth of the entrance, she stared into the darkened interior, wishing she'd had time to formulate some kind of plan. But for the life of her, she hadn't been able to come up with anything better than what she was about to do. Offering herself up in exchange for Stephanie was the only way to save that little girl's life. No matter how Erin looked at it, the simple fact remained that DiCarlo wanted her, not Stephanie. The child was merely bait. A bargaining chip. That left the ball squarely in Erin's court, and she didn't intend to squander the chance.

A shiver rippled through her as the first giant drops of rain splattered against her windshield. She usually didn't have any difficulty leaving her emotions behind when she stepped into her cop's suit of armor. But this situation was different. She couldn't get her focus. She couldn't stop thinking about Stephanie. She couldn't stop thinking of Nick—or set aside the cold, hard knowledge of how much was at stake for all of them.

If anything happened to that little girl, Erin would never be able to live with herself. She knew that as surely as she knew DiCarlo didn't bluff when it came to threats. If it was the last thing she did, she would get Stephanie out of this. Or else she would die trying.

Leaning across the seat, she picked up the .22 minirevolver and slipped it into the holster strapped to her ankle. She checked the cylinder of her service revolver, then tucked it into the waistband of her jeans. She expected DiCarlo or his men to disarm her. If she was lucky, they wouldn't find the ankle holster, and she'd have something to bargain with if things got crazy.

Erin fully expected things to get crazy.

She shut down the engine and got out of the truck. The

wind buffeted her, kicking up dust and small debris. Fat drops of rain thunked against the ground and pinged against the hood of the truck.

Another bolt of lightning ruptured the sky. Refusing to acknowledge the fear pounding in her chest, she started toward the entrance. She knew they were watching her. She felt their eyes tracking her, the malice surrounding her like a dark aura. She knew in an instant she could be dead. Just as she knew she didn't have a choice but to walk right into DiCarlo's trap.

She reached the entrance, breathless with adrenaline, every sense honed on her surroundings. Wind howled through the structure like a banshee. A dozen fifty-gallon drums lined the wall to her left. The darkened, windowed office stood to her right. A catwalk overhead offered yet another hiding place.

Erin's breaths came hard and fast as the flashback pressed down on her. She fought it, forcing it back by sheer will. *Easy. Breathe. Focus.*

"DiCarlo!" she shouted.

Two figures stepped out of the office. A surge of adrenaline sent her hand to her weapon. Every nerve in her body screamed as she drew it from her waistband. To her horror, her hands were shaking. *Easy. Breathe. Focus.* Her mind chanted the words like a mantra.

"I'm a police officer," she said.

The two men wore expensive suits. Italian loafers. They watched her with flat, emotionless eyes. Bodyguards—or hired killers—she thought, and choked back a crushing wave of fear.

"Mr. DiCarlo is expecting you," one of the men said. "Drop your gun, cop."

"Not until I see the little girl." Erin held her weapon steady on the man's chest. "Now."

The two men exchanged looks.

Erin pulled the hammer back. "A hollow-point bullet won't go through that body armor you're wearing, but it will put you down,'' she said with a calm she didn't feel. ''I won't miss a head shot. You'll be dead before you hit the ground.''

The man's cheek twitched. Raising his arm, he snapped his fingers. The office door squeaked open. Erin's heart jerked hard in her chest when she saw Stephanie being rolled out of the darkness by yet another man. The little girl's face was dirty and tear streaked, her hair mussed.

''Erin?'' Stephanie said in a small voice.

''Sweetheart, I'm here,'' Erin replied. ''Are you okay?''

''I'm scared. I want to go home.''

''Everything's going to be okay.''

''I want my dad.''

Tears burned behind Erin's eyes, and she fought for control. ''I'm a police officer like your dad, sweetheart,'' she reminded her. ''I'll take care of you. I'll keep you safe, okay?''

The little girl started to cry.

Erin looked at the first man. ''I'm taking her back to Logan Falls.''

''You're not going anywhere. Drop the gun, cop.''

She knew she didn't have any bargaining power, but she had to try. ''Not until I know this child is safe. DiCarlo gave me his word.''

''I ain't making no promises. Drop the gun.''

''No.'' Her heart began to rage. ''If I'm trading myself for this child, I want to know she's not going to be harmed. DiCarlo wants me, not her. I want her taken back to town.''

''Lose the gun, lady cop.'' The first man took a threatening step closer.

She tightened her grip on the weapon, reminding herself she had a backup, wondering if they disarmed her if she could get to her ankle holster before they shot her dead. ''Take her back to town or the deal's off.''

The man stopped three feet away from her, an ugly looking pistol aimed at her chest. ''Drop it, or I'll hurt both of you.''

Those were the words Erin had feared the most. She was outnumbered. Both she and Stephanie were at their mercy. The only thing she could hope for now was a stroke of luck or the possibility that, like some of the Mafia old-timers, DiCarlo had a code against hurting children.

Hating the sense of helplessness crashing down around her, Erin tossed her gun onto the concrete and looked the man in the eye. "I don't want her hurt," she said in a low voice.

"Get your hands up and turn around."

Fear coiled inside her like a snake as she turned. She closed her eyes as rough hands moved over her with quick, impersonal efficiency. Her legs went weak with relief when they missed the pistol strapped to her ankle.

"She's clean."

Roughly, her hands were jerked behind her back. "Tying me up wasn't part of the deal—"

"Shut up."

She tried to jerk away, but two of the thugs stepped forward to subdue her. Knowing she couldn't win, she stopped fighting and let them bind her wrists with a thin strand of wire. Erin fought down panic. She could still get to her pistol, she assured herself. It would be difficult, but she could still use it. *Easy. Breathe. Focus.*

Oh, God, Nick, I'm sorry.

"Turn around, cop."

She turned, hoping they couldn't see the fear that permeated her every fiber. The thugs seemed more relaxed now that she'd been subdued. "Where's DiCarlo?" she asked.

As if on cue, the unmistakable drone of a helicopter rose above the howl of the wind. And Erin knew the final showdown was about to begin.

Chapter 14

Panic swirled through Nick in a violent maelstrom as he drove the Suburban through the storm. Rain and hailstones pounded the windshield. The wipers couldn't keep up with the deluge, but he didn't slow down. He drove blindly, propelled by a force stronger than panic, deeper than fear.

After leaving the station, Nick had called Erin's apartment twice from his cellular, only to find the line busy. That was all it took for him to realize something was wrong. He'd walked into her apartment and spotted the dangling phone next to the answering machine. The blinking light was all he needed to know she'd left him a clue.

Dread burgeoned anew in his chest as he recalled the recorded conversation on her answering machine. God bless her for thinking like a cop and recording DiCarlo's call.

Now, pressing the speedometer to eighty, hydroplaning dangerously, Nick nearly missed the entrance to the grain elevator. He stomped on the brake. The vehicle fishtailed, coming to a stop just a few feet short of the drainage ditch.

He punched off the headlights, aware of his labored breathing even above the roar of the storm. Backing the truck beneath a stand of trees near the entrance, he shut down the engine and got out. Rain and wind pelted him, but Nick barely felt the wet or the cold. Fifty yards away, the massive structure of the grain elevator rose up out of the earth like ancient ruins.

He couldn't bear to think of the terror Stephanie must be feeling. He prayed DiCarlo wouldn't harm an innocent child. At the same time, he tried to put himself inside Erin's head. Had she traded herself for Stephanie? Or was she somehow planning to ambush DiCarlo and his men? Both scenarios sent a shiver of fear up his spine. So many things could go wrong. He should have realized she wouldn't stay at the motel. He'd been foolish in trusting her. Damn her for being so brave. Damn himself for loving her, anyway.

She knew DiCarlo was known to be particularly ruthless in the punishments he handed out to cops. If he hurt Erin...

Nick banked the thought, but not before he felt another blade of fear slice him. And he silently vowed that if DiCarlo hurt them, Nick would lay down his badge and take out the man with his bare hands.

Using the downpour as cover, he started toward the elevator at a dead run. The blue truck Erin had commandeered sat a few yards from the entrance, but she wasn't inside. An instant later, the sound of chopper blades reached him. Nick stopped and spun, spotting the Bell 206 helicopter a hundred yards away, about to land in an open area on the other side of the building.

DiCarlo.

Shock and a fresh wave of fear rippled through Nick. A personal visit from the crime boss was highly unusual. DiCarlo wouldn't waste any time with small talk.

Knowing he would be spotted out in the open, Nick sprinted toward the fence line that ran the length of the property. Brush scratched his face and ripped at his clothes, but he barely felt the pain. Mud sucked at his boots, but he didn't slow. He had to get close without being detected. Then he had to extract Erin and Stephanie before DiCarlo killed them both.

Erin watched Vic DiCarlo step out of the helicopter, angling his umbrella against the rain as he approached. Dread and terror streaked through her system like a fast-acting drug when she realized he'd probably come to handle her execution personally.

Breaking free of the two thugs, she ran toward Stephanie and dropped to her knees in front of the little girl, kissing her softly on her cheek. "It's okay, honey. These men want to talk to me for a little while, but they're going to take you home."

"Why did they tie you up?" Stephanie cried.

Erin closed her eyes and choked back a sob. She didn't know what to say. Oh, Lord, please keep this child safe. "Because I'm a police officer. They don't want me to arrest them."

Her heart broke when the little girl's arms went around her. Oh, how she longed to hug her back!

"I'm scared, Erin."

"I know, sweetheart. I'm scared, too. We're going to have to be brave, though, okay?"

"'Kay."

"Everything will be all right. I promise. Just hold on to me and try to stay calm, okay, sweetheart?" Erin didn't know that for sure. She had no idea what DiCarlo had planned for them. But she couldn't bear to let this child go without some kind of reassurance.

"I love you, Erin."

She closed her eyes, felt the tears burst through the dam. Knowing she had only a moment, she pressed her cheek against Stephanie's, felt their tears join. "I love you, too, sweetheart."

"Take the child to the limo."

Erin's heart stopped in her chest at the sound of Di-Carlo's voice. Terror pierced through her pain.

"No!" Stephanie cried. "I want to stay with Erin!"

It took Erin a moment to find her voice. "Go with them, honey. Please. They'll take you home." She forced her gaze to DiCarlo's, hoping for some kind of confirmation, but his expression was cold.

She barely felt the rough hands that jerked her to her feet. She watched as one of the thugs approached and began rolling Stephanie toward the entrance. The little girl turned in her chair, her eyes seeking Erin's. Agony filled her chest at the fear in Stephanie's eyes. Erin felt the child's departure like a stake through her heart.

"Ah, I'm deeply touched."

Breaking eye contact with Stephanie, Erin faced DiCarlo. He was standing so close she could smell his expensive cologne. He contemplated her with eyes that were as life-less as a mannequin's. She'd seen dozens of pictures of him over the years, but nothing had prepared her for the power of his presence. He was shorter than she'd imagined, just an inch or two taller than she was, but he emanated power from every pore.

Without warning his hand shot out, his palm cracking against her cheekbone like a bullwhip. The sudden violence of the act stunned her. Her head snapped back. The force of the blow sent her down on one knee.

"I've waited six months for this moment," he said.

Shaking her head against the dizziness, she raised her eyes to his. "Give me your word you won't hurt that child."

"The way you hurt my son?"

She didn't even pretend not to know what he was talking about. The warehouse. The man she'd shot six months ago in Chicago. "Your son pointed a gun at a police officer."

"My son was eighteen years old. A child. You didn't give him a chance to bargain, Officer McNeal. You didn't give me a chance to beg for his life. Why should I do the same for you?"

"That little girl is innocent. She lost her mother three years ago. She's had enough pain in her life. Dammit, let her go."

"My son is dead because of you," he said coldly. "You took from me the only thing I truly cared about in this world. I'm here now to make sure you pay for that."

Dread squeezed her chest like a giant serpent, tightening until she couldn't draw a breath. For the first time, Erin realized fully his capacity for evil, the breadth and width of his need for revenge. "You can do what you want with me—"

"Of course I can. And I plan to. Very, very slowly."

"Give me your word you won't hurt her."

Something flashed in the depths of his reptilian gaze. Something cold and lifeless that sent a chill to the depths of her soul. "I want you to know what it feels like to lose something precious."

Panic gripped her, twisted her insides into knots. Erin struggled openly against her bonds. The wire cut into her wrists, but she didn't care about the pain. All she could think of was Stephanie, and the father who loved her.

Awkwardly, she struggled to her feet. "If you hurt her, I'll kill you."

Cold amusement sparked in his eyes. "You're in no position to threaten me, Officer McNeal."

"No, I'm not. But I'm here. I kept my part of the deal. My hands are tied. I'm yours, DiCarlo. I'm a cop, and I shot your only son. Do with me as you please, but let that little girl go. Let her go, and I'll play your twisted game with you."

"You don't have a choice."

"Let her go." Her voice was low and hoarse. "Please."

Shaking his head as if she'd offended him, he said, "Ah, but I'm not a child killer."

Erin wasn't sure why, but she believed him. She believed that if DiCarlo had planned to kill Stephanie, he would have done so in front of her just to make some sort of twisted point. Just to make her suffer before he killed her. The realization made her sag with relief.

He looked at the thug on her right. "Put the child in the car." DiCarlo's eyes shifted to the other man. "I'll meet you back at the chopper when I'm finished here."

The two men stepped back, then retreated, leaving her alone with DiCarlo. For the first time, Erin considered the very real possibility that she would die at the hands of this man. The possibility that she would never see Nick again. Never hear her name on his lips. Never see him smile. She would hurt him one final time, she realized. Just as he'd feared she would. The irony made her want to sob.

Another corner of her mind, the part that thought like a cop, wondered if he'd found the recording. If he was on his way. If she could somehow get her hands on the revolver in her ankle holster.

"Get down on the ground, Officer McNeal."

He's going to kill me, she thought with an odd sense of calm. Execution style. His trademark. The realization made her nauseous.

"Get on the ground, or I'll kill you where you stand."

She stared at him, unable to move, unable to believe it had come to this. "Don't do it," she said, starkly aware of the holster pressing against her right ankle.

"Contrary to popular belief, I don't like killing, Officer McNeal. Particularly women. But I'm a firm believer in an eye for an eye. Besides, I've got an image to maintain. So, if you don't mind, get down on the ground and let's get this nasty business over with."

* * *

Nick took out the last thug just as he was getting into the limousine. Using his billy club for silence, Nick put him down with a single blow. The thug fell into the mud like a sack of flour. After disarming him, Nick cuffed him to the undercarriage of the car and left him in the rain.

Praying he would find his daughter in the limo, he swung open the door. Stephanie cried out, the sound going through Nick like his lifeblood. Dropping to his knees in the mud, he gathered her into his arms and held her tight while tears burned his eyes and waves of relief shook him through and through.

"Sweetheart." He kissed her cheek, her forehead, the top of her head. "Hey, are you okay?" His voice broke as he closed his eyes and took in her sweet little-girl scent.

"Daddy." She sobbed in his arms. "Daddy, I'm scared."

"It's okay, honeybunch. I'm here. You're safe." He tightened his arms around her. "Did they hurt you?"

"No, but those men were mean. They said a bunch of bad words."

Clenching his jaw against the emotion gripping him, he eased her to arm's length. "Where's Erin?"

"She's in the big building with another man. I think he's bad, too. They tied her up, but Erin wasn't even scared."

"I've got to go help her. I'm going to take you into the cornfield to hide. I want you to stay there until I come for you, okay?"

Wiping her nose on her sleeve, Stephanie nodded. "I'm still scared, Daddy."

"Everything's going to be fine. I promise." Loath to leave her alone, but knowing he didn't have a choice, Nick worked off his jacket and slipped her arms into it. "Here's my jacket so you don't get wet."

"'Kay."

Scooping her into his arms, he started toward the cornfield a dozen yards away. Several rows in he stopped and set her gently on the ground. His heart broke when she looked up at him.

"Don't leave me, Daddy," she whispered. "I'm scared."

Nick dropped to his knees, pulled her into his arms and held her tightly. "I love you, honeybunch. You stay put for me now, all right? No matter what happens, you stay right here. I'll come back for you."

"You promise?"

Because he couldn't speak, Nick nodded, praying he'd be able to keep his promise.

Slipping his service revolver from his holster, he broke through the rows of corn and started toward the wide entrance of the grain elevator at a dead run.

Erin stared down the barrel of DiCarlo's pistol. She couldn't believe it had come to this. She couldn't believe she was going to die.

Oh, God, Nick, I'm sorry I hurt you.

Oh, how she'd wanted to spend the rest of her life loving him. The thought ripped through her heart. He might not love her in return, but there was no doubt in her mind he cared for her. She'd seen it in his eyes. She'd felt it in his touch. Now, just as he'd feared, she was going to get herself killed.

"Get on the ground, Officer McNeal. I'll do us both a favor and make this quick for you. It wasn't the way I had it planned, but I like you—you've got guts. I have no desire to hear your screams." DiCarlo's voice rose over the drone of rain on the roof overhead. Cold. Surreal. More frightening than the gun in his hand.

He raised the pistol. "Do it now."

Her heart hammering out of control, Erin got down on her knees. Her mind rebelled against what would happen the instant she lay down. She tried not to think of everything she would leave behind. Nick. Stephanie. The dreams that would never be. She tried not to imagine the pain of a bullet. Whether her death would come quickly, or if DiCarlo would leave her to die slowly despite his words.

Gathering what little emotional strength she had left, Erin forced her gaze to his. "I'm not going to lie down for you. If you're going to kill me in cold blood, you're going to do it while I'm looking you in the eye, DiCarlo."

Her voice shook, but she didn't care. Her spirit cried out to defy him, and bound as she was, at his mercy, this was the only way she could.

"I have no compunction about shooting you this very moment. Most people don't like to see it coming."

Nausea rose into her throat, mingling with the fear in a cold, bitter mass. "I'm going to be sick," she said.

He made a sound of annoyance. "How does it feel to be so afraid? To know you're going to die? Those are all the things my son felt when you put a bullet in his chest."

"I warned your son. He shot me first."

"Liar."

"Your son didn't give me a choice."

DiCarlo stared at her as if she were a piece of cheap furniture. "You never knew that Danny Perrine was expecting my people in the warehouse that night, did you?"

Shock speared through her fear, tangling her thoughts. "You're lying—"

"He was our target that night, Officer McNeal. Not you. He'd asked for more money. It always annoys me when cops want more than they're worth. He got his just rewards, didn't he?"

Her brain couldn't digest the information. After six months of guilt, six months of blaming herself, to learn her partner had been dealing with the devil all along was too much to absorb. The sense of betrayal was bitter and acute.

"In any case, I thought you should know Officer Perrine was on the take. He was dirty and greedy. Your knowing that makes this moment all the sweeter for me." DiCarlo pulled the hammer back with his thumb. "This is for my son."

Erin sat back on her heels, her hands locked behind her, her fingers fumbling at the bulge of the pistol strapped to her ankle. Sweat pooled at the back of her neck. She closed her eyes against the terror exploding inside her, and concentrated on working the minirevolver from its holster through the impediment of her jeans. In the back of her mind, she wondered how many more seconds of life she had left. How many more breaths—

"Drop the gun, DiCarlo!"

Erin's world tilted at the sound of Nick's voice. Hope burst through the choking cloak of despair. She looked up to see him rush through the entrance, his pistol level on DiCarlo. Simultaneously, the mafioso spun. Terror paralyzed her for an instant. Then a rush of adrenaline sent her bound hands fighting the revolver from its holster. She jerked up the hem of her jeans, felt the cold steel beneath her fingers.

Two gunshots rang out in quick succession. DiCarlo stumbled back and went down. Out of the corner of her eye, Erin saw Nick go to his knees.

"Nick!" Her heart stopped. "No! *Nick!*"

A clap of thunder drowned out her scream. Ten feet away, DiCarlo rolled onto his side and leveled the pistol on her. The gun exploded.

A bullet whizzed past her ear. Erin fumbled with the .22. Her palm found the grip, her fingers the trigger. Leaning forward, she turned and fired blindly behind her back, four shots. Over her shoulder, she saw DiCarlo sink to the ground.

The pistol tumbled from her hand.

"Nick! *Nick!*"

Before she could scramble to her feet, he was at her side. He dropped to his knees in front of her, drawing her against him. Relief swept through her with such force that she couldn't speak.

"Holy Toledo, McNeal, that was some pretty fancy shooting."

The sound of his voice completely undid her. Erin couldn't catch her breath, couldn't stop shaking. Tears streamed down her cheeks, but she didn't even try to stop them. The emotions banging through her were too powerful, and not even her iron will was strong enough to maintain a semblance of control.

"Easy does it, that was a joke—"

"DiCarlo...is he—"

Nick nodded. "Don't look, honey. He's dead."

Only then did Erin notice the blood on Nick's shoulder. "You're bleeding."

"I'm all right." New concern gentled his voice. "He just winged me."

"Stephanie," she choked out. "Is she okay? She was so scared. They took her to—"

"I took her into the cornfield to hide. She's fine."

"What about the other men? There were three—"

"One is cuffed to the fence, the other two to the undercarriage of DiCarlo's limo. The highway patrol will get the guy in the chopper." Facing her, Nick wrapped his arms around her and held her tightly for a moment. "You're shaking. Easy, honey. Let me untie you." Reaching around her, he gently untwisted the wire that so brutally bound her wrists. "Your wrists are cut," he said with a grimace.

"I'm okay." Her hands were numb, but the discomfort didn't matter. All that mattered was that they were alive. Safe. Together.

Nick rose. Slipping his hands beneath her shoulders, he helped Erin to her feet. Her legs felt like wet paper, and she leaned heavily against him.

"Dizzy?" he asked.

"With relief," she said. "You saved our lives."

Surprising her, he turned her to him and wrapped his arms around her. Cocooned within his embrace, Erin had never felt so safe, so secure. Only then did she realize he was shaking, too. "I'm sorry, Nick. I'm so sorry. I almost got Stephanie killed. I almost got myself—"

"Shh." He stroked the back of her head, combing his fingers through her hair. "You don't have anything to apologize for."

"But it was my fault. You said I was going to get myself killed, and I nearly did. I put you through hell, risking Stephanie and myself like that."

"I was wrong. I've been wrong about you from the very beginning. It took honor and courage to come here and confront a man like DiCarlo. You were willing to risk your own life to save Steph."

He pulled her closer. "I've been wrong and a blind fool."

Slowly, gently, he eased her to arm's length. Their gazes locked. Erin's chest constricted at the emotion pooled in the brown depths of his eyes.

"Since Rita's death, I've been frozen inside," he said quietly. "My heart has been a solid block of ice. I've been afraid to live. Afraid to reach out and take all the things life offers. You showed me how to live again. You showed me how all those risks play into the big picture of life. You proved it to me over and over again. You proved to me Steph is young and strong and can lead a full life if I just let go a little. You proved to me that to live, to love, you must first be willing to take chances."

Fresh tears filled her eyes as she stared at the man she loved more than life itself. "I didn't ever think I'd hear you say that."

"Neither did I. And I fought you at every turn. But you're right." Slipping his hands to either side of her face, he kissed her.

The gentleness of the kiss devastated her. She closed her

eyes against the rush of emotion, the wave of physical sensation, and kissed him back.

"I know you don't want to hear this," she murmured. "But I love you, Nick. I love you, and I don't even care if you're ready to love me back—"

"I love you, too, McNeal."

The words stunned her, sent her heart tumbling into bliss like she'd never known.

He kissed her temple. Her nose. The side of her mouth. "I love you so much it scares me. But I'm willing to risk it, honey, if you're willing to take a chance on me."

"I've never walked away from a risk," she said.

"Even when walking away is the safe thing to do?"

"Especially when it's the safe thing to do."

"Ah, McNeal, I didn't think I'd ever want to hear you say that, but I'm really glad you did."

In the distance, the sound the police sirens rose above the din of rain on the roof. Pressing his cheek against her temple, Nick skimmed his hands up and down her back. "There's no policy against married police officers in the Logan Falls PD. What do you say we make it permanent?"

Erin closed her eyes and let sheer happiness wash over her. "I can probably outshoot you. And I don't mind jumping into a fray now and again. Are you sure that won't bother you?"

"I think my ego can handle the shooting part." He grinned. "And I might just keep you too busy making love for you to be jumping into frays."

"What about Stephanie? How will she—"

"She's crazy about you, Erin. Mrs. Thornsberry is crazy about you." He kissed her again. "I'm so crazy in love with you I can't stand the thought of being without you."

Erin smiled up at him through tears of joy, knowing she was the luckiest woman in the world. "Well, Chief, maybe we should go get Stephanie and take her home so we can break the good news to her."

"Home," he echoed, and pulled her close. "It's been a long time since I've truly been home."

"We're home now, Nick. You've brought me home."

"You showed me the way. I love you."

Blinking back tears, Erin looked outside. The storm had broken. Hazy tendrils of sunlight broke through the clouds like streams of wet gold. She'd never seen a more beautiful sunrise. And she'd never been happier than at this moment in her life.

Nick reached for her hand and squeezed it tightly, his gaze telling her all the things she already knew in her heart—and felt all the way to her soul.

"I love you, too," she whispered. "Always."

Hand in hand, they started toward the entrance where the future waited with a promise of happiness and light and the unending hope for tomorrow.

Epilogue

Nick paced the surgical waiting area for what seemed like the hundredth time. A dozen cups of coffee churned in the pit of his stomach, and every nerve in his body snapped like live wires. If one more nurse came through those double doors without any news, he thought he might explode. Stephanie had been in the operating room for nearly two hours, and he'd worried every second with agonizing intensity.

"Chief."

He jumped at the sound of Mrs. Thornsberry's voice. "What is it, Em?" he asked irritably.

"I'm going down to the cafeteria for coffee. Do you want me to bring you back a cup?" she asked.

"Only if it's got a doctor attached to it," he snapped. "What on earth is taking so long?"

"It's only been two hours—"

"Is he causing you problems, Em?"

Even through the stress and tension of Stephanie's surgery, Nick's heart soared at the sound of Erin's voice. He turned, and as usual, felt all his blood spiral into a slow, rolling free fall. "McNeal."

The two women exchanged knowing smiles, then Mrs. Thornsberry started for the elevator down the hall.

Erin walked into the waiting area and faced Nick. "The name is Ryan now, Chief. You're going to have to stop calling me by my maiden name."

He looked into the green depths of her gaze and felt the knot in his gut begin to unravel. That was all it took for him these days. A touch. A word. A smile. And the instant he held her in his arms, he knew everything was right with the world.

"She's going to be fine," Erin told him.

"Dr. Brooks should have finished by now."

"Dr. Brooks is the best neurosurgeon in the state."

Even in uniform, she took his breath away. They'd been married for less than a month, and he still couldn't get enough of her. Judging by the amount of love jammed into his heart, Nick figured he never would.

The need to feel her in his arms had him reaching for her. "Come here. I need to hold you."

Smiling tentatively, Erin stepped into his embrace. Nick closed his eyes and held her, felt another knot of tension unravel. "You're just what the doctor ordered," he murmured.

"I'm glad I could oblige," she said. "Maybe we could work in a little physical therapy later...."

"Ah, McNeal, you always know just where to hit a guy."

Cocooned within his embrace, she sighed. Nick knew the signs, and asked, "What is it?"

"Not now. Not when Stephanie—"

"Erin." Easing her to arm's length, Nick put his palm beneath her chin and forced her gaze to his. "Talk to me."

"For some reason Steph's operation made me think

about Danny. I still can't believe he was dirty. That he lied to me. Betrayed me…for money. It still hurts."

"I know, honey. I'm sorry."

"But even after what he did to me—all the anguish he put me through—I can't bear the thought of him going to prison."

"Frank said his lawyer is already working on a deal with the D.A. He probably won't do prison time. Probation, maybe. Or community service." Nick wasn't sure yet how he felt about that, since Danny Perrine had nearly gotten her killed, but he knew it would make Erin happy, so he'd come to terms with it.

The sound of the double doors opening spun them around. Nick's heart stopped at the sight of Stephanie's doctor, still clad in his green surgical scrubs.

Erin stepped forward. "How did it go?"

"The operation was successful," Dr. Brooks said. "We did a preliminary reflex test a few minutes ago, and she moved her right foot. That's a good sign this early in the game. We'll know more after she comes around—"

Nick didn't hear the rest of the sentence. Emotion spiraled through him with such force that he couldn't speak. He stared at the doctor, grappling for control, vaguely aware of Erin reaching for his hand.

"When can we see her?" he asked after a moment.

"In about ten minutes. We're taking her down to recovery now. She'll probably sleep most of the day."

Feeling the heat of tears behind his eyes, Nick turned away and walked to the window. His heart was doing acrobatics in his chest—flips and spins and dives, all without the benefit of a safety net. If he didn't know better, he thought he might just break down and cry.

A moment later, he felt Erin's hand on his shoulder. "Nick?"

He turned, found her green eyes bright with tears. "She's going to be okay. She's going to walk again. She's going to run again.'' A laugh broke from her lips. ''If I have anything to do with it, she's going to ride Bandito again.''

Only then did Nick realize he was crying, but he didn't care. Male pride and ego melted away as he looked at his bride and saw the same emotions mirrored in her eyes. Raising his hand, he brushed a tear from her cheek with the pad of his thumb. He smiled at her through his own tears as relief and need and a hundred other emotions barreled through him.

''We're lucky,'' he said after a moment.

''And then some,'' she agreed.

Cupping her face, he gazed into her eyes. He felt the undeniable connection between them in the deepest reaches of his heart. She was the only woman in the world who could do that to him. Leaning forward, he kissed her gently. ''You look really good in that uniform, Mrs. Ryan,'' he said.

''You don't look too bad yourself, Chief.''

''Do you think it's inappropriate for the chief of police to kiss his deputy?''

''Definitely. But you do inappropriate so well.''

''You always say just the right thing. I love you, Erin.''

''Mrs. Ryan,'' she corrected, and shot him a smile from beneath her lashes. ''While we're waiting for Steph to be taken to her room, I was wondering if you wouldn't mind explaining the police department's policy on maternity leave to me.''

The floor dropped out from under him as the words cascaded over him. ''You're…'' Emotion shook him with such force that he couldn't finish the sentence.

She grinned.

His heart thumped hard against his ribs. ''You're pregnant?''

''I'm not sure. You know how unreliable those tests are.''

''Tests?''

"The home pregnancy test I took this morning."

Nick held his breath. "What did it say?"

Standing on her tiptoes, Erin brushed her lips against his. "It told me I'm the happiest pregnant woman in the entire state of Indiana," she whispered.

Joy like he'd never known settled over him like a bright and stunning light. Laughing, he threw his arms around her and swung her in a tight circle, not caring about the tears building in his eyes again. "Just the state?" he managed to ask after a moment.

She smiled at him. "Make that the world."

"I guess that makes me the happiest man in the world."

"I love you—"

Her sentence was cut short when his mouth covered hers, sealing the words he cherished between them, and Nick knew he was not only the happiest man in the world, but the luckiest.

*   *   *   *   *

In September 2001, look for

A HERO TO HOLD

by Linda Castillo.
In this gifted author's next
Intimate Moments novel,
a rugged hero vows to protect
an amnesiac beauty
who is in grave danger!

Silhouette®

INTIMATE MOMENTS™

presents a brand-new continuity series:

FIRSTBORN SONS

Bound by the legacy of their fathers, these Firstborn Sons are about to discover the stuff true heroes—and true love—are made of!

The adventure begins in July 2001 with:

BORN A HERO by **Paula Detmer Riggs**

When Dr. Elliot Hunter reports to Montebello Island after a terrorist bombing, he never imagines his rescue mission will include working alongside his gorgeous former flame!

July: **BORN A HERO**
by **Paula Detmer Riggs** (IM #1088)
August: **BORN OF PASSION**
by **Carla Cassidy** (IM #1094)
September: **BORN TO PROTECT**
by **Virginia Kantra** (IM #1100)
October: **BORN BRAVE**
by **Ruth Wind** (IM #1106)
November: **BORN IN SECRET**
by **Kylie Brant** (IM #1112)
December: **BORN ROYAL**
by **Alexandra Sellers** (IM #1118)

Available only from Silhouette Intimate Moments at your favorite retail outlet.

Silhouette®
Where love comes alive™

Visit Silhouette at www.eHarlequin.com

SIMFIRST1

Feel like a star with Silhouette.

We will fly you and a guest to New York City for an exciting weekend stay at a glamorous 5-star hotel. Experience a refreshing day at one of New York's trendiest spas and have your photo taken by a professional. Plus, receive $1,000 U.S. spending money!

Flowers...long walks...dinner for two... how does Silhouette Books make romance come alive for you?

Send us a script, with 500 words or less, along with visuals (only drawings, magazine cutouts or photographs or combination thereof). Show us how Silhouette Makes Your Love Come Alive. Be creative and have fun. No purchase necessary. All entries must be clearly marked with your name, address and telephone number. All entries will become property of Silhouette and are not returnable. **Contest closes September 28, 2001.**

Please send your entry to: **Silhouette Makes You a Star!**

In U.S.A.
P.O. Box 9069
Buffalo, NY, 14269-9069

In Canada
P.O. Box 637
Fort Erie, ON, L2A 5X3

Look for contest details on the next page, by visiting www.eHarlequin.com or request a copy by sending a self-addressed envelope to the applicable address above. Contest open to Canadian and U.S. residents who are 18 or over. Void where prohibited.

Our lucky winner's photo will appear in a Silhouette ad. Join the fun!

SRMYAS1

HARLEQUIN "SILHOUETTE MAKES YOU A STAR!" CONTEST 1308
OFFICIAL RULES
NO PURCHASE NECESSARY TO ENTER

1. To enter, follow directions published in the offer to which you are responding. Contest begins June 1, 2001, and ends on September 28, 2001. Entries must be postmarked by September 28, 2001, and received by October 5, 2001. Enter by hand-printing (or typing) on an 8 ½" x 11" piece of paper your name, address (including zip code), contest number/name and attaching a script containing 500 words or less, along with drawings, photographs or magazine cutouts, or combinations thereof (i.e., collage) on no larger than 9" x 12" piece of paper, describing how the Silhouette books make romance come alive for you. Mail via first-class mail to: Harlequin "Silhouette Makes You a Star!" Contest 1308, (in the U.S.) P.O. Box 9069, Buffalo, NY 14269-9069, (in Canada) P.O. Box 637, Fort Erie, Ontario, Canada L2A 5X3. Limit one entry per person, household or organization.

2. Contests will be judged by a panel of members of the Harlequin editorial, marketing and public relations staff. Fifty percent of criteria will be judged against script and fifty percent will be judged against drawing, photographs and/or magazine cutouts. Judging criteria will be based on the following:

   - Sincerity—25%
   - Originality and Creativity—50%
   - Emotionally Compelling—25%

   In the event of a tie, duplicate prizes will be awarded. Decisions of the judges are final.

3. All entries become the property of Torstar Corp. and may be used for future promotional purposes. Entries will not be returned. No responsibility is assumed for lost, late, illegible, incomplete, inaccurate, nondelivered or misdirected mail.

4. Contest open only to residents of the U.S. (except Puerto Rico) and Canada who are 18 years of age or older, and is void wherever prohibited by law; all applicable laws and regulations apply. Any litigation within the Province of Quebec respecting the conduct or organization of a publicity contest may be submitted to the Régie des alcools, des courses et des jeux for a ruling. Any litigation respecting the awarding of a prize may be submitted to the Régie des alcools, des courses et des jeux only for the purpose of helping the parties reach a settlement. Employees and immediate family members of Torstar Corp. and D. L. Blair, Inc., their affiliates, subsidiaries and all other agencies, entities and persons connected with the use, marketing or conduct of this contest are not eligible to enter. Taxes on prizes are the sole responsibility of the winner. Acceptance of any prize offered constitutes permission to use winner's name, photograph or other likeness for the purposes of advertising, trade and promotion on behalf of Torstar Corp., its affiliates and subsidiaries without further compensation to the winner, unless prohibited by law.

5. Winner will be determined no later than November 30, 2001, and will be notified by mail. Winner will be required to sign and return an Affidavit of Eligibility/Release of Liability/Publicity Release form within 15 days after winner notification. Noncompliance within that time period may result in disqualification and an alternative winner may be selected. All travelers must execute a Release of Liability prior to ticketing and must possess required travel documents (e.g., passport, photo ID) where applicable. Trip must be booked by December 31, 2001, and completed within one year of notification. No substitution of prize permitted by winner. Torstar Corp. and D. L. Blair, Inc., their parents, affiliates and subsidiaries are not responsible for errors in printing of contest, entries and/or game pieces. In the event of printing or other errors that may result in unintended prize values or duplication of prizes, all affected game pieces or entries shall be null and void. **Purchase or acceptance of a product offer does not improve your chances of winning.**

6. Prizes: (1) Grand Prize—A 2-night/3-day trip for two (2) to New York City, including round-trip coach air transportation nearest winner's home and hotel accommodations (double occupancy) at The Plaza Hotel, a glamorous afternoon makeover at a trendy New York spa, $1,000 in U.S. spending money and an opportunity to have a professional photo taken and appear in a Silhouette advertisement (approximate retail value: $7,000). (10) Ten Runner-Up Prizes of gift packages (retail value $50 ea.). Prizes consist of only those items listed as part of the prize. Limit one prize per person. Prize is valued in U.S. currency.

7. For the name of the winner (available after December 31, 2001) send a self-addressed, stamped envelope to: Harlequin "Silhouette Makes You a Star!" Contest 1197 Winners, P.O. Box 4200 Blair, NE 68009-4200 or you may access the www.eHarlequin.com Web site through February 28, 2002.

Contest sponsored by Torstar Corp., P.O Box 9042, Buffalo, NY 14269-9042.

SRMYAS2

NOTORIOUS
Vicki Lewis Thompson

In August 2001
Harlequin Blaze
ignites everywhere...

GOING FOR IT
Jo Leigh

TWO SEXY!
Stephanie Bond

Look for these red-hot reads
at bookstores!

Careful: It's Hot!

EXPOSED
Julie Elizabeth Leto

"Blazing hot! It's sexy so sexually seductive you can't stop reading."
—bestselling author Virginia Kantra

HARLEQUIN®
Makes any time special®

Visit us at www.TryBlaze.com

HBINTROR

Silhouette® —

where love comes alive—online...

eHARLEQUIN.com

your romantic books

♥ Shop online! Visit Shop eHarlequin and discover a wide selection of new releases and classic favorites at great discounted prices.

♥ Read our daily and weekly Internet exclusive serials, and participate in our interactive novel in the reading room.

♥ Ever dreamed of being a writer? Enter your chapter for a chance to become a featured author in our Writing Round Robin novel.

your romantic life

♥ Check out our feature articles on dating, flirting and other important romance topics and get your daily love dose with tips on how to keep the romance alive every day.

your community

♥ Have a Heart-to-Heart with other members about the latest books and meet your favorite authors.

♥ Discuss your romantic dilemma in the Tales from the Heart message board.

your romantic escapes

♥ Learn what the stars have in store for you with our daily Passionscopes and weekly Erotiscopes.

♥ Get the latest scoop on your favorite royals in Royal Romance.

All this and more available at
www.eHarlequin.com
on Women.com Networks

SINTA1R

If you enjoyed what you just read,
then we've got an offer you can't resist!

Take 2 bestselling love stories FREE!
Plus get a FREE surprise gift!

Clip this page and mail it to Silhouette Reader Service™

IN U.S.A.	IN CANADA
3010 Walden Ave.	P.O. Box 609
P.O. Box 1867	Fort Erie, Ontario
Buffalo, N.Y. 14240-1867	L2A 5X3

YES! Please send me 2 free Silhouette Intimate Moments® novels and my free surprise gift. Then send me 6 brand-new novels every month, which I will receive months before they're available in stores. In the U.S.A., bill me at the bargain price of $3.80 plus 25¢ delivery per book and applicable sales tax, if any*. In Canada, bill me at the bargain price of $4.21 plus 25¢ delivery per book and applicable taxes**. That's the complete price and a savings of at least 10% off the cover prices—what a great deal! I understand that accepting the 2 free books and gift places me under no obligation ever to buy any books. I can always return a shipment and cancel at any time. Even if I never buy another book from Silhouette, the 2 free books and gift are mine to keep forever. So why not take us up on our invitation. You'll be glad you did!

245 SEN C226
345 SEN C227

Name	(PLEASE PRINT)	
Address	Apt.#	
City	State/Prov.	Zip/Postal Code

* Terms and prices subject to change without notice. Sales tax applicable in N.Y.
** Canadian residents will be charged applicable provincial taxes and GST.
  All orders subject to approval. Offer limited to one per household.
  ® are registered trademarks of Harlequin Enterprises Limited.

INMOM00   ©1998 Harlequin Enterprises Limited

They're Back!

The men of the Alpha Squad have returned—in Suzanne Brockmann's *Tall, Dark & Dangerous* series.

Don't miss TAYLOR'S TEMPTATION (IM #1087)!
After years of trying to get magnificent Navy SEAL Bobby Taylor to herself, Colleen Skelly had finally succeeded. Bobby was hers, if only for a few days. And she had her work cut out for her. She had to prove that she was a grown woman—and that he was all she would ever need in a man....

TAYLOR'S TEMPTATION
On sale in July 2001,
only from Silhouette Intimate Moments.

And this is only the beginning....

Tall, Dark & Dangerous:
They're who you call to get you out of a tight spot—or into one!

Available wherever books are sold.

Visit Silhouette at www.eHarlequin.com   SIMTDD01